ADVANCE PRAISE FOR STAGE SEVEN

"*Stage Seven* is a sweet reminder that love appears on its own schedule, and that being open is a gift of self-love. Delightful and touching."
~ Abbi Waxman, USA *Today* best-selling author

"Stevens has written a compassionate and moving novel about the lives we are living now. She reveals the ways that Alzheimer's challenges and changes who we are and how we love. This is a book that is an affirmation and an inspiration."
~ Marita Golden, author of *The Wide Circumference of Love*, an NPR Best Book of 2017

"A heart-in-your-throat story with the nuance and emotional resonance of some of the best accounts on family. A book so intimate I saw my own family reflected within its pages."
~ Daniel Kenner, author of *Room For Grace*

"*Stage Seven* is the story of Barbara, a caregiver, who finds love again in the most impossible of situations. But the unconventional romance she can't quit breaks cultural taboos, and Barbara (one of my favorite names by the way!) must choose. Will this 'Sandwich Generation' protagonist with every free moment dedicated to her family finally choose to allow herself to enjoy some happiness while she can? Or will she choose to let the needs of her mother, daughter, and sister suck the life out of her?

"Stevens' captivating story of Barbara's roller coaster of desire, self-doubt, selflessness, envelope-pushing risk-taking, loyalty, and standing in her truth make this book a great read I enjoyed. It emboldens the reader to reexamine priorities and refine their point of view on the meaning of life. Is everything that happens out of our control? Or can we influence our destinies by grabbing hold of opportunities and live, live, live?"

~ Dan Gasby, co-author with B. Smith, *Before I Forget: Love, Hope, Help, and Acceptance in Our Fight Against Alzheimer's*

To Christine —

STAGE SEVEN
A Novel

*Wishing you happy,
memories always!
Love,
Ruth*

By
Ruth F. Stevens

This book is a work of fiction. Names, characters, places and
incidents are either the product of the author's imagination or
are used fictitiously, and any resemblance to actual persons,
living or dead, events, or locales is entirely coincidental.

Printed in the United States of America
Print ISBN: 978-1-956019-01-8
eBook ISBN: 978-1-956019-02-5

Library of Congress Control Number: 2021915845

Published by DartFrog Plus, the hybrid
publishing imprint of DartFrog Books.

Publisher Information:
DartFrog Books
4697 Main Street
Manchester, VT 05255
www.DartFrogBooks.com

Join the discussion of this book on Bookclubz. Bookclubz
is an online management tool for book clubs, available
now for Android and iOS and via Bookclubz.com.

For Muriel

1

SWIMMING ALONE

"I'm winning, I'm winning, *Barbara, I'm winning...*" said my mother, slapping down a playing card each time she chanted the phrase.

I watched as Ma overlapped the cards face-up in four rows across the table, inventing a nonsensical version of solitaire. The placement of cards was haphazard, with no attention to sequence or suit. Then, without warning, she scooped up all the cards with both hands and flung them into the air, squealing, "I *won*," as the deck scattered like confetti. Wide-eyed, she watched the cards drop, giggled with delight, and stuck two fingers in her mouth.

I feared Ma had lost all regard for the rules of the game, and the age level of her play more closely approximated three than her actual eighty-three years. While she amused herself, I hung my mother's diplomas on the wall of her new room. I tried not to bang my thumb with the hammer in my normal clumsy fashion.

The laughter stopped, and Ma turned to me in confusion to ask, "Where the hell are we?"

As I witnessed her emotions turning on a dime, my own mood pivoted from calm to apprehensive.

The date was June 27, 2016. Three days had passed since

my mother, Dolly Gordon, moved into the memory care unit at Tropical Gardens Assisted Living in Providence.

When I called my older sister, I said, "I've been tossing and turning for three nights. I keep wondering if she's lying awake every night, too, frightened about being in a strange bed."

Vicky responded with her customary charm. "Oh, crap, Barbara. Put a cork in it. Every place is a strange place to Ma now."

"I realize that, Vick. That's why I worry about her."

This time I heard a muffled snort. "I know. Worrying is what you do." Another snort. "Anyway, it won't help matters for you to be lying awake exhausted. I wish you'd let me give you some Ambien." Vicky maintained a stash of prescription tranquilizers potent enough to fell a herd of stampeding buffalo.

"You know I don't like that stuff. I saw a scary study that said people who take Ambien are four times more likely to die."

"I thought we're all one hundred percent likely to die," said Vicky.

"I don't know how you manage to be so cavalier about all this." Her snide responses never failed to irritate me.

"That's because you've already got the worry department fully managed. Look—I know you're doing ninety percent of the work where Ma is concerned. Let me lighten your load."

Finally. I'd been overwhelmed dealing with Ma, hoping my sister might offer to pitch in.

"By helping more?"

"By *medicating* you. Since you don't like Ambien, then maybe a little Xanax."

"When are you coming to Tropical Gardens?" I asked, changing the subject to mask my disappointment.

"I'll get over there as soon as I can," she said, but her tone was noncommittal. "You know this is our busy time of year. I've got a call coming in right now on the business line. Hugs to Ma."

"Vick, one last thing, I'm trying to schedule an appointment with the nurse and—" I looked down at the "call ended" message on my cellphone and realized my sister had already hung up—leaving me alone, as usual, to deal with our mother's worsening condition.

I fought back tears. After fifteen years as a single mom, sometimes I longed for someone to buoy me up, to keep me afloat, to lighten the burden of responsibility that pressed on me from all sides with the density of water. For now, I would have to keep on swimming alone.

It rained the following day, so Ma and I spent most of our time in the family lounge off the Tropical Gardens front lobby. The room was a mishmash of institutional furniture combined with faux-tropical accents like Hawaiian seascape photos, plastic potted palms, and colorful throw pillows decorated in a birds-of-paradise motif. Inside the entrance hung a whiteboard with bold lettering that functioned as a memory aid, announcing the day's date and important reminders to the residents. This morning the board proclaimed, TODAY IS TUESDAY, JUNE 28, 2016. LUAU SUNDAY THIS WEEKEND. I tried to imagine a luau in a facility full of Alzheimer's patients.

All in all, the lounge managed to be surprisingly cheerful. The regulars included a bleached-blond lady who smiled beatifically at everyone and a thin baldheaded man who sat in the corner muttering to himself in French. Most of the time, Ma didn't seem to mind being here. But just when I detected a hint of comprehension about where she was and why, she'd turn to me and say, "Who are all these people? Can I go home now?"

As I walked down to the admitting office, the welcoming aroma of fresh-baked bread wafted from the kitchen. Nice touch. Not an odor I'd associate with a senior residence. I wanted to see if anyone in the office had reviewed the three-ring binder I dropped off the day Ma moved in. I'd organized everything using color-coded tabs to divide her information into numerous categories and lists: a recap of Ma's medications, a record of sleep and activity patterns, and notes on how she's been tracking vis-à-vis the various stages of Alzheimer's since she first became symptomatic three years ago.

Lists have always been important to me. Once, when Ma still had a busy career and active life, Vicky and I treated her to a three-day outing in Newport. "I've created an itinerary of all the places we can visit each day, arranged in geographical order," I said to my sister.

"This is supposed to be a holiday. Can't we relax? Why does there always have to be a fucking list?"

"It relaxes me to have a list."

I mistakenly believed I would wow the admitting clerk with my comprehensive record-keeping, but when I handed the binder to her the other day, she gave me a tired, nonchalant look. And when I dropped by her desk today to follow up, her face contorted with that same world-weary expression before she regained composure and said, "Better to discuss it with the nurse."

I called Vicky when I arrived back home around dinnertime. She agreed to meet me at Tropical Gardens the next morning for a ten o'clock meeting with the head nurse, Cindy. For once, I didn't even have to beg or guilt her into coming.

Then she inquired after my teenage daughter. "How's Sarah? Everything okay with her?"

"Oh, yes. She's busy with an SAT prep course right now. But I'm not worried about it. She'll do fine."

"You, not worried? *Barbara, are you in there?*" This was Vicky's favorite catchphrase for whenever she regarded me to be stepping out of character. She always dissolved into helpless laughter after saying it, as if she'd delivered a witty and original *bon mot*. She could be highly self-entertaining.

"Okay, Chicken, I'll see you at ten tomorrow," she said after I explained how to find the family lounge.

"Do you have to use that inane nickname?" I asked, bristling the way I invariably did when my sister addressed me as poultry.

"You're much too sensitive."

"At the very least, don't call me 'Chicken' in front of the new people at Ma's."

"The new people? As in the dementia patients?" I heard her suppress a giggle.

"No, Vicky. As in the staff and the other visitors."

"I'll try to remember about the nickname," she said without conviction.

I didn't admit to Vicky that I hadn't yet talked to any other visitors. In fact, except for Sunday, I was surprised by how few friends and relatives visited the memory care unit. However, I had noticed one man who came every day, feeding and tending to a frail-looking elderly woman in a wheelchair.

The aide addressed the man as "Jack" and referred to the old lady as "your wife Helen," or maybe he said Ellen. It surprised me to learn they were husband and wife. Jack appeared energetic and appealing, while the woman seemed out of it and never spoke. I wondered how the poor guy managed to remain cheerful, given what pitiful shape his wife was in.

Worse, I speculated whether that would be the shape of Ma in a year or two. I knew I shouldn't allow my thoughts to go down that path. But seeing a patient like Helen/Ellen, I couldn't help projecting into the future.

2

MISSING AT THE MALL

Every day until she retired at the end of 2008, Helen Winokur would stash her car keys in the refrigerator, to the great amusement of her husband, Jack.

The first time he'd seen this happen, Jack had said, "You know, Helen, I've read that inappropriate placement of objects around the home is an early warning sign of Alzheimer's." Never the sort of man to make cruel remarks, he'd spoken in jest—recognizing his wife's action at the time as a sign of mental clarity rather than incipient dementia.

"If you find my purse in the clothes dryer or my toothbrush in the freezer, will you report me to the Senility Squad?" Helen had asked.

Jack laughed. "That's not going to happen, darling."

She joined in the laughter.

Every weeknight until she stopped working at age seventy-one, Helen used to fix herself a healthy lunch to take to her job as creative director of a large downtown Providence advertising agency. She always packed her yogurt and salad inside a little blue cooler that she placed in the fridge for the next day's lunch—tucking her car keys in the cooler right next to the salad container.

Jack praised it as a foolproof system for remembering her lunch. Helen literally could not drive off without opening the fridge to pull out the cooler and keys. At her office later that day, she would reverse the process, storing everything in the breakroom fridge until the time came to go home. She observed this daily routine for years until retiring in December 2008.

Now, three months into 2009, Jack noticed that Helen did seem more liable to forget things. He attributed it to her newfound lack of structure. Perhaps being freed of a regimented work schedule had made her less mindful. Overall, though, she seemed like the same woman he'd loved for forty years, so Jack didn't give her occasional lapses too much thought.

Until the day she went missing at the mall.

Jack was pleased when Marge Williams, Helen's former assistant and close friend, invited Helen to Providence Place mall for lunch and shopping. He'd been so inundated lately with his graphic design work, he barely had time for his wife, and he couldn't help feeling a little guilty.

How unfortunate that Helen had chosen to retire at a time when he was at his busiest, Jack reflected. It bewildered him to see how idle she'd become—Helen had never been the type to sit still. Hopefully, she'd soon find new activities to embrace.

Well, at least she'd be happily occupied this afternoon. He pictured his wife enjoying a long lunch with Marge, then maybe stopping by the ice cream parlor to treat herself to a small cone of mint chip, her favorite. He knew her main shopping destination would be Nordstrom, where she planned to browse a sweater sale and pick up a couple of golf shirts for him. Later that day, she would arrive home laden with packages and would smile as she unveiled each purchase to him with enthusiastic commentary.

But when his wife returned home, Jack noticed she was uncharacteristically quiet—and empty-handed.

"You didn't find anything you liked at Nordstrom?"

She hesitated before replying. "I—no, I guess not."

He also noted a pale green stain down the front of her sweater. "Hmm—that looks suspiciously like mint chip ice cream to me," he said, smiling at her. "You should probably change into a different top so we can treat that with stain remover."

She nodded. "Maybe later. I'm a little tired."

"Did you enjoy your outing with Marge?"

She mused over the question as if he had posed a byzantine intellectual challenge. "I—I don't know. Lunch was okay. I browsed around, but nothing caught my eye."

"I picked up a rotisserie chicken for dinner," Jack said. "Maybe I should've checked with you first. I hope you didn't have chicken for lunch."

Silence.

"Or did you have that grilled vegetable salad you always like?"

"Yes. The grilled vegetables," Helen said in a more cheerful tone, grateful to be relieved of the burden of recollection. "You know, I think I'll put my feet up for a little while and read my book."

Jack watched with a puzzled frown as his wife headed upstairs to the bedroom and closed the door. He didn't have time to contemplate her odd behavior just now since he faced a tight deadline on a big design project. Retreating to his home office, he fired up the computer and got back to work. It seemed as if he never stopped working these days.

Twenty minutes later, a call interrupted him. Jack glanced down at his cellphone. Marge. Why would she be calling him instead of Helen?

"Hi, Marge."

"Jack. Did Helen tell you what happened at the mall?"

"Something happened?" Jack felt a little frisson of dread course through him.

"I thought she might not say anything."

"About what, exactly?"

Marge cleared her throat. "After lunch, Helen and I had separate errands to run. I suggested we stick together, but Helen pointed out it would be much more efficient to split up. We agreed to go our own ways and meet in front of Nordstrom at two-thirty."

"What happened then?"

"I arrived there at the appointed time and place—but no sign of Helen. After a few minutes, I started trying to call and text her, but she didn't respond."

"What did you do?"

"After fifteen minutes, I started looking around for her. It's a huge place, as you know. I went back to Nordstrom to wait again at our designated spot. Still no sign of her."

"Maybe Helen was there while you were off searching the mall," Jack said.

"Maybe. But if so, she didn't say anything about it later. I called mall security, and one of the guards drove me around in a golf cart. When I finally spotted Helen, she was nowhere near the Nordstrom entrance. She was sitting on a bench holding the remains of an ice cream cone. It was dripping all over her hand and onto her sweater."

"Did you ask her what had happened?"

"Yes—but she didn't respond. She just shrugged and walked with me to the car. Anyway, when I drove her home, I considered coming inside to tell you. But I decided to call instead. Helen might have been upset by my reporting on her behavior to you."

"Upset?"

"Okay, that may not be the right word. But I wanted to let you know, in light of what's been going on."

"You did the right thing, Marge," Jack said, although he didn't understand her last statement. "I'll keep a close watch on her." He didn't know what else to say.

"I know Helen is in good hands with you, Jack," she said. "I'll let you go now."

"One more thing. What did Helen have for lunch?"

Marge sounded surprised by the question. "Rotisserie chicken salad."

Disquieted by the phone call, Jack rationalized the events of the afternoon. Certainly, Helen didn't forget what she'd ordered for lunch. Her grilled veggie comment must have been a white lie to spare him the knowledge that she had eaten chicken a couple of hours ago. She knew he'd feel bad about purchasing the same item for dinner.

How typical of Helen to put his feelings first. Why didn't he see that before? Jack felt a momentary surge of relief. Yet, he couldn't deny that his wife forgot to meet Marge at Nordstrom. Or did she? Perhaps Marge confused the time and place, not Helen. That scenario seemed implausible when he compared Marge's clear and rational demeanor to Helen's muddled state on her return from the mall. Besides, Marge was young enough to be Helen's daughter.

Still, something else might be going on. When Helen worked in advertising, she sometimes became passionate about a new campaign, absorbed in thought for hours as the creative juices churned in her brain. Maybe something had been distracting her, a secret project like a novel or screenplay. Perhaps she didn't want to share it with Jack until the concept jelled in her head. There must be a reasonable explanation for what had occurred today.

He'd keep a closer eye on Helen, though, to allay his doubts. She functioned well enough most of the time, didn't she? Surely, there couldn't be anything too terrible going on. Helen was fine—merely tired, Jack told himself. Then he remembered that he really must get back to work.

3

HUNG UP ON THE STAGES

Vicky and I arrived at Tropical Gardens around the same time to meet with the head nurse, Cindy, to talk about Ma. But the nurse did not prove as punctual.

"It's twelve minutes past ten," I said to my sister, tapping my wristwatch.

"Jesus, Barbara. Is it imperative that this meeting comes off with Teutonic precision?"

Vicky knew I never arrived late for anything, nor did I tolerate people who failed to respect others' time. "I'm the one who should be watching the clock," she whined. "This was a lousy time for me to leave work. The phones have been ringing nonstop."

"It's only—I'm anxious to hear what the nurse will say about Ma."

"What do you expect her to say? 'Your mother's doing great. We should have this Alzheimer's thing licked in no time.'" Vicky flung both arms in the air with more drama than the occasion warranted.

"Of course not, Vick."

As I started to ask if she'd drive Ma to a dental appointment next week, the nurse hurried into the lounge, apologizing for her tardiness. Around five feet tall, Cindy had straight hair dyed an unnatural shade of purplish-red and a freckled, sunburnt complexion. She peered at us gravely through wire-rimmed glasses perched on a peeling snub nose. Despite her petite stature and cutesy features, something about her struck me as fierce and imposing.

Ma had gone to a physical therapy session, so we could talk without interruptions. It pleased me to note that Cindy held my three-ring binder underneath her clipboard.

"Okay. So... Mom has been here five days now," said the nurse, squinting through her eyeglasses as she examined the clipboard.

"Whoa. How crazy is that. Your mother just moved in too?" asked Vicky, feigning surprise.

Oh, God. Don't make a mockery of this meeting, Vicky.

Cindy gave my sister a perplexed look. "Pardon me?"

"You said, 'Mom has been here five days.'" Vicky found it amusing to mess with people this way. Impervious to embarrassment herself, she couldn't care less about causing discomfort in others.

"Sorry. I meant *your* mother." If Cindy recognized Vicky's unkind game, she pretended not to.

"Dolly. She's called Dolly," said my sister.

"Dolly has been here five days. Mom—Dolly—is doing as well as can be expected. She's in good spirits, and she doesn't seem to be traumatized by the move. There is confusion, but I expect that's nothing new."

"Oh, yes," I said. "She's more or less the same, and I'm here with her every day. I couldn't say how she's doing at nighttime."

"She's sleeping well and hasn't tried to leave her room," said Cindy. "If she does, we have sensors and monitors everywhere." She explained how sensors in the mattress would alert them if Ma got out of bed, and another sensor on the door would sound if she tried to open it—which she couldn't since the unit remained locked down at night. Any abnormalities would trigger an alarm both at the central nursing station and on a portable device carried by the duty nurse.

"That's a relief. Her wandering had become a nightmare." I recalled the frightening times when Ma's caregivers contacted me to report a disappearance, sometimes late at night. "We think she'll be safer here."

Cindy gave a knowing nod. "That's why a lot of families bring their loved ones to Tropical Gardens." She looked at both of us in turn with a smile that seemed more professional than warm.

"Cindy, I'd like to point out a few things in my notes." I gestured toward the binder, which she handed to me. I flipped to the second section with the red tab. "I've been keeping detailed records on her behavior. I do this to track where she is in terms of the various stages of the AD." I pronounced the individual letters: A-DEE.

Vicky gave me a puzzled glance.

"Alzheimer's disease," I said and turned back to the nurse. "These notes help me to stay on top of things. I'll be interested in your assessment, but I think she's primarily a Stage Six. Although she does still retain a few characteristics of Stage Five behavior."

Clearing my throat, I read my notes aloud. "'Dolly is

unable to recall simple personal details such as her phone number, but she still knows family members.' That's typical of Stage Five patients. But here's a whole list of Stage Six characteristics that also describe her: *'Unawareness of environment and surroundings, the need for assistance with daily activities such as toileting and bathing, inability to remember most details of personal history, loss of bowel and bladder control, and wandering.'"*

I looked up from the binder and cast an expectant glance at Cindy. Before she could comment, my ever-helpful sister chimed in, "Holy crap, Barbara." She turned to the nurse to apologize. "We're a little OCD."

Thanks, Vicky.

"I worry that our mother is close to entering Stage Seven," I said.

"And this worries you because...?"

"Hah. You obviously don't know Barbara yet," said Vicky. "Worrying is Barb's specialty."

I read another snippet from my notes. *"'While Dolly does not yet exhibit most Stage Seven characteristics, the following descriptions apply: (1) She is still able to utter words and phrases, but with no insight into her condition. (2) She requires assistance with all activities of daily living.'* I think that describes Ma."

"Yes and no," replied Cindy. "Stage Seven is the last stage of the disease, and it's broken down into six clinical substages. The final ones involve very severe decline. Dolly still walks and talks, and she does both quite well. Being limited to an occasional word or phrase is different from what your mom is capable of."

"That's true," I said, encouraged to hear Ma's dementia might not be that advanced after all.

"The other thing is, we try not to get too hung up on the stages here. As you've seen with your mother, a patient can straddle two or even more. Things can change from week to week or even day to day, occasionally getting better rather than worse. Though as you know, the overall trend is a downhill one," Cindy said, lest I become too optimistic.

By this time Vicky was scrolling through messages on her phone, bored with the direction of the meeting. She had the attention span of a newborn grasshopper.

I flipped to the next tabbed section of the binder, which listed Ma's medications.

"Ma takes a fistful of pills twice a day—heart, blood pressure, thyroid, you name it. The doctor tweaked a couple of her dosages last week. It's all in here."

Vicky looked up from her phone to say, "Personally, I don't see the point of all the meds."

I held out the binder to the nurse, but she shook her head and said, "You keep it. All we need is a copy of the medication list, which is already on file in my office. We're happy to have Dolly here." She stood to signal the conclusion of our talk. "She's cheerful, and the staff enjoys her sense of humor. Also, she's fortunate to have you with her every day. Until she settles in, it's important for family members to provide a little extra TLC."

I shot a meaningful glance at my sister, but she remained absorbed in her phone.

"We hope she'll be happy too," I said with a little sigh.

"It's been such a hard decision, moving her out of the house she's lived in for forty years."

"I'm sure." Cindy turned on the professional smile again. "She should be finished with her PT session if you'd like to go pick her up."

"That's fine. Vicky, let's both go."

"Oh, but Chicken—"

That name again.

When I was two, "Old MacDonald" was my favorite song. With each successive verse, as my family tried to interject a "moo moo" here or an "oink oink" there, I would repeatedly demand "chick chick"—wanting that famous farm to be populated only by chickens. Pigs, cows, and lambs were all unacceptable to this stubborn toddler. Seven-year-old Vicky nicknamed me "Chicken," and, almost fifty years later, she still used the unwanted moniker. I couldn't stand it when she called me that.

"I have five new texts from customers," Vicky said. "Can you get her yourself? I'll wait here."

When I returned with Ma ten minutes later, she beamed with excitement over the prospect of seeing Vicky. Her older daughter's negligence did nothing to diminish my mother's joy in her. I believed in my heart that Vicky had always been Ma's favorite, though she would never have acknowledged such a bias. Vicky and Ma had been cut from the same bolt of nubby cloth, loud with a bold clash of colors, while I'd been fashioned from a softer and much more muted fabric.

Ma maneuvered her walker slowly but steadily down the hall, her favorite stuffed animal perched in the basket—a little black Scottish terrier with the unimaginative name of Scottie. I gave her the dog as a Mother's Day present last month and took heart in observing that Ma remembered both the gift and his name without prompting. A childlike adoration of stuffed animals had emerged as her AD progressed.

Ma looked at Scottie and sang out, "*How much is that doggie in the window?*" as we entered the lounge. We did not find Vicky replying to business texts as expected but, instead, chatting it up with Jack, the man I'd seen at a distance every day. He held a plastic soup bowl and attempted to feed some sort of greenish puree to his wife. Her lips stayed shut in a tight line, rejecting the spooned offering.

Vicky jumped up from her chair. "Ma, Barbara, meet Jack Winokur," she said in the familiar tone you'd use to introduce a dear friend. One might have thought Vicky was the Tropical Gardens *habitué* and I, the interloper. My sister excelled at infuriating mind games like this.

"Vicky. My girl," said Ma. She gave Vicky a quick hug before turning to Jack. "And this is my baby girl." She pointed to me. "Isn't she pretty?"

"Ma," I said, embarrassed. I helped her into a chair.

She sank down tentatively onto the upholstered seat as if she feared her bottom would break. Seeing goosebumps on her arms, I helped her put on her favorite old beige sweater.

"She is—very pretty." Jack gave me a conspiratorial wink.

"Hi, Jack. I'm Barbara Gordon. And this is our mother, Dolly Gordon."

"I've seen you two around here these last few days. I

should have introduced myself sooner," he said. When his blue gaze met mine, I felt myself blush and turned away.

"That's okay," I mumbled, wondering why I should feel nervous and shy in the company of this pleasant man.

Jack smiled and then addressed Ma. "You know, Dolly, you've inspired me. When Helen isn't eating well, music stimulates her appetite. Will you help me sing to her?" He broke into a smooth baritone. "*How much is that doggie in the window?*"

Ma jumped right in, adding her throaty off-key voice to the chorus.

"*The one with the waggly tail?*

"*How much is that doggie in the window?*

"*I do hope that doggie's for sale.*"

By the end of the verse, I watched Helen down her food. The eating looked mechanical, with no indication of pleasure or any other emotion.

"Look at this," said Jack, grinning. "Helen is scarfing down her soup like there's no tomorrow."

I applauded, delighted that Ma had engaged with Jack in the vocals. Somehow, in clapping my hands, I snagged the clasp of my bracelet on the opposite sleeve. I tried to extricate the bracelet without calling too much attention to my awkwardness. How did I always manage to do such things? I hoped Jack didn't notice.

"She's eating because of the song? Most people throw up when I sing. Ask my girls," Dolly said.

We all laughed and chatted amiably as he continued to feed Helen.

"It's great that she knows you both."

"Oh, yes. Dolly knows her family," said Vicky. Lowering her voice, she added, "But she can't find her ass with both hands."

I felt embarrassed again—this time for Ma and for Vicky. Fortunately, Ma was absorbed with her stuffed toy, oblivious to the comment. Between Ma's dementia and her hearing loss, conversations often went over her head.

"Can you tell us the dog's name?" I asked her.

She hesitated for a moment. "He's ... Scottie."

"Well done. You remembered," I said.

"Sure, I remembered." Her brow knitted into a frown. "Remembered what?"

I glanced over at Helen, who by now had stopped eating. Jack gently arranged a shawl around her shoulders. "She gets cold so easily," he said. Rail-thin, Helen had green eyes and a head of sparse but still silky white hair. Her delicate features must have been lovely before being ravaged by age and illness.

"I guess I'll take Helen back to her room." He gave us a warm and reassuring smile. "Nice to meet all of you. Barbara, I'm here every day. If you need anything, say the word. I've been hanging around this place for a long time, so I know the ropes."

I thanked Jack for his kindness and told him I could use the guidance. He pivoted the wheelchair around and rolled Helen out of the lounge with effortless skill. He had a lean and wiry build, with neither the jowly look nor the paunch that often afflicted even much younger men. Like my ex-husband, Richard, to pick a name out of a hat.

"He was so gentle with her," I said after they'd left the room.

"His wife is in sorry shape."

"Stage Seven."

"She looks like about a stage *twelve* to me," Vicky said. This caught Ma's attention.

"Stage? Are we going to see a show?" She gave us a hopeful smile.

"No, Ma." I turned to Vicky and whispered, "Vick, that woman... I so worry Ma will end up that way."

"Don't go there."

"Go where? Are we going someplace?" asked Ma.

"Lunch," I said.

Ma's face crumpled. "I think I'm gonna die."

"Holy crap. What's wrong?" asked Vicky.

"The food in this place. It could kill anyone."

We all started to laugh. Ma didn't often surprise us anymore, but when she did, my spirits soared.

"Well, I'll walk you two to the dining room and be on my way. I've got to fly," Vicky said. With all the flying my sister did, she must have enjoyed elite status with every major airline.

"You're leaving already? You've hardly seen Ma."

"She won't care. Out of sight, out of mind." Vicky waved one arm in a dismissive gesture.

"But Vicky, remember what the nurse said about extra TLC. Can't you at least—"

"At least *what*?" Her tone grew dark and challenging.

"Forget it." I retreated in my usual wimpy fashion. Then I remembered about Ma's upcoming appointment. "Next

Wednesday an old classmate of mine is visiting from out of town, and a group of us are meeting for lunch. But the timing conflicts with Ma's dental checkup. Can you drive her?"

"Honey, I can't."

"If I could see my friends for just an hour, I'd—"

"You know summer is our busy season at the office. I'm sure you'll figure out some other way to see your girlfriends."

I heaved an audible sigh. Why did I even bother to confront my sister, knowing I would always fold my tent in the end? Hiding my chagrin, I turned to our mother and forced a smile. "Ma, they have chicken cutlet or spaghetti and meatballs today. What would you like?"

"I don't care," she said with a shrug. "It all tastes like shit." Her mood turning serious, she asked, "Can you take me home?"

"This is your home now. I think you're going to be happy here. Right, Vicky?" But my sister had grown absorbed in her cellphone again.

"Uh-huh, right," she said, not taking her eyes off the screen.

"Did you even hear what I said?"

"Sure. You said, uh... it's time to walk Ma to lunch now. With what they charge for this place, it's a pity the food is inedible crap. Let's go, Chicken."

4

SIZING UP THE SISTERS

When the weather cooperated, Jack traveled by bicycle from his house to Tropical Gardens. He enjoyed the two-mile journey down Providence's Blackstone Boulevard, a fashionable tree-lined thoroughfare with a wide, grassy central divider, jogging path, and bike lane. As he pedaled home in the late afternoon, he had time to reflect on the new family at the assisted living facility.

He'd met them when he decided to feed Helen lunch in the lounge. His wife preferred to eat anywhere but the dining room. Jack had no idea why since she hadn't spoken a single word in months. But he liked changing the luncheon venue to various locations around Tropical Gardens for his own enjoyment as well as Helen's—if it even made any difference to her. Earlier today, when Jack guided his wife's wheelchair into the lounge, a woman he'd never seen before sat on the couch, punching a message into her phone with both thumbs.

"Hope we're not interrupting anything," Jack said.

"Oh, no, it's fine. Hi. Vicky Sharpe," she said with a smile. He settled into a chair next to Helen and offered his wife a spoonful of food.

Jack noted that "Sharpe" was an apt surname for this woman. She had a tall, slender build with a pointed chin and protruding collarbones, all hard angles.

"Jack Winokur. And Helen," he added, gesturing toward the woman in the wheelchair.

"How long has your mother been here?"

"Helen is my wife."

"Oh, shit. Open mouth, insert foot. Sorry," Vicky said.

Others had made the same mistake. While Helen had aged drastically in the last five years, Jack was six years younger than his wife and by all accounts did not look his seventy-two years, contributing further to the perceptual gap.

"Helen's been at Tropical Gardens for eighteen months. I took care of her at home for five and a half years before that, from the time of her diagnosis."

"Jesus, that's rough." Vicky pressed her lips together in a sympathetic expression. "My mother moved in here a few days ago."

Now he put two and two together. The new resident Jack had noticed around the halls had the same bony build, the same pronounced chin, even the same close-cropped hairstyle—though she had silver-gray hair and the daughter, brown. "Yes, I've seen your mother. There's a blond woman who's with her every day."

"My sister Barbara."

"Ah." The sister didn't bear much resemblance to either of the other women.

Vicky gestured at a plastic potted palm and at the whiteboard that declared, FOUR MORE DAYS UNTIL LUAU SUNDAY.

"What's with the tropical theme crap? We're like five thousand miles from Hawaii. You think they'd come up with more of a New England theme, like—I don't know—Paul Revere."

Jack gave a wry smile. "Perhaps they felt a tropical paradise would be more soothing to residents than the Boston Massacre."

"Mmm." Vicky nodded. "But you can't seriously tell me they hold luaus here."

"Every single month—usually on the first Sunday, but it varies with the calendar. Though *luau* is a bit of an exaggeration. They pass out plastic leis, pipe in ukulele music, and serve pineapple upside-down cake."

"Un-fucking-believable. Though Ma will love it."

"How old is she?" he asked.

"Eighty-three next month. We kept her in her own house for as long as we could, with part-time help at first and later with live-in caregivers. Barbara wanted to move in with her, but she has a teenage daughter, and it would have been tough on Sarah."

"And on Barbara and her husband as well, I suppose."

"Oh, Barb's been divorced for years. Her ex-husband is an investment banker. Richard. *Dick* . . . appropriately." Her upper lip curled into a distasteful sneer. "He is a total dick—though I must say, he's taken care of them financially and been an okay father to Sarah."

"Wouldn't that make him more of a partial dick?" Unperturbed by Vicky's outspoken pronouncements, Jack matched her repartee with glib self-assurance.

"Touché," she said with a shrug. "Anyway... Barbara doesn't work, so Dolly has become her job and her main focal point of worry. Barb comes here every day. I run a business with my husband, but I get over here when I can."

Jack didn't know why Vicky felt compelled to impart all this personal information to a stranger, but he didn't mind learning the details. He'd been curious about the new resident and even more curious about her younger companion, who had impressed him as kind and sweet but reserved on their first meeting.

Sizing up the sisters didn't take long. They were opposites in more ways than one. Unlike Vicky with her sharp-angled slimness, Barbara had a softer, more rounded shape that fell just short of being zaftig. Her smoothly styled blond hair framed a gentle and attractive face with big, dark brown eyes.

With their contrasting personas, the two women reminded Jack of the classic female duos in old-school musicals. Barbara had the role of leading lady—pretty, earnest, and kind—while Vicky played the crusty, wise-cracking sidekick. Although with Vicky, the wisecracks sometimes crossed a line into mean-spirited territory.

Those zany sidekicks in the musicals, for all their quirkiness, had hearts of gold. Vicky's heart was made of something different. Brass, perhaps. Or maybe steel. Oh, well, he didn't expect to see all that much of the older sibling at Tropical Gardens. Barbara seemed to handle the lion's share of the caregiver duty for Dolly.

Perhaps he'd have a chance to talk with Barbara again tomorrow. Jack pedaled harder to maintain momentum as he veered his bike off the boulevard onto his own shady street, enjoying the cooling sensation of the light summer breeze on his face.

5

FEARING THE PAST

After leaving Ma, I proceeded to my usual end-of-week happy hour gathering with my three closest girlfriends: Amy and Lynne (nicknamed Red for her vibrant hair, which looked much more natural than nurse Cindy's), both married; and Carol, the youngest of our group and divorced like me. Carol still struggled to adjust to her post-marital status two years after splitting with her husband. I had been an unattached woman for fifteen years, and single life felt entirely normal.

We met at our appointed time, 5:11 p.m. A few years ago, the group agreed that five o'clock seemed too early and 5:15 a tad late, so we settled on 5:11 as a compromise. As someone who strove for punctuality in all aspects of life, I took the start time seriously, while the other three women treated it as a joke. But now, when we got together for any reason, we always engaged in a strenuous tongue-in-cheek debate about the best exact minute for us to meet.

"Let's make it 6:17."

"I can't come that early. 6:22."

"Why don't we split the difference? I'll meet you at 6:19 and thirty seconds."

I'd carried the same approach into scheduling my home life, and Sarah and Vicky now referred to it as "Barbara time."

We found a table at the crowded bar and complained, as always, about how we should gather on some day other than Friday, so we wouldn't have to buck the TGIF celebrants.

"Why don't we move it to Thursdays?" Amy suggested.

"That's worse," said Carol. "Didn't you know? Thursday is the new Friday."

We dropped the subject for now. I expected we would continue to bring it up and fail to act on it.

Amy, who tended to be the discussion ringleader, turned to Carol to ask, "Any dates lined up for this weekend?"

Carol remained, no pun intended, our "single" source of juicy gossip these days. Amy and Red were, if not blissfully married, at least placid in their conjugal relationships, with a minimum of drama. My own sex life went out more or less with the last millennium.

That left Carol—still fragile after her divorce but determined to meet Mr. Right. Or Mr. Right*stein*, as I liked to say. Carol had been utilizing JDate's online dating service in her quest to hook up with eligible bachelors of her own Jewish faith. Before signing up for e-dating, she tried volunteering at the local Reform synagogue, but she soon learned that the only unmarried male volunteers were eighty-plus-year-old widowers, and time had not been kind to them.

We could count on Carol, from week to week, to regale us with her latest dating adventures. Most recently, she'd gone out with a rabbi who seemed charming and solicitous, even sending flowers to Carol's mother (whom he had never met) for her seventieth birthday. But when he unveiled kinky sexual predilections—so kinky that Carol refused to reveal details even to us, to the immense disappointment of the group—she dropped him like a hot knish.

"Tomorrow I'm meeting someone new, for dinner. We've talked on the phone, and he has a sexy voice. And his photos are encouraging." She passed her phone around to show us a picture of the new candidate. A chorus of "oohs" and "ahs" ensued.

"What's his name?" I asked.

"Antonio."

"That doesn't sound like a Jewish name," said Red.

"Oh, he isn't Jewish. He's from Florence."

"How did he get on JDate? Is that even allowed?" asked Amy.

"Yes, you don't technically have to be a Jew," Carol said. "There are some people on the site who happen to be attracted to Jewish culture and traditions."

"So, you're willing to go out with a man who's not Jewish as long as he's *pro*-Jewish," I said.

"I'm trying to be flexible. It's slim pickings out there. Oh, I almost forgot... Antonio said his brother is hoping to meet someone too. How about it, Barb? We could make it a double date."

I didn't even hesitate before replying, "No thanks."

"Why not?" said Amy. "I know you don't like the online dating scene, but Carol's offering up an old-fashioned blind date. What's to be afraid of?"

"*Everything*. Ladies, we've been through this a million times. I'm not interested."

"Barbara, you've gotta come out of your shell someday," Red said, her voice gentle.

"Do I? I was over thirty by the time I met Richard. I hated being married to him, and my two or three serious relationships before Richard didn't have happy endings either. Maybe I was meant to be single. A spinster, as my mother would've called it."

"A spinster? Listen to you. I guess your sister Vicky didn't nickname you 'Chicken' for nothing," Carol said.

I shot her a nasty look right out of Vicky's playbook, and everyone backed off.

"How's it going with your mom at that memory care place?" Amy asked.

I paused to take a large sip of my cosmopolitan. "Okay, I guess. It's an adjustment for both of us."

Red said, "At least you'll have more people to talk to at a place like that. It must have been lonely going to her house every day."

"I could always chat with her caregivers at the house. At Tropical Gardens, the staff is too busy to engage in a lot of conversation, and the visitors don't seem to interact much. Although I did meet this nice man named Jack who gets his wife Helen to eat by singing to her. He recruited Ma to sing with him the other day. Ma loved it."

"That's sweet . . . but sad," Red said.

"I know. He offered to show me the ropes."

"Well, that's a start. I'm sure you'll meet more people," said Amy.

"Hey, I've got an idea," Carol said. "Why don't we all go over one day to see Dolly, and we can hang out with you for an hour or two?"

"Great idea," said Amy.

But I knew it wouldn't likely happen, any more than we would switch our happy hour to a different day of the week.

I had trouble sleeping again last night, so a little past midnight, I reached for my Kindle and read in bed for a while. I preferred reading on a Kindle because the e-reader always let me know exactly where I stood. I liked knowing that I'd completed 48 percent of the book, or 53 percent, or whatever the number might be. I took comfort in that high level of precision.

Sometimes the soft light of the Kindle made me drowsy, but tonight that didn't work, so I got up and watched a few episodes of *Sex and the City*. I didn't follow the show when it first aired. During those years, I was too busy adjusting to married life, then motherhood, then divorce, all in dizzying succession.

I read a column by a snarky television critic who claimed the series had grown dated since its debut in the late nineties. But I was at least a decade out of step myself, so it suited me fine. I related to the escapades of Carrie Bradshaw and her three pals as my girlfriends, and I enjoyed the same camaraderie while nursing our cosmos, lemon drops, and margaritas. But I wasn't delusional. I knew our little band of middle-aged suburban housewives and divorcees didn't measure up to the TV series' glamorous quartet of young Manhattanites.

Another thing about the show: Mr. Big, Carrie's

handsome on-and-off paramour, bore a disturbing similarity to my ex-husband, Richard. Unfortunately, not in appearance. Richard had never been leading-man material. However, my ex and the aptly named Big both projected an air of self-importance, a lack of emotional availability, and an obsession with wealth and privilege.

I sometimes wondered then, as now, what attracted a slick guy like Richard Allinson to a woman as shy and lacking in self-confidence as I. He must've sized me up as solid marriage material. I would make a dedicated wife and mother, a diligent homemaker, and a malleable mate who would not stand in the way of either his business interests or his pleasurable pursuits . . . or at least that's what he'd hoped. Richard liked having the upper hand, and I guess I struck him as a good person to have it with.

Throughout the brief years of our marriage, my husband's enchantment with the lifestyle of the rich and famous meant fooling around on the side while I stayed home caring for our beautiful baby daughter. In this matter, he overestimated my threshold of tolerance. Though I could put up with a lot from Richard, he'd crossed the line with his serial infidelity.

When divorce proceedings began the following year, Vicky lobbied for me to move out of our spacious center-hall colonial home on Providence's East Side.

"What do you and Sarah need with all those rooms?" she said, even though Richard promised to foot the bill and had the means to do so.

A stickler for economy, my sister disapproved of wasting money, time, or space. *Less is more.* Lately she focused her streamlining efforts around Ma. I recalled her comment to the nurse: "I don't see the point of all the meds..."

Earlier this evening, Vicky called me to ask, "Have you done anything about her house yet?"

"Done anything?" I was flabbergasted that she'd bring this up already. "Vicky, she hasn't even been at Tropical Gardens for a week."

"Oh, I know. But let's face it, Ma's not going back to her old house. We at least need to start clearing out all her junk so that we can list the house before too long. Summer is a good time to sell, you know. I hate to miss out on that window of opportunity."

Speaking of windows, I wanted to throw her out of one right about then, preferably from a high floor.

"When you say *we* must clean out Ma's junk, you know *we* means *me*," I said.

"Honey, I can't help how busy I am at the office."

"I know, Vicky, and I'm willing to do most of the work, but I need your word that you won't throw roadblocks in the way like you've done before."

"Oh, stop. What roadblocks?"

"Like that time when we needed to draw money urgently from Ma's account to pay her caregivers, and it took you a week to co-sign the papers."

Ma had a small trust fund that her bank controlled with a rigid hand. The bankers made me fill out a mountain of paperwork and get a notarized letter from Ma's physician as evidence that she required emergency funds for her care. I delivered the file to Vicky's office, expecting her to co-sign the papers then and there. But she begged off from the simple task, blaming a customer crisis.

"I hounded you every day for a week to sign those papers," I said to her now. "The poor caregivers had to scream for their pay. It was a nightmare."

Vicky, however, seemed amused by my recollection. "Kiddo, that's how it goes when you're OCD and your big sister is ADD. Everything worked out in the end."

I couldn't disagree with her first statement. "OCD" (that would be me) preferred to stay a couple of weeks in front of every deadline, building in a safety cushion to protect against unanticipated delays—while "ADD" exulted in living on the edge, always procrastinating until the final moment.

I dreaded butting heads with her during the eventual sale of Ma's house.

"Vicky, I've been swamped getting Ma settled and meeting with the different people in charge at Tropical Gardens. I'll start on the clean-up as soon as I can."

"Oh, I trust you. Listen, Chicken, I don't need to tell you how much this memory care country club is costing. Not to mention that fancy concierge doctor-to-the-rich-and-famous you insisted on hiring. Maybe we should rethink that strategy."

"Not an option. Dr. Sam is my lifeline."

"Okay, never mind. I guess we do get our money's worth with him the way you pester him day and night. Anyway, we could all use the money out of the house sale to help pay her bills. I know I can count on you."

No wonder I had difficulty sleeping.

By late Saturday morning, the weather had grown relentlessly hot and sticky. My blouse clung to me, wet with perspiration, as I walked into Tropical Gardens. Once inside, my body temperature pivoted from hot and sweaty to cold and clammy in the over-air-conditioned halls. It seemed appropriate that we'd be celebrating Luau Sunday tomorrow since I could almost believe we were in Hawaii.

I accompanied Ma to the midday meal and had a one-way conversation with her while she ate her tuna sandwich. I had initially hoped she might socialize with some of the other more talkative residents, and Dr. Sam had shared the same hope.

"Keep her stimulated," he said to me when I informed him of the move to Tropical Gardens. "Get her out walking, engage her in as many activities as possible, find social opportunities for her. I can't stress how important that is."

Easy for *him* to say. Let Dr. Sam come over and try to entertain her for five or six hours. You could have brought in Bradley Cooper, Dwayne Johnson, and Ryan Gosling to dance naked in Ma's room, and she still would've dozed off after five minutes.

Yes, sorry to say my dream of an exciting new social life for Ma proved to be a big miscalculation. Sadly, she had passed the stage of forming friendships. But I did think back on Dr. Sam's comments about finding activities to keep her more stimulated and give her a sense of purpose.

I pledged to become more proactive about this. Fishing

a scratch pad and pencil out of my purse, I scrawled a few notes.

Take Ma to Tropical Gardens programs: arts and crafts, story time, bingo, musical performances, therapy dog visits.

Then I got a little more creative and thought up a few personalized activities she might enjoy:

Have a treasure hunt to find "tropical" things inside the facility.

Walk around the grounds and identify trees and flowers.

Create a book of favorite old recipes. (But would she remember any of these?)

Assist with feeding Helen and singing to her. (If her husband was willing.)

Later, back at my computer, I would transfer these items to a spreadsheet, insert it in the binder, and check off the appropriate activities each day to make sure Ma kept sufficiently engaged.

After lunch Ma had an occupational therapy session, so I strolled over to the lounge, hoping to find Jack Winokur. We'd had a few brief but pleasant chats since I first met him, making me realize how starved I'd been for grown-up conversation. I found him sitting in the family lounge, listening to the Red Sox game with his phone on speaker.

The only other person in the room was the bald Frenchman, who did not allow the broadcast to distract him from his usual muttering in his usual corner. Named Alain, he preferred to be addressed as Monsieur Bonnet— unlike most of the patients, who went by their first names.

As soon as Jack saw me, he stabbed the screen with an index finger to silence the game.

"Hi, Jack. You didn't need to turn that off."

He wore a cotton knit golf shirt that brought out the color of his eyes. They were a clear, deep blue without the cloudy or bloodshot appearance you sometimes noticed in older people's eyes.

"As a matter of fact, I did. We're getting trounced—again," he said with a sigh. In Providence, as in nearby Boston, summer spirits rose and fell with the vicissitudes of the Boston Red Sox. "How's your week going?" he asked.

"Not too bad. Ma seems content if a bit mixed up."

"Well, be thankful she's content."

"Yes, it's a blessing. Even when the onset of memory loss crept up on her a few years ago, she seemed blissfully unaware. She even fooled her doctor for a while."

"Oh, I've been there. Helen excelled at charming her doctor at first. I think it was part of her initial denial." He interlaced the fingers of both hands and stretched his arms up over his head.

I watched the muscles in his tanned upper arms tauten and firm with the stretch—then turned my head away, self-conscious about checking him out.

"Same with Dolly. Dr. Sam would insist that my mother was doing great. But he didn't see her growing less and less able to function in her everyday life."

"Dr. Sam?" Jack asked.

"Samuel Fairchild. Do you know him?"

"Only by reputation," Jack said.

"When Ma started having problems, I decided to sign her up with a concierge doctor to make sure she'd have a higher level of attention."

Concierge doctors charged a quarterly fee not typically covered by medical insurance. This fee allowed unrestricted access to the physicians, who handled a limited patient load to ensure adequate time for their members.

Sam Fairchild had impeccable credentials and strong word-of-mouth recommendations, so I signed up with him. Vicky opposed the idea, disparaging it as a waste of money. Though I didn't like to make important decisions without her consent, in this case, I felt strongly enough to overrule her.

Three days before our first appointment, Dr. Sam (as he liked to be called) sent me an email detailing what he planned to cover in his initial examination of Ma. The agenda appeared as a numbered list, along with a secondary list of the information I should bring to the appointment.

Another list-maker. I could tell from day one that this man would be a godsend.

I glanced over at the whiteboard and noticed the announcement, THERAPY DOG VISIT 3 P.M.

"A therapy dog—Ma will adore that. Vicky tried to train her golden retriever Daisy to be a therapy dog, but they kicked her out of class."

"Poor Daisy," Jack said. "Why did they kick her out?"

"Not Daisy, Vicky. Rumor has it she kept showing up late, and she would swear at the instructor for taking her to task over it. My sister isn't one to keep things bottled up."

"I noticed."

"She and her husband Martin own a company that sells air conditioning and air filtration equipment. I've always said it's ironic they're in that business since Vicky has no filter."

Jack chuckled at this.

"Anyway, about Ma... I know I said she's content, but it still breaks my heart to see her in this place. It's going to take some getting used to."

He nodded. "I know. It's a bit like having a young child again. Just when you think you've figured out how to handle things, they move on to the next phase. Trust me, you'll find a way to cope with the different phases as they come."

"Will I? It helps to hear that. I feel so fearful these days."

"It's natural to fear the future."

"But I even fear the past. Sometimes I'll worry retroactively about something that *might* have happened but didn't."

Jack looked puzzled. "How does that work?"

I paused, deciding how best to illustrate the concept of retroactive worrying. "Let's suppose I host a Sunday barbecue, and the weather is fabulous. I'll remember that the previous Sunday, it poured all day long . . . and I'll say, 'If the barbecue had been last week, it would have been ruined.'"

Jack responded to this with a hearty laugh. "That sounds exhausting," he said.

I noticed he had a way of laughing with his eyes as well as his mouth.

I smiled back at him. "It *is* exhausting. I'm well-known for my worrying skills."

Just as I said that I began to worry I'd been dominating the conversation. "Is that one of your strong suits as well?" I asked.

"Oh, not so much." He paused. "For me, worry has given way to resignation, I suppose. For a long time now, Helen hasn't been speaking or reacting to anything, except music sometimes to help her eat."

I asked if Helen had been like Ma in the early stages of the disease.

"You're asking if she was unaware of the changes taking place."

I nodded.

A shadow crossed Jack's face and he stared down at the floor. "No," he replied, his voice little more than a whisper. "That's not the way it was with Helen."

"Gosh, I'm sorry. I didn't mean to stir up unhappy memories."

"No, it's okay. Helen was aware, all right. She was terrified by her memory loss back then." He managed a smile. "This is cheery, isn't it? Tell me something about *your* life. Something unrelated to dementia, please."

"I'm afraid I'm not all that interesting. Living in the shadow of two big personalities like Vicky and Ma, I grew up to be the quiet one. Since I couldn't be heard over all their swearing, I took to writing instead."

He raised his eyebrows in interest. "Novels? Stories?"

"No, more of a personal journal. I also keep a binder on Ma, where I record notes on her illness and care."

"What about your daughter?"

"Sarah? No binder, though I do keep a to-do list on her."

"I meant, is your daughter a writer too?" Jack said.

"Oh, sorry. No, she isn't."

I blushed after revealing the extent of my familial

micromanagement. Anxious to steer away from this topic, I said, "I've always wanted to write children's books—but as a single parent, I never seemed to find the time. I take care of Ma, I see my friends, and I spend time with Sarah. We like to cook together. Right now, we're focusing on Indian dishes."

"Indian is a tough cuisine. You need so many special ingredients. And the breads are a real challenge."

"Sounds like you know your Indian food," I said.

"I find time for a little cooking now and then, since retiring from my graphic design business. Helen worked as creative director at an advertising agency, and we used to collaborate on projects."

At that point, Wayne poked his head in the door. One of the aides at Tropical Gardens, Wayne had quickly become my favorite staff member. Short and stocky, with a head of thick, jet-black hair, a coffee-colored complexion, and a toothy smile that lit up the room, he had a warm and welcoming personality. He came from Indonesia, from Bali, and I was pretty certain he was gay.

When we first met, I asked if "Wayne" was his real name.

"Oh, no." He laughed, then told me an interesting story. Most Balinese families named their children based on their order of birth, and they used the same names for both boys and girls. Firstborn children were Wayan, Putu, or Gede. As the oldest in his family, his parents named him "Wayan." But when he came to the United States, he modified it to "Wayne."

He showed me a photo of his younger brother Kadek, who had the same head of thick hair as Wayne—but Kadek wore his long, tied back in a ponytail, and he also sported a bushy black beard. I learned from Wayne that many rituals existed in his country relating to the various rites of passage, and one of these rituals called for men to grow their hair out during their wives' pregnancies.

"You must miss him," I said.

He looked wistful. "I do, but it is difficult for someone like me in Indonesia," he said in his lilting accent. "There are more opportunities here."

Did his comments have to do with being gay? I didn't ask.

Today, he greeted me with his usual radiant smile. "Hey there, Barbara. Dolly should be finished with her occupational therapy by now. We can go get her."

"Okay." I rose from my chair.

"By the way, I hope you're both coming to Luau Sunday tomorrow. Be sure to bring that handsome grandson of yours." He gazed at Jack.

"My two sons and my other grandchildren live out of state, but my oldest grandson Scott is staying here in town with a college friend for a couple of months," Jack explained. "Scott's an acting student at NYU. He's got a summer internship at a theatre here. Providence Players."

"What a coincidence. My mother used to work at Providence Players."

"Did she act?"

"No, she headed the development office. Nobody could raise money like Ma. I know that sounds surprising, seeing her now. Ma's always had a potty mouth like my sister... but when the occasion requires, she knows how to behave like a lady. *Knew* how to behave."

Jack nodded.

"She secured enough donations for programs that helped put the theatre on the national map," I said. My heart swelled with pride at the memory. "She even got an honorary doctorate degree for her work."

"That's impressive," said Jack. He turned to Wayne. "I'm almost sure Scott is planning to come tomorrow, but I'll call and remind him."

"We'll be seeing his name in lights someday," said the aide.

"Maybe I'll suggest Luau Sunday to my daughter Sarah, too." Why hadn't I thought of this before? "Sarah's been a little apprehensive about visiting here. She'll feel more comfortable if she knows there are going to be other young people."

"The more, the merrier," Wayne said, winking.

"Wayne, tell me something. What happened to the blond lady who smiled all the time? She used to sit here in the lounge, but I haven't seen her all week," I said. "Is she okay?"

"Oh, yes. She found herself a boyfriend. Robert. He has one of the larger apartments here, with a separate living room, and that's where she's hanging out."

Romance bloomed at Tropical Gardens. I smiled to learn of it.

Wayne glanced down at his watch in a polite signal that time was a-wasting. "Shall we go collect Dolly?"

"Sure."

I noticed the room had grown quiet. Monsieur Bonnet had stopped his soft muttering and now sat in the corner, wide awake but silent.

"Talk to your mom about Luau Sunday," Wayne said to me as we started to leave. "If you remind her and tell her that her granddaughter is coming, something might stick in her memory. I always say to our families that it's our job to help them remember. They rely on us for that."

Wayne was right. I must help Ma with her memory. But I also wanted to help Sarah remember her grandmother and maybe even preserve memories to share with Sarah's children someday. I had an idea that excited me: I would add a new section to Ma's binder, with notable recollections about her life. It would become my job to keep her past alive.

Later, sitting in front of the computer in my study, I typed this heading:

Memories of Dolly: 1988

I stared at the screen for the next several minutes, unable to proceed. The first memory I'd hoped to describe dated back to my early twenties, and the details wouldn't come to me.

I jumped up and ran to the closet, where I pulled out a carton of publicity clips and mementos I'd moved from Ma's house earlier this year. The familiar scent of old newsprint, pleasantly musty, hit me when I opened the dusty carton. I leafed through the brittle stack of yellowed newspaper articles until I found what I was looking for. I read the article and smiled to myself as the memory came back to me.

Then, at the bottom of the carton, I noticed a box of unused writing paper. I broke the seal and opened the lid. The lined sheets were powder blue, with a screened-back image of wispy clouds in the background. Perhaps someone had given the paper to Ma as a gift. It didn't look like something she would have bought for herself. Though the design was a little cheesy, the paper was of high quality and still crisp.

I took the newspaper article and a few sheets of writing paper back to my desk, grabbed a pen, and wrote:

On a gray afternoon in December 1988, five hundred schoolchildren pour out of Providence Players' downtown theatre, where they have just seen a special performance of A Christmas Carol. *Discussing the show in animated voices, they are oblivious to the blast of bitter cold enveloping them. Mittens remain in pockets, woolen scarves in bright colors hang loosely around necks. A television reporter for one of the local network affiliates clutches a microphone and interviews the actor who played Scrooge. Clouds of vapor form around their heads as they talk in the frigid parking lot, where the children are now lining up to board a fleet of yellow school buses.*

I paused to read over what I had written. It surprised me to realize I'd been using the present tense. The newspaper story had brought back the memory in such vivid sensory detail that I must've found myself "in the moment." I was about to change everything to past tense when I decided I liked it the way it was. I continued:

This day marks the launch of a soon-to-be-celebrated program that will allow children from all over Rhode Island to experience the thrill of free live performances. It is already receiving widespread media attention and will earn Providence Players a national reputation. The woman who came up with the concept, secured the funding, and organized a team of volunteers to handle the logistics becomes the toast of the town. Her name is Dolores Gordon, but she is fondly known as "Dolly" throughout the community.

I reviewed my work one final time. I had made several cross-outs and marked a few typos, but I would transcribe the whole entry into a clean, neat script on another day. For now, I placed the sheet in a separate tabbed section of Ma's binder titled *Memories of Dolly*. I glued the newspaper article to a second sheet of paper and inserted it next to the write-up. I imagined Vicky chuckling at my amateurish effort, likening it to a fifth-grade school project.

Who cared what Vicky thought? I grinned with satisfaction at what I'd accomplished—as if, by keeping such a well-maintained binder for Ma, complete with warm recollections of her past triumphs, I could somehow hold the Alzheimer's in check.

6

A FORBIDDEN LUNCH

For as long as Sarah Allinson could remember, her mother, Barbara Gordon, had kept a detailed to-do list for her. As a little girl, Sarah assumed all mothers tracked their children's activities in a similar manner. It shocked her to learn, at around the age of ten, that most of her young friends were, in fact, listless.

Although Sarah made her own to-do list now (and she had to admit, it was in some ways a useful discipline), the list her mother maintained on her behalf was more thorough than the one Sarah kept for herself. And that didn't even include all the college-related notes that Barbara had organized with painstaking care into a separate series of documents.

One such document detailed all the things Sarah needed to do between now and application time: SAT prep, sample essay-writing, college counseling meetings, campus visits, and so on. Barbara had also formatted a spreadsheet on which she instructed Sarah to rate all colleges of interest according to several criteria: academic, extracurricular, geographical, size of school, and more.

Most of Sarah's friends wouldn't start doing anything like this for another six months or more—and, if they were lucky, never on a spreadsheet—but Barbara liked to stay ahead of the curve.

"It will give you a leg up," she told her daughter.

Today, Sarah's mother had charged her with delivering a stack of travel brochures to Aunt Vicky and Uncle Martin's townhome for a Caribbean cruise next winter. Although she seldom left home herself, Barbara maintained an information file for possible future trips that would put most travel agents to shame.

As a sixteen-year-old who had just secured her driver's license a couple of months before, Sarah jumped at any opportunity to run errands in the Toyota Camry, a generous birthday gift from her father—bestowed with reluctant agreement from Barbara, who warned against the horrific dangers of multi-vehicle collisions every time Sarah got behind the wheel.

Sarah always enjoyed visiting her aunt and uncle. The house had a chaotic atmosphere, a vast departure from her own well-ordered home environment. Like today, for instance.

When she arrived at their place a few minutes past noon with the brochures, she found her aunt eating ice cream, M&Ms, and Cheez-Its at the kitchen table, amid the clutter of unread mail, magazines, keys, purses, and other paraphernalia. Aunt Vicky offered to share this forbidden "lunch" with Sarah, and she happily accepted.

"Mom would have a fit," Sarah said as she popped a few M&Ms into her mouth. She knew her mother's more sensible and conservative approach to balanced meals—and balanced *everything*, for that matter—should be commended, but sometimes she found it a lot more fun to loosen up.

"What are you up to this summer, honey?" her aunt asked through a mouthful of coffee ice cream, a favorite Rhode Island flavor. Vicky pulled out a quart container from the freezer and a couple of bowls from the kitchen cabinet and scooped out two generous portions. She pushed one bowl to her niece across the cluttered tabletop.

"Are you expecting someone else?" Sarah asked, pointing to the second bowl.

"Oh, that's for Daisy."

Vicky placed the other bowl on the floor for the golden retriever, who ambled over to slurp the frozen dessert with the unbridled enthusiasm of a dog who lived for treats.

Sarah reached down to give Daisy a pat. The dog nuzzled her, pressing a cold jowl dripping with ice cream into the girl's palm.

"My summer's busy. I'm taking an SAT prep course and summer classes in architecture and fashion design at Frisbee." "Frisbee" was the affectionate nickname for RISD (pronounced RIZ-dee)—the acronym, in turn, for the Rhode Island School of Design, Providence's prestigious college-level art school. "And one day a week, I'm volunteering to help underprivileged kids at the tutoring center."

"Wow, you're programmed every single minute of the summer. Sounds like an agenda your mother would create," said Vicky, raising her eyebrows. "Gotta bulk out that college resume, huh?"

"Oh, yeah, that's Mom, all right." Sarah groaned and made a face. Aunt Vicky always cast a spell over Sarah that somehow caused her to see her mother through

Vicky's eyes. She knew the sisters butted heads a lot, to use her mother's words, and the girl sometimes found her loyalties torn between the two sides. But whenever she conspired with her aunt at her mother's expense, as she had done just now, Sarah felt a little guilty.

"Do you have a boyfriend on the scene these days?" Vicky asked.

"Nobody at the moment."

"Well, no worries. I'm sure someone will come along soon," her aunt said with reassuring warmth.

They went to join Uncle Martin in the TV room, where Aunt Vicky wrested the remote control from his hands to change the channel from ESPN to PBS.

"I'm going to watch an old public television documentary about a group of folksingers called The Weavers," said Aunt Vicky. "I know that sounds like a real yawner, but I think you might like it. Stay and watch with me for a while."

Vicky loved folk music. She had a lot of interests, and Sarah found her aunt funny and entertaining, though her husband was kind of a lump. Uncle Martin's whole life consisted of four basic activities: eating, drinking, working, and vegging in front of the television. As his wife and niece watched the PBS program, he withdrew to the bedroom, where he could continue to enjoy his summer entertainment menu of baseball and golf without further interruption.

Sarah found herself drawn to the documentary. Naturally, she knew about Pete Seeger—who didn't? But she hadn't heard of the other three members of the group, who'd joined Seeger for a reunion performance show-cased in the film. These Weavers looked pretty ancient. One of them even used a wheelchair, but Sarah could tell they didn't think of themselves as old. They played and sang and talked with amazing energy and animation, their minds as alert and engaged as ever.

Then Sarah recalled her grandmother, who could move around well but behaved like a goofy little kid. Which would be the lesser of two evils, she wondered—an intact body with a failing mind or an intact mind with a failing body? She favored the latter, though the girl didn't relish either alternative.

After the documentary ended, Vicky switched the channel and broke into a wide grin when she saw Billy Bob Thornton on the screen, wearing a lopsided Santa hat and clutching a bottle of booze as he staggered across a parking lot.

"*Bad Santa.* I frickin' love this movie. I watched it last night for maybe the fifth time."

"Why are they showing it in the summer?"

"The station's running a Christmas-in-July promotion all week."

Sarah smiled to think that Aunt Vicky's favorite holi-day movie told the story of a raunchy and dissolute mall Santa who drunkenly pissed himself as innocent kiddies sat on his lap—while Barbara's top pick was the funny-sad rom-com, *Love Actually.* She mentioned this to her aunt, saying, "The two couldn't be more different."

"Are you talking about the two movies? Or about your mother and me?"

Sarah paused before answering, "Both, I guess."

"Hah." Vicky emitted a loud laugh and slapped one hand on the coffee table, rattling the antique brass tray that sat on the tabletop and dislodging a stack of magazines, which now cascaded haphazardly across the floor.

Vicky resumed her channel surfing. Now Ellen DeGeneres appeared onscreen, talking with a tearful guest about her recent divorce. They watched in silence for a moment.

Then Sarah said, "What happened between my parents? To cause their divorce, I mean. I wonder about it sometimes."

For once, Aunt Vicky had to fumble for words. "Maybe it's better to ask your mother about this."

"I've tried. Mom said she initiated the divorce, but she never told me why. I've always wondered if Dad cheated on her. But when I ask her, she always says something vague, like 'We wanted different things from marriage,' or 'Your dad and I weren't well-suited.' *Duh.*"

"She won't give you a straight answer?" Vicky said. "Don't get me wrong; you've got a wonderful mother, but sometimes I wish she didn't act so goddamn uptight. Anyway, you were a toddler when your folks divorced. How could you suspect he cheated?"

"Dad always has a woman. At least for as long as I can remember."

"I don't know a lot of the details myself. But since you've apparently figured it out, I'll tell you what I do know. They *did* have some big blowup over another woman. And after your dad moved out, he acquired a live-in girlfriend right away, though I don't even know if she was the same woman. I think he had a few other relationships after that. You just about needed a scorecard."

This news did not shock Sarah. "He's like the opposite of Mom. She's never had a real boyfriend, and she hardly even dates anybody. Sometimes one of her friends tries to fix her up, but it never goes anywhere." Her brow furrowed. "Do you think Mom could be gay?"

Vicky's eyes popped.

"What the fuck... Two minutes watching Ellen DeGeneres, and this is what you come up with?"

Sarah blushed. "No, no. That's not why I said it."

"J-Jesus Christ." Vicky's response came out as a strangled cough. "Why, then? Did something happen?"

"Not really." She explained to her aunt that when she started high school at Classical, a public magnet school known for academic excellence, she became more aware of gay and lesbian issues through the on-campus Gender and Sexuality Alliance club. "Mom seems so *off* men. It occurred to me that maybe she likes women. I mean, I'm pretty sure she doesn't. But I'm curious if you know—if you think—if Mom has ever—" She looked at Vicky unhappily.

"Hell, no, honey. Your mother may be off men, as you put it, but I'm a hundred percent sure she's not a lesbian. I wouldn't give it another moment's thought. I really wouldn't."

Sarah gave a solemn nod. Vicky's reply should have placated her, but instead, she felt guilt-ridden and disloyal. Mom would die of embarrassment if she knew Sarah had initiated a discussion about her sexuality and asked Aunt

Vick all those prying questions about the divorce. True, Vicky could have refused to answer the questions. But her aunt never held back demurely, as Sarah well knew when she broached the subject.

To assuage her feelings of remorse, Sarah texted her mother.

—*Can we hang out for a while later this afternoon?*

Barbara's response was immediate.

—*Love to.*

—*What time will you be home?*

—5:23.

Sarah smiled at this latest example of what she and her mother had come to refer to as "Barbara time."

As she prepared to leave, Sarah asked her aunt, "Are you going to that luau thing tomorrow at Tropical Gardens?"

"Well, there's a chance, but . . . probably not. Gotta catch up on paperwork over the weekend. Besides, I saw your grandmother a few days ago."

Sarah recognized this as a sore subject for her mom, who went to see Grammy every single day. She had to agree it didn't seem fair for her aunt to do so little when Barbara did so much. But then, Aunt Vick worked at her company and had a husband. Barbara only had Grammy and Sarah.

"I'm going tomorrow," Sarah said. "I haven't visited Grammy since she moved there."

"I'm sure she'll be happy to see you, sweetie."

Sarah had to admit she didn't look forward to visiting Tropical Gardens. She still couldn't fathom that Grammy now lived in some depressing senior home for people with memory problems.

Maybe, later at home today, she would talk to Barbara about her apprehensions. Even though her mom drove her crazy, Sarah liked to have grown-up discussions about feelings with her mother, who showed surprising calmness and reassurance in these situations.

They would have their chat about Grammy and Tropical Gardens, and maybe after that, they'd watch *Sex and the City*—the expurgated version that aired in syndication on cable television.

When mother and daughter watched the show together, even with the censored version Barbara sometimes blushed to a deep shade of pink and said, "Honey, maybe you shouldn't watch this scene." A couple of times, she even stuck a hand over Sarah's eyes. Aunt Vicky had nailed it about Mom being uptight.

Sarah knew her mother drew pathetic comparisons between her own happy-hour clique and the women in the TV series. Given how little opportunity Barbara had to party, though, Sarah couldn't begrudge her this small Friday indulgence, lame as it might be.

Sometimes Sarah wondered what her mom would do in two years' time when she went off to college, and Grammy—well, who knew how long things might go on with Grammy. It made her feel a little sad sometimes, picturing her mother rattling around in their big house. But then she forced herself to shake off the image.

Sarah couldn't help that her mom had remained alone all these years. Barbara would need to figure out her own life. As Sarah intended to do for herself.

7

SKIDDING ON BLACK ICE

Throughout the Winokur boys' childhood, despite Helen's demanding work schedule, Jack marveled at how his wife had managed to be as caring and attentive as any stay-at-home mom. Later, when they became empty-nesters, she would juggle multiple clients and new business pitches plus a large staff and still keep up with cooking, reading, exercise, and hobbies. Jack always boasted that she made it all appear effortless.

But things were different now.

Half a year had passed since the day Helen got lost at the mall. At first, Jack made excuses to himself and others for her increasingly forgetful behavior, but he could no longer write off his wife's actions as mere absent-mindedness.

In the fall of 2009, he accompanied her to see their long-time family physician and friend, Ned Miller. The doctor examined Helen and called them both into his office afterward for a consultation. Jack and Helen settled into two adjacent chairs facing the doctor's desk. Jack reached out and gave his wife's hand a reassuring squeeze.

In his late fifties, Dr. Miller had a bald dome of a head and a salt-and-pepper beard that he sometimes fiddled with the way an actor might use a prop. Right now, he stroked his beard as he addressed the Winokurs with a relaxed smile.

"Helen, I've got your lab report up on the computer screen, and I do not see anything alarming in the bloodwork."

"Well, that's good," said Jack, inspecting the monitor and pretending the jumble of onscreen medical terms made total sense to him.

"I'm going to ask you a few questions now. Nothing to worry about; this is standard procedure," Dr. Miller said to Helen.

She gave her husband an apprehensive glance. Jack responded with a quick nod of encouragement, but in truth, he felt frightened for Helen and for himself. He squinted up at the overhead fluorescent fixture as if fearing the bright light would somehow expose their thoughts and secrets.

"Where do you live?" asked the physician.

"At 152 Laurel Road," Helen replied without hesitation.

"Good. And who is the president of the United States?"

"Barack Obama—thank heavens." She rewarded the kind doctor with her most charming smile.

"Great. Now I'd like you to count backward from one hundred, as fast as you can."

Helen started to recite, very fast indeed, "One hundred, ninety-nine, ninety-eight, ninety-seven, ninety-six, ninety-five, ninety-four, ninety-three—"

"Okay. You can stop counting."

"Darn. I was enjoying this one," she said.

Jack gave his wife a wink, relieved to see her relax a

little. The doctor went on with the questioning.

"Can you tell me today's date and what day of the week it is?"

This time, Helen hesitated. "Oh, dear. I think it's . . . Tuesday?"

"And the date?"

"Um . . . well, I'm almost sure it's still September. Or maybe it's October now." Helen started to blink rapidly. Perhaps she, like her husband, found the intensely bright light disturbing.

"Which one do you think it is?"

After a long silence, she gave a random guess. "October."

"Today is Wednesday, September 23."

Helen sighed. "I could always recall the date in a heartbeat, but not since I retired."

Dr. Miller looked up from his paperwork. "Helen, I know you've had a remarkable career. How long since you retired?"

"Let's see . . . a month or two? No, maybe it's been a little longer than that."

"How much longer?" Now Dr. Miller pulled at the tip of his beard with one hand, waiting for Helen's response.

She shrugged. "I—I don't remember. Jack?"

"The end of last year," he said to the doctor.

"Ah. How do you like retirement, Helen?"

"It's not too bad. Though I guess it's a little boring. It's kind of strange, too... I don't feel like myself." Helen lifted both hands as if to inspect them and started picking at her index fingernail.

"It's a big adjustment," Dr. Miller said.

"Oh, yes. A big adjustment," she parroted, nodding her head but still keeping her eyes trained on her manicure. To Jack's surprise, Helen started to cry. "I have a lot of things I want to do, but I haven't been able to get organized. I wake up in the mornings and I—I feel so sad, and . . . and useless. I can't find the energy to do anything." Large silent tears streaked down her cheeks.

Jack felt in his pockets for a handkerchief but came up empty. Dr. Miller reached over to the credenza behind his desk for a box of tissues, which he passed to Helen. She pulled out the top one and honked into it noisily.

The conversation continued for a few minutes longer, during which the doctor also ascertained that Jack had been working long hours, leaving Helen alone with a great deal of empty time to fill. He jotted notes on a prescription pad and addressed them both.

"I'm going to prescribe Zoloft for Helen," the doctor said. "I believe this may be depression."

The two Winokurs exchanged glances. Though they knew many people on anti-depressants, neither of them had ever tried the drugs before.

"It's common for feelings of depression and anxiety to follow retirement," Dr. Miller said. "Retirement is one of the biggest transitions in the life of an adult. When we work hard every day in our chosen profession, our career defines us to a large extent. It can be a tough challenge, losing that sense of identity and having to reinvent yourself."

"But what about the memory loss?" Jack wondered if they'd become sidetracked.

"I was getting to that," Dr. Miller said. "Depression can manifest itself in a number of different ways, but memory loss and confusion are both common symptoms. I'm thinking that may be what's going on with Helen."

"Really?" said Jack.

"We won't know for a while. It takes time for antidepressants to work. But let's give it a try."

At last, some good news. Jack had felt as if he and Helen were skidding out of control on black ice. Now the vehicle had come to a safe stop. His pulse still raced, and he couldn't yet assess if they would emerge unscathed, but at least he could hope that Helen's memory issues might be temporary and reversible.

Dr. Miller gave them the prescription with further instructions on how to take the medication and what to expect. Jack prayed the drug would have the desired effect.

It did not. Her memory loss continued to worsen on the Zoloft, and she also experienced side effects of fatigue, insomnia, and occasional dizziness. After two months, Dr. Miller weaned her off the drug and started her on a different antidepressant.

"Don't be discouraged," he said to husband and wife in a reassuring tone. "Treatment of depression is tricky. It can take time to find the right medication and the right dosage. This is a common situation."

Helen felt even worse on the second drug, suffering pounding headaches and other incapacitating side effects.

After several more weeks in which the symptoms subsided only a small amount, the doctor supervised gradual weaning off this medication as well, concluding that depression did not appear to be the root cause of her problems.

Jack gave up the graphic design studio he'd rented for years and started working from home to keep a closer watch on his wife. He said nothing about Helen's condition to their two sons, Michael in Baltimore, and Paul in Los Angeles. He didn't know how to frame it to the boys.

He had another reason for maintaining silence. Jack feared, irrationally, that if he acknowledged the truth about Helen's behavior, the disclosure would somehow make it more real. He remembered when his own mother died many years ago, and his father called him with the news. Jack wanted to shout, "No. No. Take it back," as though his father's words had killed his mother instead of the fatal aneurysm that erupted in her brain without warning.

Jack did, however, inform both sons that he'd moved his design business into the house, positioning it as a cost-saving strategy since the retired Helen no longer generated a second income. Neither one questioned the move or had reason yet to suspect their mother had a serious health problem.

The older son, Michael, had troubles of his own. He'd separated from his wife Anne the previous year. Though the breakup of a marriage never came as happy news, Anne was a difficult and negative person who didn't get along well with anyone in the Winokur family, not merely her husband. As a result, Jack and Helen tried to view it as a positive move and remained hopeful that Michael might someday find a more fulfilling relationship. The split proved tough on their teenage son Scott, but arguably not as tough as the years he'd spent living in a toxic environment with two parents forever at loggerheads.

Paul had not married until well into his thirties and had a two-year-old son, a five-month-old daughter, and a wife named Elise, whom Jack and Helen adored. Elise taught at an inner-city elementary school, and Paul held an administrative position at a Los Angeles counseling center that provided affordable mental health services to those in need. They were both busy people doing good work. Between their jobs and the care of their small children, however, they had little time for cross-country trips to Rhode Island.

There had been many occasions when Jack wished his children lived closer. But for the present, the distance shielded them from Helen's problems, which Jack preferred—at least until they figured out the cause of her memory loss.

They had ruled out depression. Now, Helen's concerns seemed to run in the direction of a physical cause. Every day she posed a different theory: a sleep disorder, vitamin deficiency, stroke, brain tumor.

"Maybe I've got the disease that folksinger had," she said one day. "Woody... Woody..." She strained to remember the name.

"Guthrie."

"Yes."

"Helen, he had a genetic condition called Huntington's disease. I think it presents with physical symptoms at a much younger age, and it's a hereditary condition. Nobody in your family has had it."

"Oh," she said, looking disappointed that Jack had debunked her theory.

Dr. Miller referred them to a specialist for further exploration. This time there would be no softball questions lobbed by the family doctor. Instead, Helen underwent a comprehensive battery of cognitive tests, along with more bloodwork, a thorough physical examination, and an MRI.

Helen and Jack received the devastating diagnosis of mild Alzheimer's dementia. She gasped upon hearing this and started to cry, her shoulders shaking. Jack kept his own emotions in check for his wife's sake, giving her arm a consoling squeeze as he asked the specialist if it wasn't unusual for a woman of seventy-one to be thus diagnosed. Helen seemed too old for early-onset Alzheimer's and too young for the other kind.

Speaking in an apologetic tone, the doctor assured them he had diagnosed many patients in their late sixties or early seventies with the disease. Jack nodded in a calm, matter-of-fact way, hoping his modulated reaction might somehow lessen the impact of the bad news.

The Winokurs left the office armed with prescriptions, a stack of pamphlets, and referrals to programs and services from which Helen might benefit. That evening over dinner, she became angry and dismissive about the doctor's findings.

"He might say it's mild Alzheimer's, but he can't know that for certain, can he, Jack? I've read that they can't be sure until they do an autopsy after you're dead. And even if he's right, I'm not too bad most of the time. I mean, *mild* is good, right? I think I'm doing pretty well, don't you?"

"Of course, darling," he said, to reassure himself as much as Helen.

"Okay, I did get lost that day at . . . at the . . . you know, the place with the stores. But only the one time."

Jack found it interesting that the mall incident with Marge from several months back remained entrenched in Helen's memory. Since then, she'd been lost several more times on walks right in the neighborhood, but she had no recollection of the more recent episodes. Once, a neighbor had to bring her home. Another time, a policeman patrolling the boulevard rescued her from her wandering. Last week, Helen managed to find her own way back to the house after an apparent period of memory loss.

"I was worried about you," Jack said when she returned, collapsing into a chair the moment she entered the kitchen. "You've been gone two hours." Helen never took two-hour walks.

"I don't know why you should be worried. I'm fine."

Woefully overdressed for the warm afternoon, Helen wore a thick cotton hoodie that clung to her with dark patches of perspiration spreading under the arms. Jack took in Helen's flushed cheeks, the moisture that dampened her brow, the expression of alarm in her green eyes. He thought she didn't seem fine at all. She appeared to be on the brink of physical and emotional collapse.

The memory issues weren't the only thing, Jack reflected. Helen's demeanor had changed too. One day he had an epiphany as he poured a cup of leftover coffee from yesterday's pot and heated it in the microwave. It'd occurred to him before that rewarmed coffee always tasted muted and bland. You wouldn't call it downright undrinkable—yet it lacked the robust flavor and complexity of a fresh-brewed cup. And it dawned on him, with horror, that his wife's personality these days could be likened to a cup of reheated coffee. Not bitter or unpalatable . . . but one-dimensional, flat.

Yet, a few days after the Alzheimer's diagnosis, Helen seemed improved—more upbeat, more energetic, sharper. When Jack emerged from his home office for a mid-morning coffee refill, he found her sitting in the kitchen with the pamphlets from the doctor fanned out across the table. She glanced back and forth between the pamphlets and the screen of her laptop, also perched on the table.

"Jack, listen to this," she said, her manner bright and attentive. "I've been reading about all the things I can do to keep my brain sharp. Like chess, and puzzles, and memory games. And there are, you know, pills I can take. Not only the ones the doctor prescribed, but vitamins and supplements and things. I'm making notes right now on what I need. I'll order the pills online and start taking them every day." Her long, pale pink fingernails danced on the computer keys with a rhythmic click as she composed her notes.

"Darling, that's a wonderful idea," said Jack.

"Dancing, too. Did you know dancing is good for the mind?"

"I did not know that."

"Well, it is. It's one of the best things you can do for cognition. They did a study about it. To follow dance steps, you have to keep creating new . . . new . . . I can't remember the word, but they're like pathways or roads in the brain. When you drive on those 'roads,' it keeps your brain firing. And if you can keep your brain from . . . from . . . what?" Her expression darkened. "Damn. I lost my train of thought."

"It'll come back to you. I've been doing a little research of my own. There's something called the mind diet, where you eat certain foods that help with brain function."

Helen made a face. "Which foods?"

"Most of them are things you already eat: salads, vegetables, berries, nuts, poultry and fish, olive oil . . . oh, and wine," he said.

"Sort of like the Mediterranean diet."

"Yes . . . but there are some no-no's, too."

"Such as?" she asked, her tone apprehensive.

"Things you dislike anyway: red meat, pastries, fried foods, processed snacks. But you're also supposed to avoid dairy."

Cheese and yogurt had always been favorites of Helen's, foods she enjoyed eating every day. "Oh, dear," she said. "I'm not sure life is worth living without cheese." She gave him a sad smile.

"I need to do further research, but I think goat cheese

and yogurt are safer than the products that come from cows. Maybe sheep dairy is all right too, but I'm not certain. I promise to check into it for you."

"Oh, thank you, darling. I'm going to fight this," she said with a defiant toss of her silvery blond hair. "We've been through some rough patches before. We always find our way through things together. If I try very hard, and you help me with my memory, I'll have lots of good years left. *We'll* have lots of good years—won't we, Jack?" Now her green eyes clouded over with worry, and her tone sounded a touch less confident. He nodded and wrapped her in a reassuring embrace.

Helen had always said, "Knowledge is power." In her advertising work, whenever she met with a new client, she insisted on learning everything she could about the company and the products or services they offered, rather than blithely accepting the sugar-coated sales pitch. She demanded to know the weaknesses along with the strengths. The more she knew, the better equipped she'd be to strategize the best positioning for the company. Now Jack understood that his wife would tackle Alzheimer's with the same zest with which she had created successful marketing campaigns.

Knowledge is power. After months of uneasy speculation and the initial misdiagnosis, Helen at last knew the nature of the specific threat facing her. Now she could come up with a plan. It dawned on Jack that his wife had lacked a sense of purpose and intellectual focus since her retirement. Helen was back in the saddle with something important to concentrate on. A new challenge. A new campaign.

Her good spirits continued through the evening. And when they climbed into bed that night, she snuggled up to Jack, first nuzzling her face into his chest and moving up to his throat and then to his mouth to bestow slow, sweet kisses. This had not happened in a long while. Jack responded to her overture, hopeful at this turn of events. As he started to explore her still firm body under the covers, he found himself wondering if the doctors had been mistaken. Maybe some rare virus had been affecting her brain all this time, and now she'd started to emerge from the illness. Stranger things had happened.

All at once, she said, "Oh, Jack. My diaphragm. I forgot to put it in."

Through his desire, he laughed softly at this. Even her old sense of humor had returned. But when she sat up and started foraging through the top drawer of her bedside table, Jack realized with a sinking feeling that she had not been joking.

"Darling, it's okay. We don't need the diaphragm."

"No, no, we agreed—" She snapped her fingers. "Wait. You must have one of those—you know, one of those thingies to cover yourself with . . . "

"A condom. A rubber."

"Yes, that's it."

"I don't have any condoms. We haven't needed birth control for years. Trust me, it'll be fine."

"No, we mustn't be careless about this," she said with an insistent shake of the head. She jumped out of bed. "I need to pee."

When Helen returned a couple of minutes later, she'd

forgotten all about the romantic encounter. She picked up a book on the nightstand and opened it to the book-marked page, puzzling over it as she attempted to focus. "I don't remember these characters," she said. "This isn't what I was reading."

It appeared to Jack that she had spoken to herself, not to him. His presence had become irrelevant.

Helen dropped the book with a thud and rummaged through a pile of dog-eared catalogs, selecting one at random. It was a collection of cheesy holiday knick-knacks from last year, but she didn't seem to care. She leafed through it noisily.

Every turn of the page set Jack's nerves further on edge. He found himself skidding on black ice again, but this time down a treacherous hill that left him no opportunity to regain control.

Jack didn't want her to sense the panic he felt building inside him. He rolled over on his side, turned his back to Helen, and pretended to be asleep.

8

REMEDIES UP HER SLEEVE

Klutz *extraordinaire* that I am, I managed to spill coffee all over myself a few minutes after Sarah and I joined Ma in her room at Tropical Gardens. In my haste to rub out the stain with a damp paper towel, I scratched my forearm with a broken fingernail, drawing blood.

When she saw me bleeding, Ma gave me a disapproving frown and said, "Barbara, that's disgusting. Blood makes me sick."

I felt absurdly wounded by her lack of compassion. As a woman over fifty, how could I expect a mother with Stage Six AD to kiss my boo-boo and make it better? I couldn't expect it, but I could still *want* it.

I had plenty of time to make a quick trip home to change my top and return for the Luau Sunday celebration. I left Sarah in charge. As I drove home, I kept checking the scratch on my arm and noted that the bleeding had slowed to a trickle. It caused me to recollect an incident from my childhood, something I knew I must add to Ma's binder.

At home, I traded my coffee-stained gray cotton shell for a white one. Glancing at the clock, I decided I could spare another ten or fifteen minutes to write down my thoughts while they were fresh in my mind. I went to the study, pulled out a clean sheet of cloud paper, and wrote:

Memories of Dolly: 1974

Dolly Gordon is serving as toastmaster at a banquet to honor the retiring artistic director of Providence Players. Since her husband is out of town, she will take her teenage daughter Vicky in his place. However, when the babysitter for nine-year-old Barbara cancels at the last minute, Dolly offers Vicky double pay to stay home with her younger sister. Vicky threatens to run away from home and leave Barbara unattended if forced to do this.

I laughed aloud at this last sentence. Some things never changed.

Dolly relents, departing for the banquet with both children in tow. Barbara is too young to understand most of the jokes and speeches, but she can see that her mother is a relaxed and polished toastmaster who receives frequent laughs and applause from her audience. At the end of the evening, Barbara bolts from her seat to run and embrace her mother, falling and scraping an elbow along the way. Dolly folds the girl in a comforting embrace and leads her to her own seat at the head of the table, where she tends to her daughter's wound with soothing ointment and Band-Aids.

Hot tears pricked my eyes as I recalled this scene with a fuller and fresher appreciation for the tenderness and the significance of my mother's actions. Even with the last-minute change of plans, even with the rush to drive to the banquet, even with her responsibilities as emcee of the event, Ma remembered to stash first-aid remedies up her sleeve—or to be literal, inside her sequin clutch bag—for her accident-prone younger daughter.

I added these observations to the entry before heading back to Tropical Gardens.

9

I WANT ONE OF THOSE

Sarah opened the door to the family lounge for her grandmother. Dolly glided along on the walker, her stuffed Scottie dog in tow. Inside the lounge, a dark-haired man spoke in a loud, agitated tone to a fragile old lady in a wheelchair. He faced the woman with his back to Sarah and Dolly, so he couldn't see them as they walked in on his rant.

"Don't deny it, sweetheart. We all know what a god-damn whore you are," he shouted in an affected British accent. "You've been cheating on Jimmy for the last twenty years. Not only with strangers . . . with the husbands of your closest friends, and your children's teachers, and even your grandchildren's camp counselors, for Christ's sake. And you wonder why no one in your family will have anything to do with you."

The bizarre harangue shocked Sarah, and she couldn't think what to do next. "Grammy, let's get out of here." She whispered this into Dolly's ear, hoping the raving madman wouldn't overhear her. "We'll find someplace else to sit."

"*I can't hear you,*" Dolly said in a booming voice that could likely be heard across the river in neighboring East Providence. The man who'd been screaming wheeled around to face them.

What happened next stunned Sarah even more than his outrageous remarks. Sarah almost reeled back when she found herself face to face with the most gorgeous guy ever. Drop-dead gorgeous. She took in his wavy dark hair, piercing blue eyes, prominent cheekbones, and perfect aquiline nose. Perfect *everything*. She guessed him to be in his early twenties. When he flashed his dazzling white smile at her, she expected to melt into the floor.

"Wait—no. It's not what you think. I was just rehearsing a scene in front of my grandmother."

"Uh—sure," Sarah said, skeptical.

"It's true. You must think I'm an asshole."

She was thinking, instead, that this guy was scary-cute. She noticed he held some sort of book in his hand. A script.

"Here, read this. Second paragraph from the top." He thrust the script in her face, and she scanned it. Sarah found the tirade he'd just delivered, printed on the middle of the page.

"Oh—I guess you *were* rehearsing," she said, relieved to learn she would not be obliged to flee the company of this Adonis. "Come on, Grammy. I think it'll be okay." She led Dolly over to one of the couches and helped her take a seat, arranging a tropical throw pillow behind her grandmother's head.

"Hi, I'm Scott. I must've been damn good if you didn't realize I was acting. I'm a senior at Tisch."

"What's Tisch?" she asked, thinking there was no false modesty with this guy.

He didn't bother to hide his surprise. "You don't know

Tisch? It's part of NYU. It's like Harvard for actors. I guess you're visiting your grandmother, too. You must be here for Luau Sunday, same as me. They ought to rename it Grandchildren's Sunday."

"Yep. This is my first time visiting here. It's nicer than I expected. Oh, I'm Sarah. My grandmother is Dolly."

"And this is Helen." Scott gestured toward his own grandmother. "She doesn't talk anymore. But deep inside her head, I think she knows what's going on. You knew I was acting just then . . . right, Nana?" He leaned in and planted a light kiss on the top of her head.

It seemed to Sarah as if the young man had to summon his best acting skills to appear cheerful and lighthearted in the presence of this pitiable old woman.

"I tried to show that woman my doggie, but she won't talk to him either," Dolly complained, examining Helen with curiosity. She addressed the woman in the wheel-chair. "Hey, lady, what's your problem? Why don't you answer us?"

Sarah removed the stuffed dog from the walker basket and handed it to Dolly. "Grammy, Scott has the same name as your dog."

This concept perplexed Dolly. "I don't understand how he got my dog's name." Dolly looked back and forth from the canine Scottie to the human one, attempting to figure out this puzzle.

Sarah remembered now. Her mother had mentioned a man she saw here every day tending to a patient with bad dementia. "I think my mom is friends with your dad."

"Not my dad, my grandfather."

"Oh, right. What's the deal with this play?" She pointed at the script.

"It's the fall production at my school. A student-written drama called *Instability*."

"What's it about?"

He explained that the action took place a hundred years in the future, in a world where cancer no longer existed, and people lived to be a hundred and fifty years old. But climate change had wreaked havoc with everything, and as a result, nobody on the planet was having much fun.

"Sounds like an interesting story."

"To tell you the truth, it's kind of dumb. But futuristic dystopian drama is way popular nowadays. I've been cast in one of the main roles, a character named Robert," he said. "It's very challenging because I'll be playing against type."

"What do you mean?"

"Most times, they give me the romantic leading man roles, but Robert is supposed to be an old, funny-looking dude. But he's witty and sarcastic and all."

Sarah nodded.

Then Scott said, "Hey. It would be a big help if you could read lines with me sometime."

"Sure, I guess I can do that," she said, feigning nonchalance as if she received offers from handsome men all day long. "So, you're training to be a professional actor."

"Yeah. Tisch has an incredible program." Scott's blue eyes shone with enthusiasm. "Lots of famous people have gone there. Woody Allen, James Franco, Lady Gaga..."

He had a deep, sexy voice that made Sarah wonder if

he sang as well as acted. "Wow—that's cool. It must be nice to know what you want to be."

"Well, you're young yet."

For a moment, the girl felt chagrined by Scott's condescension, but she recovered her composure. "Not so young. I'll be a junior at Classical High this fall."

Scott did the math. "That makes you, what? Sixteen? Seventeen?"

"Sixteen. This is the year I have to figure out where I'm applying to college," Sarah said, to emphasize she played in an arena of mature decision-making. "Ugh. My mom's already driving me crazy with that. She gave me a spreadsheet to fill out."

"A spreadsheet?" Scott gave her an incredulous look.

Sarah explained how her mother had entered the names of the colleges that she liked (*she* meaning her mom, not Sarah), and she had then tasked Sarah with listing positive and negative aspects of each school in a series of vertical columns extending across the spreadsheet.

"Jesus."

"I *know*. I haven't decided what I want to be, the way you have—but I know who I want to be *like*." Her dark, thoughtful eyes peered at him warmly from beneath a soft fringe of light brown bangs. "Have you heard of Beryl Markham?"

Scott hesitated. "Sorry, no."

Sarah felt pleased with herself for stumbling onto a topic about which she knew more than this confident young actor. "She was, like, a racehorse trainer in Africa, and later she became a bush pilot. Beryl was the first woman to fly solo across the Atlantic from east to west. She wasn't afraid to do anything. Also, she was beautiful and had affairs with famous men."

"Then, you want to be a horse trainer . . . or a pilot? Or maybe you just want to have a lot of hot affairs?" They both laughed.

"Oh, none of those things. I mean, that's not the point. Beryl's more of a role model. I want to be like her, living life and having all kinds of adventures. Not like my mother."

"What's wrong with your mother?"

"She's a nervous wreck . . . always worrying about stuff. 'Don't do this; you might fail the exam. Don't do that; you'll get in an accident.' She's basically a huge scaredy-cat. My aunt Vicky calls her 'Chicken.' It started as a nickname when they were little girls, kind of a pet name, but it turned out to be like crazy accurate."

Sarah continued, "And that's not the only funny thing to do with her name. My mom's full name is Barbara Gordon. Did you know that's the real-life identity of Batgirl? It's so ironic she has the same name as this cool, really brave crime-fighter."

"I never followed Batgirl. Isn't that more of a chick thing? So, you and your mom don't get along?"

"Oh, that's not it. Don't get me wrong. Mom's a good person, and she's sweet. My folks split up when I was little, and she's had to deal with being a single parent all these years. But I don't want to be frightened of life the way she is. Women like Beryl Markham aren't afraid of being single, or divorced, or . . . well, anything."

"My parents are divorced too. Since I was thirteen."

Sarah nodded in empathy. "Do you have a role model?"

"Well, for acting, too many people to name. But my real-life role models are . . . my grandparents."

Sarah looked over at Helen, slumped in her wheelchair, and felt surprised by Scott's revelation.

"I don't mean now. I'm talking about how they were a long time ago," Scott said. "I used to spend summers with them at their place near the beach in Narragansett. Nana and Grandpop always had a great time together. We all had a great time. Everybody liked and—I guess, *respected*—each other. Sometimes they would let me collaborate with them on their advertising projects, and we had a blast." He paused, then shook his head and hunched up his shoulders as if shaking off an unpleasant memory. "Nothing like that ever happened with my parents. They were too busy fighting to act like a real family . . . or to pay much attention to me, for that matter."

"That's sad."

"Yeah, well . . . Once they got divorced, I had to stay home with my mom because she would have been too lonely spending summers by herself. Nana started to— you know, have problems around the same time—so our visits together at the beach probably would've come to an end no matter what."

At this point, Jack walked into the room and bellowed a general "hello" to the group, startling Dolly, who had dozed off next to Helen.

Dolly opened her eyes wide and fixed her gaze on Scott. "You're pretty," she smiled, pointing at him.

Scott beamed back and took the compliment in stride.

"I see your grandma hasn't lost her good judgment."

Sarah knew her grandmother used to work in the-atre, and it had been one of her great loves. Five years ago, Dolly would've launched into an animated dis-cussion with Scott—firing questions about his acting experience, exploring what types of roles he preferred, and comparing which playwrights they most admired. But now, the best she could manage was a two-word generic compliment. Still, Scott didn't seem to mind being stroked.

"Hey, Grandpop." He greeted Jack with a high-five.

"How's everyone today?" Jack placed a kiss on Helen's forehead.

"Wonderful. I love you," Dolly said with a crooked smile. Jack patted her shoulder in response, then shook hands with Sarah.

"I'm Jack. You must be Barbara's daughter. She told me you'd be here today. You resemble your mother." Sarah had a taller and lankier build, with darker hair that hung long and straight, but she had inherited Barbara's lovely brown eyes.

"Nice to meet you," Sarah said, polite but less than thrilled with the comparison.

"Has Nana been sleeping for long?" Jack asked Scott.

"Not long. But most of the time, she's been acting out of it."

"Let's take her for a walk on the grounds. It's beautiful outdoors."

"Can't you take her? I'm kinda busy." Scott stole a glance at Sarah.

"'*Kinda busy*'? Scott, I thought you came to visit with us," said Jack. "Take a short walk with us. I scarcely see you these days."

"Oh, all *right*." Scott did not bother to hide his irritation. "Rehearse with you later if you're still around," he said to Sarah.

"Uh . . . sure, why not." She tried to sound as casual as possible.

"Bye-bye, Mister Pretty," Dolly called after him.

Right after the two men had wheeled Helen out of the room, with Scott the last to leave, Dolly pointed in his direction and informed her granddaughter, "I want one of those."

"So do I, Grammy," said the teenager with a dreamy sigh. "So do I."

Sarah's cellphone buzzed with a text message. Her best friend Dory.

—*My stepmother made chocolate chip cookies and I just ate seven. I hate myself.*

Another child of divorce, Dory was in Connecticut for the summer with her father and his second family.

—*Don't beat yourself up. I ate ice cream and Cheez-Its for lunch at my aunt's yesterday.*

—*You can afford it. My thighs are already expanding.*

Dory had the face of a cheerleader, pretty in a conventional way, with light wavy hair and a slim waist—but she constantly berated herself for her pear-shaped body. Sarah texted back:

—*Stop it. You're gorgeous.*

But she knew it wouldn't make any difference.

—*I'm stuffing myself out of sexual deprivation. I miss Nick.*

—*At least you have a boyfriend.*

—*Nothing going on with you?*

—*Well, I did meet a GORGEOUS boy named Scott today. Acting student from Tisch.*

—*What's Tisch?*

—*It's like Harvard but for actors. I'm gonna rehearse with him.*

—*Nick's driving down to see me next weekend. If we don't get some time alone, I'll either die of frustration or gain 15 pounds.*

Nick and Dory had been going out for a year now, and things had gotten physical and close. They even planned to apply to the same colleges in the fall. Dory recently described herself to Sarah as a "TV"—explaining, "That's short for Technical Virgin."

Sarah had said, "I'm a POV."

"What's that?"

"Plain Old Virgin. Boring."

Incredibly boring.

10

THE RULE OF NOCDAR

Yesterday they served apple pie to Ma in celebration of July Fourth, and they forgot to give her sugar-free. I'd have to speak to the staff and remind them of her diabetes.

If they couldn't get Ma's diet right, maybe they were making mistakes with her medications too. Oh, God, another thing to worry about. She had so many prescriptions.

In the mornings, she took Namenda, Simvastatin, Losartan, Synthroid, Furosemide, Digoxin, Lexapro, Metoprolol, Metamucil, Protonix, and a multivitamin for good measure. Evenings were simpler: Aricept, more Namenda, Coumadin, and Metformin. I had listed all her meds in the binder with the dosages prescribed by Dr. Sam.

When she started requiring help with her meds a few years back, I almost needed a seminar to keep all the pills straight. These folks purported to be professionals, however. Accurate medication delivery should've been a walk on the beach to them.

But then I recalled the rule of NOCDAR.

My friend Red and I, like-minded in our view that incompetence reigned in almost every area of life, often lamented that No One Can Do Anything Right, which we shortened to the acronym NOCDAR.

I'd walk the staff through the medication list again, to be on the safe side . . . and the dietary restrictions as well. Carol and I had planned a rare overnight getaway to the Cape on Saturday, and I didn't want to be worrying about this.

But three days later, on Friday morning, I found another reason for concern over the weekend plans.

Sarah stomped into the kitchen and said, "Mom, listen to this. Dad just told me he's staying in Boston all weekend and he won't be able to see me. I can't believe he waited till this morning to cancel our plans." She paced the kitchen, agitated.

"Why can't you take a bus up to Boston and visit Dad there? Does he have to work?" I asked. Richard now split his time between his house in Providence and a pied-a-terre near his new office in Boston.

Sarah stopped pacing long enough to roll her eyes for dramatic effect. "I think this is about a woman." A couple of weeks ago, Sarah had intimated that her father had girlfriends in both cities. I avoided discussing Richard's social life with her, but not only had he upset his daughter, he'd thrown a monkey-wrench in my plans as well.

I called Richard's cell and, as usual, he didn't pick up. Whenever instructed to "leave a message at the tone," I experienced a sensation of mild panic that inevitably led to voicemail diarrhea—running at the mouth and overexplaining myself. I recognized when I did it, but I couldn't seem to stop.

"Richard, I don't understand what's going on. Why

can't Sarah spend the weekend with you in Boston? I'm supposed to go away Saturday night. This is the one time in months that I made plans to get away now that Ma is settled in her new place. I'll have to cancel my trip, and it's not fair to my friend or me. Besides, our hotel booking for Saturday is nonrefundable. And Sarah is so disappointed. Call me, and we can discuss this."

Ten minutes later, my phone buzzed with a text from Richard. How typical of my ex to dodge a bullet this way, avoiding direct confrontation.

—It won't work out for this weekend. Something came up. Why can't she stay with Vicky or someone? If not, I'll pay for your hotel cancellation. Tell Sarah I'll make it up to her.

I felt like a cornered animal, my pulse racing. It was just like Richard to throw money at every problem. Write the ex-wife another check, buy your daughter the latest iPhone. Adding insult to injury, I felt certain Sarah had nailed it. The "something" that came up must be a woman.

I had to say this much for Richard, though. He'd become less dishonest. Back in the days of our marriage, he would have lied straight away and blamed it on work.

This spotlight on Richard's current two-timing and his latest act of selfishness hurtled me back in time to the still painful memory of the final deal-breaker in our short marriage.

A storm had raged all night, with lightning bolts splitting the sky and thunder loud enough to frazzle my nerves. Even louder than the thunderclaps were my baby daughter's relentless screams. She had a high fever and what turned out to be her first ear infection, and she wailed in abject misery.

I tried in vain to console her and bring the fever under control while attempting to call Richard, who had stayed at the office for a late meeting. Not unusual for an investment banker. When I failed to reach him on his cell, I called his office phone and let it ring. After maybe fifty rings, one of his colleagues picked up the phone. When I asked for Richard, he put me on hold while he checked around the office or at least pretended to check. He came back on the line and said, "He's not here."

"Not there?" I asked. "He's supposed to be at a meeting."

"I guess he must have stepped out," came the anonymous colleague's lame reply. "I'll tell him you called."

I wanted to believe Richard's story about working late, but I knew in my heart he was lying. It had happened too many times before, though never when I'd needed him with such urgency. I'd grown accustomed to that nervous roiling in my gut, that awful feeling of not knowing my husband's whereabouts or when he might come home. Sometimes I felt I'd prefer to be alone than keep experiencing this wretched anxiety.

I'd also come to realize that any woman who had a suspicious nature or who suffered from low self-esteem should never marry an investment banker. They routinely worked past midnight or later when closing a deal, making it difficult for an insecure spouse to distinguish the cheating from the legitimate late working nights.

Richard arrived home at two-thirty in the morning to a crying wife and daughter. He ignored our unhappiness, grousing instead about his late night in the office. It was obvious he'd been drinking, though, and—it didn't get any more clichéd than this—I noticed a lipstick stain near the top button of his shirt, a dark purple shade I had never worn in my life.

"Seriously?" I said, jabbing at the stain with my index finger. "Do you still want to stick to the late meeting excuse?"

Richard glanced at himself in the mirror, inspecting the stain. Then, to my total disbelief, he broke out into the song, "Lipstick on your collar, told a tale on yoooo-uuu." He slurred the words in a deep voice meant to mimic Elvis. Maybe it seemed amusing to him in his drunken and disheveled state, but to me, every word sounded like a cruel mockery.

When I tearfully reported this encounter to Vicky on the phone the next morning, she said, "Elvis, huh. Well, I guess you couldn't expect him to mimic Connie Francis," referring to the vocalist who had first popularized the song. She added, "I'd like to kill the fucking prick."

That night marked the beginning of the end for Richard and me.

In the Tropical Gardens lounge on Friday afternoon, still smarting from my ex's latest effrontery, I watched as Jack massaged lotion into Helen's reddened and brittle-looking hands and forearms with a gentle touch. They too must have had their share of arguments during their long marriage. At least the angry days were over for them as a couple. Every day as Jack fed her and sang to her and tended to her needs without even a glimmer of a response, I marveled at how he still managed to treat her with such tenderness. And I thought nobody was more alone than that man.

Lately, observing his patient ministrations to Helen, I'd experienced a feeling of—how to describe it? Envy? Regret? Yearning? Maybe a combination of all three. I sensed something missing that I'd never missed before, and I felt compelled to find it. But first, I would need to figure out what "it" might be.

11

THE CHOWDER CHALLENGE

In June 2007, at the age of eleven, Scott Winokur flew up from Baltimore to spend his fourth summer in a row with Helen and Jack, his dad's parents, at their cottage in Narragansett Pier, Rhode Island. His grandparents commuted at least once a week to their Providence offices, but most days, they worked from the cottage or sometimes took it easy. Those four summers with Nana and Grandpop, from the ages of eight through eleven, remained the happiest ever for Scott, who ranked them higher even than the subsequent years at theatre camp.

Every year they rented the same little house. It had an ideal location, about a ten-minute walk to the beach.

"This place is no mansion, but it has everything a beach house should have," said Nana.

"Like what?" Scott asked, curious.

"Well, let's see. For starters, old linoleum floors that feel gritty under your feet with the sand from five summers ago."

Scott knew without her saying so that they'd all be expected to build on this. "Clammy bedsheets," the boy said.

Nana clapped her hands together in approval.

"That wonderful musty, salty smell you only find this close to the ocean," said Grandpop.

Nana's turn again. "No dishwasher."

"Why is it good *not* to have a dishwasher?" Scott asked. A reasonable question.

"Much easier. It provides an excuse to eat on paper plates and then throw them out," said Grandpop. The whole green movement hadn't yet gained full momentum in 2007.

"You are brilliant. We are brilliant," Nana said with satisfaction.

Scott's mother, Anne, disliked visiting the Winokur summer digs because of the very shortcomings that Jack and Helen regarded as assets. Scott preferred that his parents stay in Baltimore anyway. He liked having Nana and Grandpop to himself. He didn't bother telling his grandparents how his mom felt about the Narragansett cottage, though he suspected they already knew.

"Who wants some posh, air-conditioned, fancy-ass place where you always have to worry about tracking in sand and dirt?" Jack said, further supporting their case. "That would suck all the joy out of summer."

The rest of the year, in Providence, his grandparents lived in a house off the boulevard that *could* accurately be described as posh, air-conditioned, and "fancy-ass." It shone as an example of stunning contemporary architecture. The house had an artful design with vaulted ceilings and big custom windows in odd geometric shapes.

Though not one of the largest homes in Providence's fashionable East Side, it ranked as one of the most interesting, featured in the design pages of two local publications when Scott's grandparents first built it. Framed copies of the stories still hung on the wall. Scott found it fascinating to study the photos of Nana and Grandpop in those articles—seated together in the big open-plan living room, working at the granite-topped kitchen island, and looking way younger than their present-day selves. Younger, and yet very much the same.

All three Winokurs enjoyed the Narragansett town beach. They liked to wait until the day-trippers had departed in the late afternoon when Jack and Scott could boogie-board in the cool, clear ocean without the constant worry of plowing into other swimmers. Scott liked the way his grandfather wore boardshorts and fitted t-shirts that set him apart from the other older men at the beach. Jack's curly hair had hardly thinned at all and still looked more dark than gray, especially when his head got wet from ducking under waves.

Helen seldom ventured into the water unless the weather was sizzling and, even then, only under calm conditions. She preferred relaxing in a beach chair with a good book, wearing one of her brightly colored tank suits, her shoulder-length silver-blond hair tied back with a matching ribbon.

Even more than the beach, Scott treasured the intimate family rituals they repeated every summer. Visits to the oceanside clam shack remained a favorite. Scott couldn't wait to eat lunch there, although they didn't find time for this until their third day in Narragansett.

They took their seats at a well-worn picnic table as Jack distributed Styrofoam bowls of steaming chowder and a big basket of fries. The day was breezy, with more clouds than sun, and the gunmetal gray expanse of white-capped water appeared bleak yet luminous at the same time. Helen shivered and pulled her red windbreaker tightly around her.

"New England chowder is still the best," Scott said. Every summer, they had the same spirited discussion. "The cream and butter and flour make it rich and delicious." He held up a spoonful of thick, creamy white soup and slurped it down, licking the spoon so as not to miss a drop.

"Those ingredients also make it *fattening*," said Helen. She always opted for Rhode Island chowder, a local recipe that used clear clam broth without the addition of thickeners or dairy products. "Clear chowder is the healthiest, it's the simplest, and it's the best because you can taste the clams and onions better."

Jack shook his head. "Nope. Manhattan chowder is healthy too. But the tomato broth gives it more balance, less of a fishy aftertaste."

"Red chowder should be illegal," Helen said, standing her ground.

"Clear chowder is the color of yesterday's dirty bathwater," countered Jack.

Scott found this hilarious.

And so it went.

"Is everyone up for the chowder challenge again this year?" asked Scott. Every summer, the boy conducted an informal survey of local chowder enthusiasts to determine the most popular type: red, white, or clear. He did not make the results public until the end of the season.

"Bring it on," said his grandfather. "The contest begins right here, right now."

"At this point, it's a dead heat—as usual," Helen added.

On the following day, the weather improved, and the ocean sparkled with sapphire brilliance beneath a cloudless sky. Gulls shrieked and soared exuberantly overhead as if in celebration of the spectacular summer morning. Scott and his grandparents set out on a hike along the rocky shoreline off Hazard Avenue.

"Grandpop, did you check the tide chart?" the boy asked as he hopped from boulder to boulder across the rough weathered granite.

"Yes. The tide's going out. We're about two hours from low tide, so we should be good."

A popular area for rock-climbing, Hazard Avenue was not without its dangers, as the name implied. The combination of salt spray and algae growth made the rocks closest to the water slippery and treacherous. At high tide, rogue waves had even been known to sweep unwitting tourists out to sea, sometimes to their deaths.

Jack and Helen exercised an abundance of caution on these treks. While many of the climbers wore flip-flops, Helen insisted on hiking shoes to prevent slips and falls. Jack even carried a coil of rope that he used to help secure the others as they climbed the steeper rocks. Scott suspected the rope served more as a theatrical prop than a true hiking aid, but he found it fun to pretend they were on a serious expedition.

They hiked across the rocks toward the ocean, eventually reaching the edge of a tall rocky promontory, Scott's favorite part of the climb. To get over to this outcropping, they first had to allow the water to subside. They waited as a wave rushed in, swirling noisily around the rocks and making the channel in front of them too deep to cross safely. By high tide, it would be totally impassable. But now, the seawater ebbed, making a deep gurgling sound as it drained out. Jack said, "The coast is clear—literally."

Jack crossed first, as always, and extended a hand to Scott and Helen to help them across one by one. They proceeded uphill and then climbed back down to the far side of the promontory, where they spread out a striped beach towel in their secret spot—a flat V-shaped boulder tucked away between two rock walls about six feet high. It boasted a dazzling view, yet it was sheltered, dry, and safe. No matter how many people hiked Hazard Avenue on a given day, the Winokurs always had this tranquil spot to themselves.

Helen reached for her backpack and pulled out a bagful of sandwiches: peanut butter for Scott and Jack, brie and sundried tomatoes for herself. The fresh-baked whole wheat bread had a delectably sweet, yeasty smell that whetted their appetites. They chomped their lunch in amiable silence, washing down the sandwiches with cool bottled water as the bright sun warmed their heads and shoulders.

After eating, they retreated from the outcropping of rocks, and Jack helped Scott back across the narrow passageway. Jack and Helen still moved with agile competence for people their age—she would turn seventy next year. In her usual summer garb of cotton sundresses or white jeans with cropped pastel designer tees and colorful jewelry, she didn't seem like an old lady.

But today, as she crossed the rocks, Helen lost her footing and went down, twisting her right ankle. Jack had a tight grip on her hand when she slipped, and he managed to lessen the impact of her fall but not prevent it. He squatted down to examine her as Scott rushed to her side.

"Nana, are you all right?"

"Darling, I'm fine," she said, forcing a cheery smile. But when she tried to stand, her hand still clutching Jack's, she grimaced and quickly lifted her right foot to take the weight off.

"Helen, lean on me, and we'll take it slow and easy."

"I *was* leaning on you, and I fell anyway." Her tone sounded uncharacteristically harsh. She dropped her husband's hand and hobbled up the rocks on her own.

"Helen, please—" Jack extended his hand toward her.

"I *told* you I'm fine." She continued to hobble along without looking at Jack.

During their slow progress toward the car, the silence felt heavy and ominous. By the time they reached home, however, Helen had begun acting more like her old self again, joking around with her grandson, to the boy's relief.

Rain returned the following day. "Shall we brush up on our acting skills?" asked Helen. In inclement weather, Scott and his grandparents enjoyed reading and performing scenes from plays. Nobody could remember how this tradition began, but without question, it helped to pique Scott's interest in acting and live theatre.

Scott and Jack sloshed over to the town library on foot while Nana stayed home off her ankle on the pretext of needing to call the office. The men returned with a tote bag filled with old Kaufman and Hart comedies. Their first selection, *You Can't Take It with You*, featured a large ensemble of zany characters, which would necessitate double or even triple casting.

"We can do this," Nana said.

Scott asked which role he should play in the first scene.

"Tony Kirby, of course."

"Why, of course?"

"Tony's the leading man. Jimmy Stewart played the role in the film version. With your looks, you need to get used to playing leading-man types, my dear boy."

The night before, Scott had overhead Jack saying to Helen, "I wish you wouldn't pander to Scott's ego with comments about how handsome he is."

Nana had defended her comments. "Scott's been embarrassed by his own appearance for such a long time that he needs help restoring self-confidence. That's all I'm trying to do, darling."

Over the past year, Scott's transformation from ugly duckling to swan had been nothing short of miraculous. The previous summer, he'd been a geeky middle schooler— chubby, with a round face dotted with boyish red pimples on his forehead and chin. His tight-lipped smile concealed a mouthful of metal braces. The boy never once took off his shirt all summer, even on the beach, being far too self-conscious to reveal his roly-poly stomach.

Then, all at once, it seemed, he grew six inches, and the baby fat melted away. His braces came off to reveal a perfect white smile; his skin became smooth and clear; his features matured into an impressively chiseled profile that made him look older than his age. People who had not seen Scott for six months literally failed to recognize him.

Though he wouldn't turn twelve until September, Scott had grown—facially, at least—into the person he would be for the next twenty-five or thirty years, maybe even longer, with good care and good luck. And that person was uncommonly handsome.

"Your grandmother loves you for who you are, but during your life, you'll meet a lot of people who will only love you for how you look," Jack cautioned his grandson, trying to neutralize the impact of Helen's effusive praise. "One of your biggest challenges will be to tell those two types of people apart."

Scott knew this statement contained a gem of wisdom somewhere—but still, it sounded boring to him and a little preachy. He preferred to bask in the glow of his beloved Nana's unconditional admiration.

The rain continued with periodic thunder, lightning, and heavy downpours. The beds, the curtains, the upholstered chairs, *everything* inside the house felt saturated with wetness, almost as though it had rained indoors.

"Let's go see an old chestnut tonight," Grandpop said, referring to the local summer playhouse a few miles away. The plays and musicals featured there were the same tried-and-true crowd-pleasers being performed in a hundred other summer venues across the country. But to Scott's inexperienced ears and eyes, the old chestnuts dazzled every time. He adored the energy and excitement of live performance.

Over the next few days, Helen continued to hobble around until the swelling in her ankle subsided. In the meantime, she pretended she wasn't limping, and Scott and his grandfather pretended they didn't notice.

Another thing about summers with Grandpop and Nana was that even work seemed like play. Scott's grandparents collaborated professionally on advertising campaigns, and they included him in their collaborations as often as possible.

Sometimes they made a kind of game of it. Nana said that to come up with a good ad campaign for a product, you had to brainstorm the *worst* ideas you could think of, then work backward from there. They would invent all kinds of crazy, terrible ad concepts, some of them so stupid they would all howl together. It didn't seem possible this game could lead to bold, creative, successful campaigns. But many times, that's what happened.

This summer, Scott's role as the junior member of the creative team took on an added dimension. Helen's agency had been hired to brand and promote a new line of children's toys. The as-yet unnamed objects were multicolored plastic bricks with interlocking pieces, similar in concept to Legos. Since Scott fell into the target age group for the new building toys, Helen unofficially appointed him to test and evaluate the product. He became a kind of ad-hoc technical consultant as well as a copywriter.

The morning Scott received his new research assignment dawned gray and foggy, with the threat of rain in the air. He set about his task with industrious zeal, spreading the colorful bricks across the dusty living room floor and planning what to construct first.

It didn't take long for Scott to recognize the inferior quality of the bricks. The plastic felt flimsy, and the interlocking pieces didn't snap into place as they were supposed to. When he managed to jam a couple of dozen bricks together, attempting to stack them into an erect tower, they collapsed into a pathetic pile on the floor. His success rate did not improve over time. The same sequence kept repeating itself: jam, stack, collapse.

After an hour had passed, Grandpop and Nana both popped their heads in.

"How are things progressing in the test lab?" asked Jack.

Scott directed a sad frown at his latest failed attempt and shook his head. "Permission to swear," he said, raising a hand to one eyebrow in a military-style salute. It was something they said to each other.

"Permission granted." Jack returned the salute with mock formality.

"This toy," said Scott, "is a piece of shit."

His grandparents traded solemn looks as if struggling

to mask their amusement at Scott's critique.

"Nevertheless, the show must go on," Nana said. "Any suggestions on a name for this wretched product?"

"How about we call them . . . *Suckos*. I think the slogan should be, 'A lot like Legos, except they suck.'"

"I like it." Grandpop nodded in agreement. The three of them explored other names and taglines—first, silly ones and then more serious contenders—but in the end, Helen said, "The best advice we can give this client is to go back to the drawing board. This product will be a laughing-stock, and we will all suffer by association."

Most of her professional colleagues shared a wide-spread adman tendency to approach every challenge with a "can do" attitude, rejecting any negative thinking as too—well, negative. But Helen could not tolerate dis-honesty to clients. After much discussion, she convinced the creative team at her agency as well as the account managers (or "suits," as she called them) to advise the toy maker against going to market with this product in its current state. Her colleagues insisted that Helen lead the meeting, so she trekked into town later that week to break the bad news to the client.

When she related the events of the day to Jack and Scott over dinner that night, Scott responded, "Wow. All this happened because I said the product sucked?"

"Darling, it wasn't only you. Our research department conducted a focus group that came to the same con-clusion. The product didn't do well in an analysis of the competitive market data either. But your findings were important, trust me."

"Who knew you carried that kind of clout," Grandpop said, smiling.

Scott beamed at his grandparents, the two people with whom he connected much more closely than he did with his own mother and father.

At the end of every summer, Jack spent a day driving Helen and Scott around to say goodbye to their favorite haunts in and around Narragansett. The Farewell Car Tour, named by Scott after his first summer at the cottage, included the town beach, the library, the summer theatre, the rocks at Hazard Avenue, and several other picturesque stops along the coast.

The three Winokurs ate their way around the tour, starting with homemade breakfast pastries in the quaint little town of Wakefield. For their lunch destination, true to tradition, they chose the clam shack.

While enjoying their favorite chowders one last time, Scott announced the results of this year's challenge. "Forty-four people voted for white chowder, twenty-seven for red, and eleven for clear."

"How is it that *your* favorite chowder wins the contest year after year?" Nana asked.

"I think Scott's sampling methods may be suspect," said Grandpop. "Last week, I saw him interviewing a French poodle."

After lunch, they followed the scenic coastal drive north up Route 1A toward Jamestown to stop at the ice cream parlor for generous scoops of homemade mint chip and chocolate peanut butter.

Nana said, "We should rename it the Farewell *Carb* Tour."

They didn't know it at the time, but this would be a true farewell tour. Just before the following summer of 2008, Scott's parents separated. Michael lobbied to accompany Scott to Narragansett and spend a few weeks there with Helen and Jack. But the newly single Anne balked at being alone for such a long stretch of time so soon after the separation.

A disappointed Scott remained in Baltimore with his unhappy mother, where they spent an altogether miserable summer together. Scott tried on occasion to introduce some of the activities he had enjoyed with Nana and Grandpop—like a crab cake contest (the Maryland equivalent of chowder) or the simple game of picking a topic and taking turns building on it.

But Anne would say, "I can't think of anything," or "Time to watch *Jeopardy!*" And the game would screech to an abrupt halt.

Then, in 2009, the owner of the Narragansett cottage decided to sell the property, and Grandpop claimed he couldn't find a suitable replacement. Another couple of years passed until Scott understood that back in 2009, his grandparents had begun their long struggle with a problem much greater than any real estate challenge— the heartbreaking problem of memory loss that would compel them to keep their oldest and dearest grandchild at arm's length.

12

SO WHAT ELSE?

Jack wore my favorite shirt again, the blue one that matched his eyes. Wait—suddenly I had a "favorite shirt" for Jack? How did that happen? Though I did like the way his chest hairs curled out above the open collar.

He fed Helen her midday meal and told me he had to leave for an appointment with his doctor. "I won't be back today, but Wayne promised to give Helen a little extra attention in my absence," he said.

"I'll be happy to feed Helen her afternoon snack."

"Thanks, Barbara. I'd appreciate that."

I hoped he'd be seeing the doctor for a checkup and not an illness. He looked fit and healthy enough, but you never knew.

The afternoon loomed long and empty without Jack to keep me company. I tried to engage Ma in conversation without success. Although she could crack the occasional joke, to my delight when it happened, most of her dialogue had become generic. Ma had a couple of stock phrases in her repertoire, the only words she could summon to keep the conversation flowing.

"So, what's new with you?" Ma asked me over lunch.

"I took Sarah shopping for a new bathing suit."

"That's nice. So what else?"

"I went to the East Side market."

"So what else?

"I picked up some crackers and cheese."

"So what else?"

"Then Sarah and I went over to that strip club in Cranston where we got hired as pole dancers, and we danced topless for three hours."

"So what else?"

Needless to say, it didn't happen exactly like that.

I decided to take Ma for a walk. As we strolled along, she slowed down every few steps, distracted by anything in her path: a picture on the wall, the big whiteboard in the lounge, a vase full of marigolds on the lobby table.

"Those marigolds are pretty," I said. She stared at the floral arrangement, mouth agape, with the fascination of an infant entranced by a colorful mobile rotating over her crib. Bad idea to start a conversation about the flowers, I realized. Ma's walking had deteriorated from snail's pace to dead stop.

Simply stated, Ma could no longer walk and chew gum. She started exhibiting this behavior months before we noticed anything else wrong with her. Perhaps we should have recognized it as an early warning sign of dementia.

Ma and I didn't break any land speed records on this little expedition. When we made it outside to the garden, after what seemed like about a year, she pronounced herself ready for a catnap. She collapsed into a patio chair and tilted her head back, enjoying the sun on her face. She dozed off at once, and her mouth drooped open a little, a smile playing at the corners of her lips.

Though helpless in many ways, Ma still insisted on applying her own lipstick, a task she performed with poor accuracy. As a result, her bright pink mouth always had a lopsided tilt, especially when she smiled as she did now. She also liked to slather on her favorite gardenia-scented perfume, causing her to smell like an overeager bridal attendant.

Ma had always loved the sun. How many times I had witnessed her in repose, with that same serene expression, while sunning herself at the beach or on the back lawn of her house. Content, I sat and observed her for several minutes. I could almost believe that when she awoke, she would be the old Dolly again. I closed my eyes and brushed my hair away from my forehead to bask in the warmth of the July afternoon.

The next thing I knew, Ma stood in front of me saying, "I can't get over how hot it is in this garden today, can you? Why, it's downright sultry. I feel like a character in a Tennessee Williams play. Blanche Dubois, maybe. Yes, I do declare I'm feeling a whole lot like Blanche." She affected a heavy drawl as she spoke. With a dramatic flair, Ma swooned a little on her feet and gave her best Southern belle laugh. She posed before me without her walker.

Had my wish come true? Did a miracle occur here in Tropical Gardens, returning the old Dolly to me?

My head jerked forward, jolting me back to consciousness. I had drifted off to sleep. This had been no miracle, only a dream—and Dolly's chair was empty.

I sprang up from my own seat, my heart crashing in my chest.

"Ma. Ma, where are you?" I turned in a clockwise arc and spotted her several feet behind me, plodding along on her walker in the direction of the road.

We retreated to her room to watch TV. For the next couple of hours, I watched, and she napped again, waking every now and then to stare mindlessly at the screen and swallow a few sips of water at my urging. I had the television tuned to MSNBC, which featured their usual nonstop coverage of the upcoming presidential election. At one point, they zoomed in for a closeup of Donald Trump stumping on the campaign trail. Ma pointed at the screen and snapped, "I don't like that man. He's ugly, and he looks mean."

Just when I believed my mother had lost it, she came back to surprise me.

Sarah had gone to spend the night at a friend's place, so when I arrived home, I decided to mix myself a festive drink. I took my little martini shaker out of the freezer and poured in a shot of vodka. Then I hand-squeezed the juice from half a lemon and added that to the shaker, followed by a packet of stevia sweetener and a handful of ice cubes. I shook it hard and strained the liquid into a chilled martini glass, adding a curlicue of lemon peel as the finishing touch. *Voila*—a refreshing and low-cal summer cocktail.

While I sipped on the silky-smooth lemon drop, I cobbled together a salad and settled in to watch a little *Sex and the City*. Tonight, I viewed the episode in which

Samantha hooked up with a much older man named Ed—a wealthy and generous man. Samantha warmed up to the possibility of a relationship with this septuagenarian . . . until she caught a glimpse of his saggy, naked old-man butt. She fled in horror.

I switched off the TV and jumped out of my chair, ready for a less salacious pursuit—eating ice cream. As I savored the rich mocha chip direct from the container, it reminded me of Helen. This afternoon, true to my promise, I had fed her a cup of vanilla pudding, which she devoured. Jack would be pleased to hear it. Sometimes she ate apathetically, if at all, though it still seemed to help when he serenaded her.

Feeling drowsy in the aftermath of video and ice cream overload, I crawled into bed, settling into the coolness of the cotton sheets. My thoughts returned to Samantha and Ed. I wondered, if everything else about a man seemed right and good, would drooping geriatric buttocks be sufficient cause for a woman to reject him? I pondered this weighty existential question for several minutes before I at last drifted off to sleep.

Monsieur Bonnet, the French mutterer who habitually sat in the corner of the lounge, died unexpectedly.

Wayne gave me the news after I arrived Wednesday morning. When he set out to escort his patient to breakfast, he found the old gentleman slumped over in an armchair next to his bed.

"This is how it goes sometimes. One day, they're at dinner. The next morning, they're gone," said Wayne.

It never occurred to me this might happen to Ma. Maybe something would take her from us with no warning, and all my diligent efforts to chart and anticipate the various stages of her decline would have been irrelevant. Had I been worrying for nothing?

But the phrase *worrying for nothing* was not in my personal lexicon.

According to Wayne, Monsieur Bonnet had only one nearby family member, a nephew with a home in southern Massachusetts. All the other relatives lived in France. Wayne said he doubted there'd be any kind of funeral service, which made me sad.

Later, I filled another page of cloud paper with this recollection:

Memories of Dolly: 2004

(I couldn't be sure of the correct year—2004 or 2005. But for this particular entry, it didn't matter.)

Dolly's love affair with the theatre has given her an unerring sense of timing. Nothing annoys her more than an overlong performance, whether the cause is slow pacing or poor script editing. She will invariably grumble, "I didn't realize we were seeing Long Day's Journey into Night."

This impeccable sense of timing extends to all kinds of events. Dolly attends a colleague's memorial service with daughters Victoria and Barbara. As friends and relatives parade onstage one by one, droning on tediously about the deceased in an open-mic forum, Dolly turns to her daughters after about ninety minutes to complain in a ferocious whisper, "We will all die of boredom if someone doesn't stop this endless stream of banalities. Promise you will never, ever let this happen at my funeral."

It is a promise her daughters intend to keep whenever that sad day arrives.

13

HER GUILTY SECRET

Sarah had returned three times since Luau Sunday to visit her grandmother, and Barbara heaped praise on her daughter for being attentive to Dolly as she adjusted to her new environment. Sarah felt a tad remorseful about this, knowing a desire to run into Scott again had been the real driving force behind her frequent trips to the memory care facility. She wondered if her mother had any notion of her guilty secret.

Finally, on her third time back, she ran into him. Scott asked if she had time to help him rehearse. They went outside to sit on one of the patios.

"I've been memorizing my scenes, and I think I'm ready to get off book," he said. "You follow the script, and if I flub a line, I want you to correct me, okay?" He handed her the script, which he'd opened to a scene about halfway through the play.

"Sure." Sarah took the pages from his hand.

As they prepared to start, Scott's phone buzzed with an incoming text. He made a face.

"Goddamn. I wish she would leave me alone for once."

"Who?" asked Sarah, wondering if it was one of his many female admirers.

"My mother. We talked on the phone about an hour

ago, and I got pissed off at her. She called my father a shit. Can you believe that?"

"That's kind of harsh."

"He would never say that about her, even though my mother *can* be a shit, no question. She has a good job, but right now, she's trying to extort more alimony out of him, and she wants me to take her side."

"That sucks."

"Yeah, no kidding. Now she's texting to try and make nice to me. She's always pulling this kind of crap. Your parents are divorced too. Do they do stuff like this?"

"No, not exactly."

"So, they like each other?"

"I wouldn't go that far," Sarah said. "They avoid each other as much as they can. But they don't put me in the middle of their issues."

"Well, you're lucky." Heaving a sigh, Scott pointed at the script. "Why don't you start at the top of this page? You'll be reading Elena. She's this warm, touchy-feely, earth-mother type that everyone is crazy about at the beginning. But as the play goes on, she turns out to be a phony and a nymphomaniac who's been screwing every man and woman in sight for years. I play Robert, a close friend of Elena's husband, and I'm her latest victim."

They read through the scene together. Scott knew most of his lines—Sarah only had to correct him in a couple of spots. Then they came to a stage direction that caused Sarah to pause, unsure of how to proceed. *Elena reaches for Robert and kisses him on the mouth.*

She held up the script and showed him the direction,

giving him a questioning look.

In response, Scott grinned and leaned forward, brushing her lips lightly with his own before drawing back. He smiled and said, "Keep reading."

Sarah did as he asked, though she felt rattled by what had occurred. Scott might have handled that situation in any number of ways. He could have given her an air-kiss or skipped over the stage direction. But he chose to make direct contact, even if she could scarcely feel his lips on hers.

Upon parting, Scott asked for her phone number and said he'd text her about getting together the next time he had a day off. This sent her soaring into the stratosphere.

She needed to share this development with Dory at once. Sarah texted her friend and said:

—*Scott kissed me today! And he got my phone number.*

She omitted the part about the kiss being more of a peck, as well as the part about it being mandated by a stage direction. Dory responded immediately.

—*OMG, that's great. I have big news too. No more TV.*

—*Wait, what? Why did you stop watching television?*

—*No no no. I'm not a Technical Virgin anymore.*

—*Do you mean what I think you mean?*

—*YES. It finally happened with Nick. I love him like crazy.*

—*I'm SO happy for you, Dory. But how did you manage it?*

—*The usual way.*

—*LOLOL. I meant how did you manage to be alone with him?*

—*My dad and stepmom took my little brother to a*

birthday party. Nick and I left at the same time and pretended to be going to a movie, but then we drove right back to the house. I knew they'd be gone for hours.

—WOW. That's amazing.

—Hey who knows . . . Maybe this summer it will happen for you with Scott.

—Oh, I'm not ready for anything like that.

But then, realizing her friend had reached womanhood in every sense of the word, Sarah didn't want Dory to regard her as too much of an innocent. She added:

—Then again, I could change my mind. Scott IS pretty awesome!

14

FREEFALL

As the Winokurs adjusted to life with Alzheimer's, Jack came to understand that Helen's decline was not linear. She would follow a straight path for a while but then take a step downward—sometimes a tiny step, other times a freefall from a steep precipice. The plateaus could last for weeks or even months. In fact, throughout 2010, her condition had remained stable. Perhaps the memory drugs and the supplements were helping to keep the dementia at bay? Jack became hopeful and even a little complacent. With luck, it wouldn't get any worse than this.

But in 2011, things took a decided downhill turn, and Helen's decline accelerated. One spring afternoon, Jack walked into the kitchen and found his wife holding a pair of pruning shears and facing out the window.

"Where did those gardeners go?" she said, gazing outside and speaking more to herself than to Jack. "They didn't prune the hedge like I told them to. The grass is overgrown. There are weeds in the garden. Now I'll have to do it all myself."

"What's wrong?" he asked.

"The gardeners. Nothing's been done," she said, turning to face him.

"No worries. Today is Tuesday. They come tomorrow." He gave her a consoling back rub.

Helen shook her head in violent disagreement. "No, no, Jack. Today is Wednesday, I'm sure." She returned her gaze to the window and stood there with a fixed stare as if trying to conjure up the gardeners through sheer concentration.

Then she turned around and, with a strange look on her face, said to her husband, "Please instruct your crew to take care of this right away. And they need to clean up better. Last week one of your men left a soda can on the driveway." Her tone had become impersonal, formal.

Jack hesitated, not knowing how to respond. In his most gentle voice, he said, "Helen. It's me, Jack. Your husband. I'm not the gardener." He removed the pruning shears from her hand and placed them on the kitchen table.

She stood in silence, a confused expression in her eyes. After a minute or two, he could sense her returning to reality.

"I—I know it's you. The baseball cap made a shadow across your face, and you looked different for a moment." Helen pointed to the Red Sox cap on Jack's head and gave a forced laugh. "You must've thought I'd lost it."

"Never, sweetheart. Don't worry." Jack hugged her to him.

"I only mistook who you were for a moment, I swear. Only the briefest moment. I'm okay."

Jack wanted so much to believe her—even with all the other issues, she had always recognized him until now.

"I'm fine, I promise. But I need you to help me remember

things." She started to cry, burying her face in his shirt.

"Shhh," he said, at a loss for words of comfort when he himself felt so desolate.

"You'll keep working with me on my memory, won't you?"

"You know I will. The same way we used to work together on ad campaigns. It will be a collaboration."

She forced a little smile at this. "Yes. A . . . a . . ." She struggled with the pronunciation. "Co . . . coll . . . collab . . . co . . . I can't remember the word." She collapsed against Jack's shoulder and started to sob.

He encircled her with his arms and kissed her hair lightly, but she continued to weep until she had trouble catching her breath.

"Maybe you'll feel better if you lie down and rest."

"No, no. I don't want to be alone." She shook her head, still sobbing, her green eyes now panicky behind the heavy film of tears.

"Don't worry. I'll stay with you. I promise."

He led Helen upstairs to the bedroom, and she stretched out cooperatively on the bed, with Jack beside her, one arm still cradling her. Within a few minutes, her raspy breathing smoothed out, and sleep overtook her.

Jack watched his wife's resting profile, tranquil now in the aftermath of her torment. He felt a sob rise in his own chest and struggled to contain it. He wouldn't have minded curling up into a fetal ball right then and crying until he had no tears left, as his wife had just done. But he needed to remain straight and strong to deal with Helen.

He tensed his limbs, squeezed his hands into a tight

ball, and inhaled all at the same time. Then he relaxed his legs, arms, and fists as he emptied his lungs. He continued to repeat this exercise in a methodical pattern, focusing on his breath to bring his anguish under control.

Helen's crying jags became a regular event as she grew more confused about her whereabouts, her activities, her husband's identity. Eventually, she came back to the present, but it always ended the same way—with her weeping and Jack consoling her in his arms, promising to try and help her remember things.

One day the following fall, Jack stood in his office talking on the phone when, from the corner of his eye, he noticed Helen tiptoe into the room to listen to his conversation.

"What time did you expect her? I see. And you say she missed last week, too. I'm sorry about this. But in the future, it's best if you make Helen's appointments with me, at this number. I'll be sure to deliver her to you on schedule. Yes. That's right. Thank you very much." He put down the phone.

"Who called?" Helen asked.

"Your manicurist. You missed your appointment this morning. And she said you missed last week as well."

"Why did she call you?" she asked, suspicious.

"She left a message on the landline. I called her back."

"I could've handled it if she'd had the sense to call me instead," said Helen, indignant. She studied the screen of her cellphone. "Oh—there are three text messages from her. They must not have shown up on the phone before." Her face flushed with anger, and she glared at Jack. "You're supposed to help me remember my appointments. Why didn't you remind me?"

"Helen, I can't remind you of an appointment if I don't even know that it exists," Jack said as gently as he could.

"Oh, then you're saying this is all *my* fault."

"No, darling, it's nobody's fault. I'm simply trying to work out a better system for managing the schedule."

"But I wrote it down."

"I didn't see it on the wall." Jack gestured toward the big wall calendar where they posted all Helen's appointments and reminder messages.

"Well, I wrote it . . . I wrote it . . . somewhere. I don't appreciate you colliding behind my back with the people from the nail salon."

"I wasn't—colluding—with anyone," Jack said, reluctant to correct her malapropism yet also unwilling to repeat it. "I wanted to make sure you don't miss any more appointments. You know how you hate it when your nails get all chipped."

Helen looked down at her hands and examined her fingernails with distaste.

"Yes, I do hate it, Jack. I don't know how you could allow this to happen." By this time, she'd grown upset. "You can't keep letting things slip through . . . through the . . . you know what I mean." Her lovely eyes shone with anger, and she started to weep in frustration.

"Helen." He spoke in a soothing tone as he put his arms around her.

"No, no, *no*." She wrenched herself free from his

embrace. "I'll be damned if I'm going to put up with this sort of treatment from you." She wrinkled her nose and pursed her lips into a hideous expression, then jerked her head sharply.

Jack didn't realize what had happened until he felt the cool, sticky wetness on his right cheek.

Helen had spit on him.

As Jack would later recognize, that hostile gesture marked the moment when Helen first stopped seeking solace from him, when she ceased viewing him as the beloved partner who shielded her from pain and heartache. His ability to provide comfort had been one of the few remaining forms of intimacy between them. But it was clear Helen now viewed him as an adversary.

He saw in his wife's eyes that she suspected him of talking about her behind her back, of conspiring against her somehow. He didn't mean to make her feel even worse about herself, but he couldn't keep ignoring the missed appointments and mental confusion. Every time he tried to correct a difficult situation, she treated it as a personal betrayal. With distrustful looks, with coldness and with harsh words, Helen let Jack know she did not appreciate his so-called help.

15

LIPSTICK AND LIES

I couldn't stop obsessing about Sarah and her deep infatuation with this boy Scott. Well, at twenty years old, Scott qualified as a man, not a boy, which only heightened my concern. Four years struck me as a huge gap at this age.

In addition, I'd noticed that *Scott* seemed infatuated with Scott. I worried that Sarah would get hurt, that she'd do something she shouldn't. How could I protect someone so young and vulnerable?

Yesterday, she helped him rehearse and floated home from Tropical Gardens. "Mom, I had no idea theatre could be this much fun."

"Maybe you should try out for one of the plays at Classical this year." It *might help to round out the college resume*, I reasoned to myself, always trolling for new angles.

"Oh, that's different," she said. "I don't think I'd be good at acting."

"You don't have to act. What about costume or set design? Your summer classes at RISD are good preparation for that."

She shrugged. "But the boys in the drama club at school are all geeky."

"So, this isn't about your newfound passion for theatre; it's more about meeting a cool guy?"

Sarah rolled her eyes. "The thing is, I'm having fun doing these scenes with Scott. He's got me playing a character named Elena. She's this huge slut, and she sleeps around with everyone in sight."

Terrific. "Is there anything . . . you know, inappropriate, in this play?" I asked with forced casualness, trying to hide my distress.

"Like what?"

"I don't know, sex scenes, or nudity . . . anything like that?" My question came out as an embarrassed squeak.

"Mom—jeez." This time, not only her eyes rolled but her entire head, her long hair tossing like a horse's mane. "There's nothing like that." But then she described a stage direction that involved a kiss.

"Okay and did you and Scott . . . uh . . ." I knew she could read the worry written all over my face.

"He didn't say anything; he just kissed me."

I tried not to freak out in front of her, but I felt myself starting to lose it. Then Sarah said, "But it wasn't a real kiss. Here—I'll show you." She simulated the kiss with me.

That didn't seem too bad. Yet I couldn't help wondering, what next? Maybe a more soulful kiss, or even . . .

Then my daughter said, "There's something else I need to talk to you about."

Oh, dear God, something more *did* happen with Scott. But she said, "It's about Dad."

"Dad?"

"Yeah. I told you I thought he's been seeing two women

at the same time, but now I'm certain."

This didn't surprise me. "Oh, honey. I don't think I'm your best audience for this."

"But it involves me, and I'm not sure what to do."

Now she had my attention. "What do you mean?"

"I think one girlfriend lives in Providence and the other lives in Boston. But last time I went to Dad's, the Boston lady was visiting Providence."

"Ah, the ill-advised geographical cross-over. Big mistake on his part," I said. "Sorry. Go on."

"Anyway, Fran—her name's Fran—picked up a tube of lipstick from the kitchen counter, and she said, 'This must be yours,' and handed it to me. I told her, 'This isn't my lipstick.' Then Dad jumped in, like, all nervous, and said, 'Sarah, don't you remember? It's from that cosmetic kit I gave you for your birthday.' I got kind of flustered, and I said, 'Yeah, remember now.' But I think Fran wanted to kill us both."

"*Did* your father give you a cosmetic kit?" I asked.

"No, Mom. He gave me a car, remember?"

I'd expected her to add "duh."

"Just asking."

"Well, the two of them went into the bedroom and closed the door, and their voices were muffled so I couldn't hear most of the conversation. But I could tell she sounded angry, and Dad kept trying to calm her down. He shushed her a couple of times to keep me from overhearing. Then he came out and told me not to worry. And he said, 'Do me a little favor, will you, honey? Be sure to wear that lipstick in front of Fran . . . you know, take ownership of it. You can do that, can't you?'"

"'Take ownership'? He said that?" I asked in disbelief.

"Yeah. I didn't say no, but I didn't promise to wear it either." She produced the offending lipstick, a glossy stick of dark Chinese Red.

"Does this color look like me?"

I shook my head. "It does not." I noticed the lipstick was well-worn. If Boston Fran bought into the alibi about a forgotten birthday gift, she would have to be a major idiot.

"What should I do, Mom?"

"I think you need to tell your father how you feel about all this. How *do* you feel?"

She considered the question. "I feel bad that I got in the middle of their problem. But Dad's the one who put me in the middle."

"That's absolutely right. It's not your job to cover up for your father's mistakes. Or for my mistakes, either." I hoped that would make my argument appear less biased.

"So, should I wear the lipstick or not?"

"Honey, this isn't about the lipstick."

She nodded. "I guess I should tell Dad that it's not fair to involve me, and if he does something like this again, I'm not going to lie for him next time." She gave me an uncertain look. "Does that sound good?"

"That sounds perfect." I couldn't believe this whole conversation. And here was something even more incredible: Years after what I had dubbed the marriage-ending "Elvis incident," my ex-husband continued to get into trouble over lipstick.

I felt I had helped Sarah resolve the problem with her father but not the problem with Scott. Then again, *she* didn't see Scott as a problem, which may have been the biggest problem of all.

I weighed whether to tell Jack about what had happened between the two young people during Scott's rehearsal, but what would I say? I didn't know how to voice my concerns without appearing to accuse his grandson of something. I decided to let it go, at least, for now.

Today, when Jack and I sat in the lounge with Helen and Ma, Wayne came in and mentioned he'd seen Sarah and Scott rehearsing yesterday. "That Scott is to *die* for," he said, addressing Jack. "I know he's going to be a star." Then Wayne turned to me. "Your daughter's pretty too," he added, but more as a polite afterthought.

I thanked him for the compliment, feeling a mixture of amusement and worry. Judging from Wayne's starstruck appearance, I guessed Sarah wasn't the only one smitten with Scott Winokur.

16

NO COSMO FOR YOU

Around five-thirty on a warm Thursday afternoon, Jack stood outside the Tropical Gardens entrance, preparing to head home. He had just unlocked his bike from the bicycle rack when he noticed Barbara emerging from the front door on her way to the adjacent parking lot.

Barbara often poked fun at her own clumsiness, but Jack found her movements to be fluid and even elegant in their own way. Today he admired how she swiveled her hips and swung her arms as she headed toward her car. They waved to each other and, spur of the moment, he called, "Barbara, if you don't have any plans, how about joining me for a quick drink someplace?"

She stopped and hesitated for a moment. "Sure, Jack. That would be nice."

"I'm sorry to say I'm at your mercy, however," he said, pointing at the bicycle. "But if you do the driving, I'll treat the drinks."

"It's a deal."

Jack resecured his bike to the rack and walked with Barbara to her black Prius. By mutual agreement, they drove a couple of miles over to Thayer Street, a busy commercial artery close to Brown University and RISD.

A lack of street parking challenged visitors to this

popular neighborhood, so as soon as she saw an empty spot, Barbara claimed it. Laughing, she warned Jack, "I'm not the most competent parallel parker. By the time I finish parking the car, happy hour may be over." She spun the steering wheel hard to the right in a failed attempt to back accurately into the spot. After three tries, she managed to maneuver the Prius into the tight space.

"Did you have a particular place in mind?" Barbara asked as they walked south to the area where most of the restaurants and bars were concentrated.

"Not really. I tend to go downtown most times, but parking there is even more of a hassle. Let's keep walking in this direction and see what catches our eye." Jack found himself stealing glances again at the gentle swaying of Barbara's hips and at the way the afternoon sunlight caught her hair.

First, they passed a new, unfamiliar place, nearly devoid of customers. The tables sported crisp white linens and small crystal vases containing fresh pink-and-white alstroemeria. The bill of fare posted on the window looked formal and pretentious, with fancy calligraphic script. Perusing it, Jack saw that the menu featured French bistro-style bar and dinner offerings at unconscionable prices.

"Are they kidding? Seventeen dollars for a glass of house wine," Barbara said.

"No wonder it's empty."

They continued walking. Next, they encountered a large bar that might be better described as a saloon. It had sawdust on the floor, three big video screens tuned to different sporting events, and a rowdy young crowd gathered around the bar area. A pungent odor of cheap beer floated through the open doorway, and Barbara wrinkled her nose.

"Student dive," Jack said, and she nodded in agreement. They kept on walking.

In another two blocks, they came to an establishment that billed itself as a wine bar but also offered a full cocktail menu and an interesting assortment of tapas. It had a contemporary ambiance with teak tables and an abundance of chrome and glass. Around two-thirds full but with several tables still empty, the place seemed festive but not too noisy.

Impressed, Jack and Barbara spoke at the same time. He said, "This is it," just as Barbara pronounced it "perfect." They laughed briefly at this, and their eyes locked.

As inconsequential as it all seemed, Jack at that moment felt a connection to Barbara that hadn't existed before—a feeling something had progressed between them, though he couldn't articulate what that might be.

Jack pointed out a selection of wine flights on the menu, each flight comprised of five different wines of the same varietal or theme.

"Five glasses of wine? I'll never make it back to Tropical Gardens."

"Don't worry; they'll be very small pours. We could share one flight between us. But only if you enjoy wine."

"I *love* wine," Barbara said, a little too quickly.

"I love it, too." Jack smiled wistfully. "It's not only the taste of a fine wine—it's the nose, and the feel of it in your mouth, and the way it makes food taste so much better.

It's a whole different experience from drinking some icy blend of sugar, flavoring, and alcoholic slush."

Though Jack spoke from the heart about wine, with warmth and enthusiasm, he wondered if he had come off sounding like one of those commentators on an effete Travel Channel special. He peered across the table at Barbara and tried to gauge her reaction. She appeared nervous and shy to him, much the way she'd acted when they first met. But then, Barbara admitted to being nervous during most of her waking hours, so perhaps he shouldn't take it personally.

Not wanting her to think him an insufferable snob, he added, "But sometimes on a summer day, there's nothing like a frozen margarita or a tall glass of beer, is there?"

Barbara smiled back with what struck him as an expression of relief in her eyes. "I agree. But I like your idea of sharing a wine flight, Jack. Whatever you choose will be fine with me."

He suggested the featured special, a flight of five Malbecs.

"Malbec comes from Argentina, doesn't it?" Barbara asked.

"You're right. But a lot of people don't know it originated in France. A French agriculturalist exported the grape to Argentina in the nineteenth century, and now most of the world production comes from that country. It's a tricky grape to grow—not terribly hearty—and it isn't as popular in France as it used to be."

The flight they shared consisted of two Malbecs from Argentina, one from Chile, one from California, and one from France. Jack pointed out differences among the various wines as they tasted them. Barbara asked questions and showed interest in his well-informed discourse, though she didn't seem to know a great deal about Malbec herself beyond the Argentina connection. Jack explained that you could find respectable Malbecs from countries other than the selection they'd just sampled: New Zealand, Brazil, Italy, even Mexico.

"The Valle de Guadalupe in Baja Mexico is producing all kinds of varietals and unusual blends. It's an up-and-coming region with more than a hundred wineries and terrific restaurants. And it's a quick drive down from San Diego."

"You've been there?" Barbara asked.

"No, but I've read articles and heard about it from friends," he said. "I plan to go there after"—he stopped and corrected himself—"when I'm able to travel again."

Jack's sons had been urging him to give himself a week off to go away on vacation somewhere. As they pointed out, it seemed unlikely that Helen would know the difference in her current state. But he still felt committed to his wife's care for the foreseeable future.

Jack steered the conversation away from wine, and they moved on to other interests and hobbies, losing track of time as they chatted. Neither of them brought up Alzheimer's or Tropical Gardens. They had time enough to do that on the long afternoons when they sat together in the lounge or out in the garden with a listless Helen and an increasingly lethargic Dolly.

After an hour had passed, a red-headed woman approached their table and clapped Barbara on the back.

"Hey, sweetie. Fancy meeting you here," said the woman by way of greeting. She surveyed the row of wine glasses on the table, all five of them now empty but for a few residual drops of the reddish-purple liquid.

"What's up? This is a change. No cosmo for you tonight?"

"Oh, is a cosmo usually your drink of choice?" Jack asked Barbara. He couldn't help noticing how she stared down at the empty wine flight and blushed at this, as if embarrassed to be revealed as an unsophisticated drinker.

Barbara introduced the other woman to Jack as Lynne, explaining that her friend belonged to the Friday happy hour clique.

The redhead grinned and commented, "Oh, *you're* Jack."

He watched Barbara blush again, more deeply this time. Jack made a mental note that Barbara had been discussing him with her friends. It did not displease him to learn this.

Lynne excused herself, but not before saying, "You must try one of the cosmos here. They are divine."

After she walked away, Jack turned to Barbara and said, "I think we *should* order the cosmos next time. That would be fun."

"Yes, it would." Barbara nodded, and that unmistakable look of relief crossed her face once again.

Her cellphone buzzed. "It's Sarah, wondering where I am," she said, reading the incoming text on the screen. She tapped a brief reply. "This deviates from protocol."

She smiled. "Most times, I'm the one investigating *her* whereabouts."

"We'd better get you home, then. I'm sure I've droned on much too long about varietals, and vineyard management, and all manner of sleep-inducing topics."

"No, not sleep-inducing at all. I enjoyed it."

Their eyes locked again, this time in an affectionate glance that gave Jack cause to believe Barbara *had* enjoyed their time in the wine bar, despite the few awkward moments here and there.

They drove the short distance back to Tropical Gardens together. After Barbara pulled the car up to the curb alongside the bicycle rack, Jack leaned into her and he kissed her on both cheeks, European style, as befit the occasion.

17

THE DATING EQUATION

I think Ma just achieved a new personal best (or would it be a personal *worst*?) for time clocked napping in a single day. She only stayed awake for her meals and a short walk. She exhibited signs of a mild head cold, sniffling and clearing her throat nonstop. Perhaps that contributed to her drowsiness.

At least it left me with more time to read, and I even started making notes for a children's book. But as soon as I began noodling ideas, I would become distracted by one problem or another.

To make matters worse, my sister had been even more absent than usual, blaming the recent heat wave and the subsequent high demand for air conditioning products for her negligence.

"This is the silver lining of climate change," she proclaimed on the phone. "The world suffers, but Martin and I triumph. July will be a record month for V&M. Even so, it's good news-bad news. Our emergency cooling department is working 24/7, and Martin and I are beyond exhausted."

Given Vicky's flightiness and blatant disregard for deadlines, I puzzled over how she managed to run a successful business. I guess that's where Martin came in. If they were a pair of chefs, I envisioned Martin handling all the food prep, the measuring, and the step-by-step execution, overseeing the recipe and cooking the stew to perfection—while Vicky did nothing but stir the pot. This might explain why I always found Martin collapsed in his lounge chair in the TV room, with all the energy of a deflated balloon.

They called their company V&M Solutions. The initials stood for "Ventilating & Mechanical," the words spelled out below the logo on their letterhead and delivery vans, right below a graphic swirl meant to depict a fan blade. But the letters also stood for "Vicky & Martin." My sister came up with the name and regarded it as devilishly clever, despite the problem that nobody "got" the *double entendre* without a detailed explanation.

"I guess it's good to be busy," I said.

"Yes, but I feel like a cad for neglecting poor Daisy." Interesting that Vicky should feel guilt-ridden about her golden retriever but not about her own mother.

"Are you bringing Ma for dinner tomorrow night?" she asked me. We planned to gather in honor of Martin's birthday. Vicky had organized a lavish catered party for him in the office last Friday afternoon, and this dinner would be a secondary celebration for immediate family. My sister and Martin had no children, so the only other participant would be Daisy, who would receive a small bowl of ice cream to feel included in the festivities.

"Given Ma's cold and general lack of energy, I'm not sure it's wise for her to come."

Vicky agreed at once. "Yeah, better not to wear her out and confuse her with a disruption in routine."

"To be honest, Vick, I'm relieved to have an excuse not to bring her. It's becoming harder to take Ma anywhere."

"I know. Ever since that incident last fall."

Every October after Ma's retirement, Providence Players held an annual "Drama for Dolly Night" in her honor—a staged reading of a new dramatic work in front of an audience. Ma always loved being in the limelight and reconnecting with old friends and colleagues at this annual event.

But by last year, she couldn't focus on the performance and fell asleep after a short time. Before long, she was snoring, and when I nudged her shoulder to wake her, she said in her loudest stage voice, "*What?* Where the hell am I?"

I think every other person in the theatre cringed with embarrassment at her outburst, but Ma remained clueless, which was the only good thing you could say about it. After that incident, Vicky and I agreed with reluctance that Dolly had taken her final bow at the playhouse.

For Martin's birthday tomorrow, I'd offered to make angel food cake with mocha whipped cream icing and shaved dark chocolate bits, his favorite. "Happy to do it if that won't be an infringement on your wifely duties."

"Fuck, no," Vicky said with a throaty laugh. "The last thing I want to do is stand in a hot kitchen, up to my ass in flour and cream and egg whites or whatever the hell you use." Since Vicky loathed any form of food preparation, for the main course she always served pizza from Federal Hill, a historic district of Providence long celebrated for its authentic Italian restaurants and markets.

With his favorite unhealthy dishes on offer, Martin would be a happy man tomorrow night. I'd bake the cake first thing in the morning before heading over for my day of fun and excitement with Ma.

After we finished our second helpings of angel food birthday cake at Vicky's townhome, Sarah excused herself to go to a friend's house. The rest of us retired to the den to watch a little television. This marked the final night of the Democratic National Convention, with Hillary slated to deliver her acceptance speech later in the evening.

"This election is such a shit show," Vicky said. "And the polls have gotten way too close."

"Everyone says the convention will give her a bounce. I'm not worried about it."

"What? Barbara, are you in there?"

"I mean, Hillary's going to win. She just *is*," I said.

Truth be told, the upcoming election terrified me. Or, to express it in Vicky parlance, I was scared shitless. But whenever I admitted to Vicky the extent of my anxiety, she either poked fun at me or attempted to ply me with Xanax. Trying to outmaneuver Vicky proved a no-win situation.

Sated with pizza, beer, and cake, Martin snored loudly in his favorite chair. I viewed it as a busman's holiday for me—watching Ma sleep all afternoon, only to witness Martin engaged in the same act a few hours later.

Vicky and I retreated to the kitchen where we could talk without waking up Martin. Daisy padded along behind us, and my sister spooned some ice cream into a bowl and put it down on the floor. The dog lowered herself down slowly to rest at my sister's feet, and Vicky scratched her thick golden ruff with affection. Daisy licked the frozen treat without enthusiasm.

"Barb. I need you to worry about something for me." Vicky gave me a little wink.

"Sorry, Vick, the dance card is full. I'm booked solid for the rest of the month."

She peered down at Daisy, and now her expression became grave.

"Wait—I thought you were joking just now. Is something wrong?" I asked.

"It's this old gal. She's slowing down big-time, and her back legs are starting to give out. Arthritis."

"Oh, dear." It dismayed me to hear this. Something else bothered me as well. "Why is she acting blasé about the ice cream? It used to be her favorite treat."

"It still *is*," Vicky said, and her tone sounded bitter. "We've been assigned to a new doctor at the veterinary office, and she lectured me that ice cream is terrible for Daisy, and I might as well be feeding her rat poison. I've had to switch to this crap called Freezy Paws, 'formulated with your pet's health in mind.'" She sarcastically mimicked the promotional copy on the freezer carton. "You can't fool Daisy."

With a dramatic swing of her furry head, the dog averted her mouth from the bowl of uneaten doggie dessert as if to confirm Vicky's statement.

"That new vet is a bitch on wheels."

"But if you've been giving Daisy ice cream all her life with no ill effects, maybe you could disregard the vet's order," I said. "Remind me how old she is."

"Daisy's thirteen. Our last one didn't make it to twelve. Oh, I can't stand to think about it," said Vicky, her voice choked with emotion. "Of all the dogs we've had, Daisy is my all-time favorite."

"Can't the vet give her something to help with the arthritis?"

"She's already on two medications, but the meds give her stomach trouble, which is a whole other problem. Speaking of meds . . . maybe I'll pop a teeny chip of Ativan. You know, to take the edge off."

"Oh, God." I groaned as she jumped up to retrieve a pill bottle from the kitchen counter. She sat back in her chair and popped a not-so-teeny chip with a quick swig of water.

"Vicky, let me update you on Ma."

"Sure, honey. Tell me what's doing with her."

"I think she's holding at Stage Six. Except the naps are getting longer and more frequent." I retrieved the binder from my tote bag. "I'll read you some notes."

I flipped it open to the page where I had logged Ma's activities for the day and summarized, "Nap, two hours . . . nap, ninety minutes . . . nap, forty minutes . . . nap, seventy-five minutes. She slept all day except for lunch and a short walk." I snapped the binder shut. "When Ma's asleep, I've been starting to make notes for a children's book, but I haven't gotten very far."

"Too busy documenting the naps? Sometimes I wonder why we're paying all this money for her to lie around and snooze."

"It's not an investment strategy, Vick. It's for Ma's safety. You and I agreed we would find a way to manage the cost between us."

"But who knows for how long . . ."

"Well, yes." I had to agree. "She's still out-and-out frisky compared to Helen Winokur."

"You know, when Ma moved to Tropical Gardens, I expected the other residents to be like her. But they're not."

"And this is based on your in-depth observations from visiting the place—let's see, *one* time?" I said, and she gave me the dirty eye. Vicky enjoyed being at the delivering end of zingers, not the receiving end.

"You're right, though," I said. "Jack said if you've met one person with Alzheimer's, you've met one person with Alzheimer's."

"Interesting."

"He also said people could change as they get sicker. I guess Helen has given him a rough time over the years. Jack says we don't know how good we've got it with Ma."

She narrowed her eyes. "I get the impression you've been spending a lot of time with this man."

I shrugged. "We're both there every day. I've enjoyed his company this past month. After all, Ma isn't the most scintillating conversationalist."

"Not unless you're entertained by someone shouting 'I love you! You're pretty!' to anything that moves," said Vicky, and we both laughed. She slouched down into a relaxed pose. Could the Ativan be working this quickly?

"Jack's an interesting man," I said, warming up to the subject. "I'm learning a lot about wine from him. The other day he introduced me to a French Malbec."

She squinted again, the frown lines between her eyebrows deepening. "How did *that* go down?"

"It tasted nice, but tart . . . not fruit-forward like the Malbecs from Argentina." I flaunted my newfound knowledge.

"Hah. My sister, the sommelier. But that's not what I was asking. You can't tell me they serve Malbec at Tropical Gardens."

"No, not there. We went to that new wine bar on Thayer Street."

"Are you fucking kidding me?" Vicky shot up in her chair, assuming a pose of rigid attention. Given the depth of her consternation, you might think I had just announced plans for gender change surgery, or perhaps a defection to Russia. "I cannot believe you are dating this man."

"I'm not dating him. We both left at the same time one day and decided on impulse to have a glass of wine together. Anyway, I don't get why you have to sound so—disapproving."

"For one thing, he is, uh, married." She spoke in that same tone Sarah always used whenever she said "duh."

"Technically, yes. But not when you consider that the woman is almost completely unresponsive."

"Married or not, he's too old for you," she said, pressing on with her case. "He must be in his seventies."

"Seventy-two. But come to think of it, he's still within the dating equation."

"What the hell is that?"

"Okay, you take the man's age . . ."

"Seventy-two," said Vicky.

"You divide by two . . ."

"Thirty-six."

"And add seven," I said.

"Forty-three."

"I'm fifty-one, which puts us well within the guidelines. If we were dating, which we are not."

She remained skeptical. "I don't think I get this."

"If a seventy-two-year-old man dated a woman of thirty-five or forty, that would be inappropriate. But forty-three or older . . . and it's all good," I said with a little smile.

"I see you *have* been thinking about this," said Vicky in a "gotcha" tone. "Anyway, leave it to you to reduce romance to a numerical formula." She gave me a cynical smirk.

"I have not been thinking about it. All I did was share a little wine with the man. You're the one who brought up this whole dating topic."

"Well, I hope we can both put it to rest. I mean, what do you need with a guy that age? In time, something would happen to Ma, and before you know it, you'd be stuck taking care of an old man. Sounds like a busman's holiday to me."

Funny she chose to use the same old-fashioned saying I had silently applied to her husband. "Aren't we getting ahead of ourselves? I told you we're only friends. Anyway, there is nothing old about Jack."

"Listen, Chicken—"

"For the hundredth time, I'm asking you not to call me that."

"Sorry, honey." Her voice softened. "You've got a lot on your shoulders, with Ma and Sarah. The last thing you need is a man with his problems. It's a darned good thing you're not involved with Jack."

I hadn't intended to share this next bit of information, but somehow, I blurted out, "He invited me to his house next Saturday night to cook an Indian dinner together."

"Holy crap. Sounds like he's flying right past the first date and heading straight into romantic candlelit dinner at home . . . to 'cook' together?" Vicky made little air quotes with the fingers of both hands. "I won't even ask what—or who—is on the menu."

I paused to contemplate this. "You may be right. Intimate Saturday night dinner at his place. It doesn't leave a lot of room for interpretation, does it? Maybe I shouldn't go." As usual, I wavered in the face of my big sister's superior logic.

"That's my girl. I knew your good sense would prevail." She bestowed her warmest smile on me.

"Then again—what's the harm in having dinner?" I said, thinking out loud.

"Maybe you should create a spreadsheet to analyze this. You could list all the reasons in favor of a relationship in column A and the reasons against in column B."

"That's not a bad idea. I could use one of the blank forms from here." I reached for the binder.

Vicky threw her hands up in the air. "It's a terrible idea, Barb. I was joking. You can't let an Excel program decide your life for you." She groaned. "I'm sure Jack is a great guy. But you can't expect me to jump for joy over you getting involved with a man who's more than twenty years your senior and who is caring for a gravely sick wife. It could mean a world of hurt for you. Besides, Ma needs your attention—now, more than ever."

The flaps of my tent started folding inward yet again. "I guess you're right. But maybe I'm agreeing only to please you. Why does my big sister's stamp of approval still matter to me after all these years?"

"What are you talking about? You disagree with me all the time."

"Yes, but it upsets me when I do. I can't shake things off the way you can."

She gazed up at the kitchen clock and said, "Look, I don't have time for this discussion. I need to go through my work emails before bed tonight. And I don't want to miss Hillary's speech."

I got up to leave. "One more thing before I go. The nurse would like to meet with us tomorrow afternoon. It's Ma's one-month evaluation. You name the time."

"No way, Chicken. We're doing inventory tomorrow, and it will be a madhouse."

"But Cindy said it's important for both of us to—"

"Cindy and the rest of the staff need to understand the division of labor in our family. You manage Ma, I manage my company."

"The real issue is you can't bear to be around Tropical Gardens."

"Well, I admit hanging out with the 'inmates' is not my favorite pastime ever. Though it may be my most expensive."

Vicky never missed an opportunity to grumble about the fees.

"Do you think I find it amusing there? I do it for Ma."

"I know, Chicken, and I stand in awe of you for that. I truly do. The eldercare gene is not in my DNA," Vicky said. "If I spent a full day there, I think my head would explode."

"And your solution is to put it all on me."

"Honey, it's not like that. It's a time issue. In addition to a demanding business, I've got Martin. I've got Daisy. I've got a million things on my plate. Like it or not, that's my life."

"Oh, right, that's your life; excuse me for losing sight of that important fact. There's only one thing I'd like to know, Vicky. When do I get to have a life?"

Back home, I slammed cups and plates into my dishwasher, still fuming at my sister. Yanking a load of clean towels from the dryer, I folded them on the table with almost violent purpose while I watched the convention on my little countertop TV. The housework calmed me down, but then my brain started racing again as I contemplated the dinner invitation from Jack for Saturday night. I replayed the whole conversation with Vicky in my head. I had no idea what to do.

Why did my sister have to make a federal case over my grabbing a drink with a man? In a month's time, without question, I had already gotten to know Jack well and to value him as a dear friend and confidante. But the two of us joined as a couple in a romantic involvement? It was a preposterous notion.

And yet.

18

A STRANGER IN HER MIST

By the summer of 2012, Helen's memory had continued to slip at a distressing rate. Jack decided to make a last-ditch effort to see if his wife could reconnect with her past by taking her to Narragansett for a week. After studying the Airbnb website, he'd found a little studio to rent for seven nights, a couple of short blocks from the old summer cottage they had leased until five years before. He hoped it might help to immerse her in the environment she had loved for most of their married life.

It proved to be a terrible mistake.

Their first night in the studio, as they settled into bed together, she turned to Jack and asked, "Where are we?" She had posed the same question repeatedly since they arrived.

"In Narragansett, Helen. We're renting this cottage for a week. It's been a long time since we've had a vacation."

Then, a few minutes later, she said, "The bed feels lumpy. This isn't our bed."

"You'll get used to it, darling."

"Where are we?"

Helen's state of confusion disrupted her sleep and aggravated her incontinence. During the night, they were both up for a couple of hours after Jack had to change the bed and mop up the floor. Good thing he'd remembered to pack lots of extra sheets and towels.

The next morning, as he put on a pot of coffee and attempted to navigate the unfamiliar kitchen in a groggy haze, Jack sighed. He had only been on "vacation" one day with his wife and he already felt exhausted.

They made it to the beach by late morning and staked out a good location for their umbrella and chairs. Helen dug her hands into the warm sand, sifting it through her fingers, and stuck three fingers into her mouth experimentally, recoiling in disgust from the gritty taste and texture of the sand. She cried like an inconsolable toddler when this happened. Jack laid an old blanket under her chair to avoid a recurrence of this ill-fated game. But when he held her hand and led her to the water's edge to cool their toes, she became terrified and planted both feet in the damp sand, refusing to continue.

"Maybe an ice cream will cheer you up," he said, conceding that the beach expedition hadn't been a resounding success.

"Oh, yes. Ice cream, I want ice cream."

At the ice cream parlor, she changed her mind several times as to what she wanted. The boy behind the counter sensed something strange about this woman, but he treated her with kindness and patience, letting her sample several flavors. When Jack convinced her to go with mint chip, her long-time favorite, she wrinkled her nose after a couple of bites and snapped, "This isn't what I ordered. I don't like it."

The boy appeared sympathetic to their plight, and Jack

escorted Helen back to the car, throwing a generous contribution into the tip jar before departing.

Jack knew from experience that restaurant dining was no longer a good option with Helen. But they did venture over to the clam shack one day for lunch. With its informal atmosphere and outdoor picnic tables, he figured they could safely manage a cup of clear chowder (Helen's old favorite) and an order of clam cakes, a Rhode Island specialty consisting of chopped clams in a doughy batter formed into balls deep-fried in oil. Since these tasty treats were hand-held and easy to chew, Jack assumed they would be on safe ground. But Helen refused the chowder altogether and ate only half a clam cake without enthusiasm, finally dropping it on the ground—he did not know whether by accident or on purpose.

Saddest of all, Helen mistook this vacation as her first in Narragansett. They walked past their old cottage, which had not changed in appearance except for a fresh coat of paint. Helen pointed and said, "Oh, look, Jack. That's such a cute place. Maybe we can stay there sometime." They drove to Hazard Avenue, where they parked by the rocks to watch the hikers. But these once cherished sights had become unfamiliar now.

Discouraged and remorseful that he had put his wife through what turned out to be a trying and unpleasant ordeal, Jack decamped and drove Helen back to Providence three days early.

The following week, Scott and Michael spent a night at Helen and Jack's en route to Boston for a schedule of college tours. Helen had not improved after they returned from the beach to their Providence house. Though she recognized her son Michael most of the time, Scott had matured in the past year, and she did not know him at all. Jack could see in his grandson's face that the boy was devastated.

Jack struggled to contain the irritation he felt toward Helen during Michael and Scott's brief stay. Couldn't she manage to act a little more cheerful when everyone had bent over backward to cater to her? How could she disappoint Scott this way? Jack knew he was being irrational and unfair, Helen couldn't help it—but sometimes, lately, he grew so damned weary of the whole situation.

Michael and a subdued Scott said their farewells early the next morning. Helen sat at the kitchen table, holding a coffee mug in both hands and staring out the window. When Scott gave her a bear hug and said, "See you, Nana," Jack saw the tears well up in his grandson's eyes. Though moved by this sight, Jack himself could only feel frustration and bitterness right now.

After they drove off and the sound of the car engine faded, Jack said, "I'm going to run outside for a moment to pick up the morning paper."

Helen frowned into her coffee but didn't respond.

"Helen, how about walking with me to the end of the driveway and we'll get the paper together? We could both use a breath of fresh air."

She shook her head.

"All right, then. I'll be back in a minute."

Jack headed out the kitchen door. As he came back up the steps with the paper, less than a minute later, he heard the unmistakable metallic sound of the door being bolted shut. He could see and hear Helen through the open kitchen window.

She had locked him out.

"There's a stranger out there," he overheard her say aloud to herself. "What's he doing?"

Now she shouted out the window, "What do you want?"

Jack made a fruitless attempt to open the back door, knowing the bolt would not give way. He knocked on the door and called out to his wife.

"Helen, it's me. Jack."

"Go away."

"It's Jack. Your husband." He knocked again.

She paused, took another look through the window, and said, "I don't have a husband. Go away, or I'll call the police. I don't let strangers in."

"Helen, please. I know your name. That proves I'm not a stranger, right? Please let me in."

"I told you to leave. I'm calling the police—right now."

Jack watched her pick up her cellphone and study the jumble of icons on the screen, uncertain of what to do next. She rarely used the cell anymore and had forgotten how it worked.

"Helen, let me in." Jack knocked again.

Helen ignored his pleas, and now he saw her walk across the room to the wall-mounted landline a few feet away. A note taped next to the phone displayed Jack's name and cell number in large print and, below it, *Emergencies: Call 911*. He'd posted it last year, recognizing it might be easier for Helen to place a call from a conventional wall phone.

Helen picked up the receiver. The mist in her head apparently cleared long enough for her to succeed in dialing 911, fingers trembling.

"Hello. Hello?" Jack listened to Helen's side of the conversation through the open window. "A man is breaking into my house . . . No, he's outside. I—I think I locked the door. I don't remember . . . You want to confirm my address? I'm not sure. Oh, wait. It's . . . 42 Gibson Road, Providence. Please come quickly." She hung up.

Helen had given the wrong information to the 911 operator. Gibson Road had been her address as a young girl. Jack expected them to ascertain her location regardless, knowing that landline-based emergency calls could pinpoint the whereabouts of the caller with instant accuracy. But he retrieved his cell from his back pocket and made his own 911 call.

"My wife has Alzheimer's, and she's mistaken me for a burglar and locked me out of the house. She just called 911 from our landline."

The dispatcher advised him to stay on the line until the police arrived. He waited in silence, recognizing that his repeated shouts to Helen through the window only fueled the fire of her panic.

A police cruiser pulled up to the curb a few minutes later, and two officers jumped out and strode toward Jack. How fortunate that he'd been carrying his cellphone and had the means to place his own emergency call. Jack recollected those terrible stories in the news about innocent people getting arrested or shot because they'd been mistaken for intruders.

He greeted the officers. "My wallet is inside the house, but I have a copy of my driver's license on my phone." He handed it to the police to confirm his identity.

"Has this happened before?" one of the policemen asked.

"Sometimes my wife doesn't recognize me, but she's never locked me out. I just walked to the end of the driveway to get the paper. I never imagined something like this could happen so quickly."

"Let me borrow that phone for a minute," said one of the officers. Then he spoke in a calm voice to Helen through the window, holding up his badge. "Mrs. Winokur, I'm here to help you. Would you please let me inside so that we can talk? My partner will wait outside with this gentleman."

Helen opened the door cautiously. The policeman showed her Jack's photo ID, pointing out the address.

"This is your husband Jack, Mrs. Winokur. I think maybe you got confused for a minute. He'd like to come in and talk to you."

She examined the picture of Jack's license and gazed out the window at her husband, who stood next to the second policeman. "I—I guess it's okay," she said. But she gave Jack a distrustful look when he walked into the kitchen.

"Helen, remember this morning? Our son Michael visited us with our grandson Scott. They came to see you."

He thought he saw a glimmer of comprehension.

"Yes, I—I do remember something about that. They're not here now, are they?"

"No, that's right. They had to drive to Boston."

"Oh. Yes."

Helen walked back to the kitchen table and took a seat, grasping her coffee mug in both hands. She stared down into the mug and started sipping the cold coffee, now oblivious to the others around her. Jack thanked the officers, who retreated politely from the house.

As the days wore on, Jack focused on the hundred quotidian tasks required for Helen's care. Check her Depend once an hour to make sure she remained dry. Drive her to appointments—the doctor this morning, the hair salon on Wednesday, the dentist on Friday. Take her to her Alzheimer's music class in the afternoon. Shop for groceries and other supplies. Figure out the meal plan. Would she eat salmon again? Wash a load of laundry—unbelievable how fast she could go through clothes and bedding.

In the evening, after putting her to bed, Jack rewarded himself with a glass of good wine from his cellar. Too busy to indulge in self-pity, he reviewed the day's accomplishments. Helen hadn't locked him out of the house; she'd cooperated with her bathing; she'd even had a bowel movement in the toilet—a rare triumph. He felt pleased with all the boxes he'd checked off.

But on other days, hopelessness washed over him like

a powerful wave. He was sixty-eight years old and felt younger than that, but the future appeared bleak. Most of his friends were retiring and enjoying travel, golf, boating, and active social lives. But Jack had forgotten what it felt like to experience pleasure. And when he allowed the negative thoughts to take over, he despaired that feelings like hope and joy would never again be within his grasp.

19

THE DECIDING VOTE

I kept thinking about poor Daisy and how my sister got them both kicked out of therapy dog training because of her profanity. And *that*, in turn, triggered a downward spiral of worry that Ma might be kicked out of Tropical Gardens because of all her foul language. By the time I met with the nurse on Friday afternoon to review my mother's first month, I'd convinced myself that Ma's expulsion from the facility was imminent.

But to my relief, the subject never even came up.

My mother got a good evaluation. The nurse pronounced her "stable," though she still declined to assign an AD stage to her. The sole black mark had to do with her incontinence, which had worsened. I asked if the change in environment had caused it. Cindy said maybe, but she'd expected it to happen sooner or later anyway. Then she launched into a description of this "Extra Care" program they had for the Highly Incontinent, where you paid a supplemental fee for additional toileting help and laundry services. When she pitched it to me, it sounded like an optional add-on, but no such luck. If we wanted Ma to stay, we had no choice but to ante up.

I considered it fortunate, after all, that Vicky hadn't come to the meeting. I must inform her of the added cost, regardless, and I could already hear her bellyaching.

Extra Care or not, thank goodness Ma could stay put. I breathed a huge sigh of relief that the one-month review had gone well. I felt reassured to know the staff here looked on my mother with fondness, and they couldn't care less if she swore like a long-haul truck driver.

After leaving Ma for the day, I headed to the weekly happy hour with my girlfriends to get their input on my potential "date" with Jack. I had emailed all three women earlier to confirm that everyone planned to go. Attendance had fallen off, what with summer vacations. I'd hoped to get all their feedback on this.

Amy replied first:

—*I'll be there.*

But she responded only to me. I hated when people forgot to reply to all. Then I had to respond to Amy and the other two, saying:

—*Amy's in, how about the rest of you?*

—*I'm in.*

This was from Carol—who, to my annoyance, also failed to reply to all. Her careless response necessitated yet a third email from me to the group. Red, with her unfailing attention to detail, correctly replied to all that she would be there too.

I sent off a quick message to Red alone, groaning about the unnecessary confusion surrounding the previous email conversation.

She shot back a one-word response:

—NOCDAR.

No One Can Do Anything Right, indeed.

After the server delivered our tray of drinks, I stared thoughtfully at my cosmo. "You know, that day I went to the wine bar with Jack, it brought back memories of Richard."

"Now that's a good argument for *not* going out with him," Carol said.

"Let me finish. They both love good wine. But when Richard used to talk about wine, he mostly bragged about how much he'd spent on this or that bottle. Jack seems passionate about it."

"When Jack went on about wine, did you feel awkward?" Amy asked.

"Well, at times—partly because I don't know much about it, and partly because Richard used to make fun of me for drinking sweet cocktails. But when I remember that day with Jack, I felt like he tried his best to put me at ease."

"It sounds like this guy *gets* you," said Red.

"Maybe he does. I don't know, though. My sister's making a big fuss about the age difference." I related our discussion about the dating equation.

"That formula is irrelevant," said Amy. "Chronological age is overrated. It's the biological age that counts." As the oldest member of our group, and the most pampered, it didn't shock me that she should take this position. Red nodded, but Carol scoffed at this assertion.

"Does Jack *seem* his age?" Amy asked.

"Definitely not," said Red without hesitation.

Carol challenged this. "How do you know? You met him for, like, what? Two minutes?"

"Doesn't matter. That's all it takes."

Amy said, "When my college roommate turned thirty, she fell in love with a man twenty-five years older."

"And?"

"They got married."

"Tell us how they're doing. Are they still happy?" I asked hopefully.

"Oh, he's dead now."

"See," said Carol. "Age does matter. You can only keep yourself fit for so long, but at some point, everything goes to hell in a handbasket."

Amy gave her a withering look.

"Present company excluded," Carol said.

"Well, I think you should go to his place for dinner," said Red. "I don't see what the big deal is. Nobody's getting married here."

"That's right, because Jack already is married," Carol reminded us. Then she turned to me and asked, "Have you lost sight of how it felt when Richard was unfaithful to you all those times? Have you forgotten how you used to cry on our shoulders?"

"But when Richard cheated on me, I was a young woman with a new baby. That's different." I uttered this last remark with a little uncertainty, glancing first at Amy and next at Red for validation.

"Barbara's right," said Amy. "The wife sounds about a hundred and ten years old, and she's totally out of it."

Red said, "I think you should go. I agree with Amy. Besides, he's cute. Nice eyes."

"Can you be cute at seventy-two?" Carol sounded doubtful.

"Certainly, you can. There's no expiration date on cuteness," said Amy, who, in all our years together, had never revealed her own age. I suspected she was sixty-two if she was a minute.

Carol, however, still smarted from her own ex-husband's infidelities and stood her ground. She said in an uncompromising tone, "Cute or not, cheating is cheating. And married is married."

After I left happy hour, I tallied up the votes as I drove to the supermarket to pick up tonight's dinner and a few staples. I counted two votes in favor of the date with Jack (Amy and Red) and two against (Carol and Vicky). Oh, and one abstaining. Because I still had not cast the deciding vote. I realized with some trepidation that the polls would be closing soon. I'd promised Jack an answer by dinnertime tonight, and the hour had nearly arrived. I needed to shop, prepare shrimp stir-fry for Sarah and me, and call Jack with my answer.

I've considered hanging a sign on my back to warn fellow shoppers: *Do not get behind me in line.* I was almost certain to pick the slowest checkout aisle every time. I invariably found myself behind an elderly retiree whose sole activity that day was to chat it up with the cashier, or else I'd be stuck with a trainee who'd started that same morning and was struggling to punch in the codes.

Today, the shopper in front of me happened to be one of the six remaining people in America who still paid for groceries with a personal bank check, requiring approval by a manager who had gone out on break. As aisle five came to a complete standstill, the customers who'd streamed past me on the fast-moving aisle four with its super-efficient checker were no doubt at home with their families by now, purposefully unpacking their purchases and settling in for the evening.

This afternoon, however, all the waiting paid off because it gave me an opportunity to mull over my dilemma. By the time the clerk handed me a receipt and asked, "Do you need help with your bags, ma'am?" I'd decided whether to vote yea or nay to Jack's invitation.

20

FIRST HELEN, NOW BARBARA

A little after seven o'clock on Saturday evening, Jack looked out his window just in time to see Barbara pull up in the Prius. She sat in the car for a few minutes, and Jack wondered if she was uncertain of the address. The modern wood and glass structure with its multiple intersecting roof planes often took new visitors by surprise. He started to go outside to tell her she'd found the correct house when she finally stepped out of the car.

"I've never seen a house like this," Barbara said as she entered. The early evening light filtered through the large windows and skylights, accenting their unconventional shapes. "Is that a trapezoid or a rhombus?" she asked, pointing to one of several high windows in the foyer, which had a vaulted, open-beam ceiling. "Geometry has never been my strong suit."

Jack poured them each a glass of a dry, salmon-colored French rosé and gave Barbara a house tour as they sipped their wine. Numerous paintings and drawings—all original art—covered the walls in the living areas. Next, they passed through a long hallway lined with laminated print advertisements mounted on plaques awarded by a society of local marketing professionals.

"Helen created some of these ads, I did others, and the two of us collaborated on the rest," Jack said as they walked.

"It's wonderful, Jack. The whole place has a look of high design, but it's so warm and welcoming, not pretentious. I can't imagine how it must feel to live in such an interesting home."

Jack had invested a great deal of himself in designing and building the place with Helen twenty-six years before. In the office, they stopped as Barbara examined two framed articles about the design of the house, hanging side by side. He watched her study the photos of Helen and himself. He'd been around forty-six and Helen in her early fifties when the articles came out. They looked like an age-appropriate couple back then, both fit and attractive.

Barbara gave a sad smile.

The tour ended back in the kitchen, where she admired the expanse of gleaming countertops, the enormous cooking island, and the abundance of natural light even at this late hour.

"Have you remodeled the kitchen since the original construction?" she asked.

"No. Except for replacing some of the appliances, it's the way we built it in 1990."

"Well, in that case, you were ahead of your time. This is still a very modern, state-of-the-art kitchen."

"I appreciate the compliments. Why don't we get started with the cooking now?"

They had agreed to prepare a simple Indian menu together: a chicken curry, the popular lentil side dish known as *dahl,* and a pre-purchased whole wheat flat-bread or *naan.*

On the island, Jack had placed fresh wine glasses, a tray with small saucers of ground spices and other cooking ingredients, and a selection of bowls and saucepans. An uncorked bottle of white wine, nestled in a cooling collar, sat on a side countertop across from the island. Perched on the same counter was a silver-framed picture of a young Helen.

"With dinner, I'm planning to serve a California viognier," Jack said, pointing to the bottle in the collar. "It's got the right balance for Indian food—not at all cloying, but sweet enough to pair well with the spicy dishes."

"Sounds perfect. Now, what can I do to help?"

"Let's start with the chicken dish. First, you can check to see if the ingredients are ready to go. I made a list on my cell." Jack handed his phone to Barbara.

"A list. Oh, wonderful." But Barbara frowned as she scrutinized what Jack had written, and she read aloud, "Turnover? Graham mass? Jack, this doesn't make any sense."

Jack shared her confusion before saying, "Sorry. I forgot for a moment. I tried typing the recipe into my phone before I went shopping, but autocorrect changed all the Indian ingredients to unrecognizable words." He sighed.

"I hate when that happens. Two weeks ago, I texted a group of friends suggesting a place to meet for cocktails. I told them it had 'pretty ample bar seating.' But somehow, autocorrect changed 'ample' to 'American.' My friends wondered why on earth I wanted to meet at a place with pretty American bar seating."

They laughed together.

"I love pretty American bar seating. But it's not easy to find," Jack said.

"I know. A lot of the bars in Providence have that dingy Irish pub seating."

"Or tacky nautical bar seating."

"Ha. Remind me how we got onto this subject."

"Autocorrect," said Jack. "After autocorrect garbled my shopping list, I resorted to the old-school approach and wrote it out in longhand." He retrieved a scrap of notepaper from the counter and unfolded it. "Here you go. Try this one." He handed the paper to Barbara. "And here's the recipe." He passed her a computer printout.

"Ah. Turmeric, garam masala, curry powder. That's more like it. But . . ." Barbara glanced with uncertainty between the recipe and the ingredients on the island. "I'm not certain what's what. Basically, we've got *yellow* powder, *orange* powder, and *yellow-orange* powder."

They both paused, staring down at the spices. "Not sure if I know either," Jack said.

Barbara snapped her fingers. "Go and grab the spice jars, and we'll match them up."

Another pause. "No spice jars." Jack sighed.

"No spice jars?"

"I bought these from open bins at the market and spooned them into plastic baggies."

"Let's check the baggies, then. You must've labeled them," said Barbara.

"I did."

"Great."

Jack went to the pantry, opened the door, and retrieved three small bags half-filled with the colorful spices. He rejoined Barbara at the island, held up the baggies one by one, and read, "163, 184, and 172."

They paused yet again—spice identification having reached a dead end.

"We could call the market and ask them to look up the names of the spices," Barbara said but with less confidence this time.

Jack gave her a doubtful look.

"I suppose that's a little obsessive, even for me."

"We'll figure it out."

Then Barbara asked, "Where's the garam masala? I happen to know that one is a brownish color. I don't see that here."

"Oh, I couldn't find any of that at the store. No big deal. We can use a little extra of the other spices instead."

"Well, I don't know. I guess maybe we could do that."

Jack transferred a heaping spoonful of each of the three spices into a large shallow dish and handed Barbara a measuring cup containing chicken broth.

"Now, pour the broth almost to the top of the rim, and whisk it carefully."

She hesitated. "This is an awfully shallow dish for mixing."

"Ah, but it's important to use a shallow dish," Jack said in a professorial tone.

"Why is that?"

"It adds an element of *danger* that makes the whole process much more exciting."

She cast him another doubtful look, not sure what to make of this. The two of them laughed at the same time.

"Okay, if you say so." Barbara continued to laugh as she poured in the broth an ounce at a time.

But when she glanced down at the bowl, which indeed seemed precariously full, she froze. Jack moved closer to her, positioning a wire whisk in her right hand. He continued to hold his hand over hers. She looked up at him, their faces close together.

"When you stir it, you need to be gentle yet decisive at the same time. Uncertainty will only lead to failure," Jack said, still using that tone of breezy self-confidence. His blue eyes sparkled with amusement.

Barbara turned her head away from Jack, focusing on the bowl again. They started to whisk the liquid together, his hand still atop Barbara's, but most of the contents sloshed over onto the granite island countertop.

"Uh-oh." Barbara looked down in despair at the mess. She held up the whisk in her right hand. "I should have told you I'm left-handed. Oh, dear. Now we won't have enough broth for the recipe."

Jack grabbed a dish towel and mopped up the countertop. "No, no, *my* fault for introducing recklessness into the proceedings. We have plenty more of the spice powders. And I'm sure I must have broth somewhere." He went back to the pantry, his eyes scrolling up and down the shelves.

"I only have beef broth," he said, pulling out a quart container. "You're okay with eating beef products, I hope."

"Yes, but . . . beef broth in a chicken recipe?"

"That is a dilemma. The best way to solve it is . . ." Jack

grabbed the viognier bottle from the counter and pulled out the cork.

"Oh, pour wine into the broth. That might work."

"No—pour wine into the *cooks*." Jack poured a generous amount into two fresh glasses, which they clinked together before taking their first taste.

"Mmm . . . nice. And perfect for this weather."

"Okay, Barbara, it's confession time. I've never made Indian food before."

"But you've been telling me—"

"I know," he said with an apologetic shake of the head. "That was me trying to impress you."

"It's all right, honestly. The fact is, I have a confession as well."

"You do?" Jack said, curious.

"Yes. I—I've been trying to pass myself off as a big wine enthusiast like you."

"And you're not."

"Oh, I enjoy wine on occasion, and the ones you've served tonight are lovely . . . but wine has never been a favorite beverage. Maybe if I knew more about it, I'd feel different."

"You knew Malbecs hailed from Argentina," Jack said.

"Dumb luck I happened to remember that. If you asked me to recap everything I know about wine, I think my entire narrative could be measured on an egg timer."

Jack grinned at this. "It seems our true colors have been exposed. I am not a gourmet cook, and you are not an oenophile."

"Guilty as charged."

"I can live with it if you can."

This time, Barbara grinned. "Shall we try to salvage the curry?" she said, turning her attention to the recipe printout. "The next step is to sauté a chopped onion." She grabbed an onion that Jack had placed among the cooking ingredients and started to reach for a cutting board. But Jack politely took the onion from her hand and guided Barbara into one of the high-backed stools along the opposite side of the island, stationing her wine glass in front of her.

"No, wait. You sit and relax. I've got a better idea."

Around ninety minutes later, Jack and Barbara sat together in the breakfast nook adjacent to the kitchen. This cozy area had a tile-covered table large enough for four, bordered on two sides by comfortable built-in banquettes. Open Chinese food containers, dinner plates, and rice bowls cluttered the small tabletop.

"I hope you liked that. I may be deficient at cooking Indian, but I'm a genius at ordering Chinese." Jack grinned and waved his chopsticks in the air.

"It was excellent—but hot," Barbara said, fanning herself with her napkin to emphasize the point.

"I've got mango sorbet that should help to cool the palate." Clearing the dirty dishes and food containers from the table, Jack deposited them in the sink and walked over to the freezer, pulling out the frozen dessert and spooning it into two small bowls as they talked.

"You must think I'm a lunatic. The whole cooking

experiment has been one misstep after another. In your hands, I'm sure we would have had a better outcome. You're extremely methodical."

"Ouch." Barbara grimaced at this comment.

"Did I say something wrong?"

"Oh, it's not your fault. It's only that Richard used to accuse me of being obsessively methodical, and that was on a *good* day. On a bad day, he used terms like controlling and neurotic."

Jack wrinkled his brow in disapproval. "I would never say that to you."

"Even if it's true?"

"Even then." He walked back to the table and set down a dessert bowl at each of their places. He picked up a small bag from the restaurant and pulled out two fortune cookies, handing one to Barbara and keeping the other for himself.

"Here. Have this with your sorbet."

Barbara started to crack the cookie open but stopped herself and said, "Read yours first."

Jack broke his cookie in half, extracted the thin white slip of paper, and read, "'Something you lost will soon turn up.' Intriguing."

Barbara followed suit, reading, "'Follow your smile and you won't go wrong.' Well, technically, that isn't a fortune. And I have no idea what it means."

Jack leaned toward her and said, "I'd like to follow your smile. You have a magnificent smile, Barbara."

"Oh, gosh," she said, embarrassed.

He took both her hands in his and said in a soft voice,

"You are so lovely."

She returned Jack's gaze but did not speak. Then he leaned in closer to give Barbara a gentle kiss on the mouth. After he pulled back from her, she turned her head away but not before Jack saw an expression in her eyes of—*what*? Uncertainty? Fear? He only knew it wasn't the look he'd hoped for.

Barbara cleared her throat. "Jack, I—"

"What's wrong?"

"I—I think . . . My stomach is screaming at me after all that spicy food, and it doesn't have anything nice to say."

"That's not good. Let me get you some club soda, or antacid, or something."

"No, no. When this happens, the best remedy is to go home and get a good night's rest. I think I'd better do that now," she said, the nervous words of excuse tumbling out much too fast. She rose from the table.

"I understand." Jack nodded and rose alongside her.

"I—I'm sorry to be a party pooper. But thank you for tonight. It's been a fun evening." She attempted a smile.

"I imagine I'll see you tomorrow," Jack said as he walked her to the front door. Trying to lighten the mood, he added, "I can't believe Luau Sunday is rolling around again."

"I know. Good night, Jack," Barbara said, hurrying out the door as if she couldn't get away fast enough.

"Good night," Jack said—addressing the empty foyer since Barbara had already fled the premises. He let out a long sigh and went back into the kitchen, where he picked up the wine bottle to pour himself another glass, then changed his mind and set it down. He picked up the framed picture of Helen on the counter and addressed it aloud.

"Hey, Helen, what an evening I've had. I thought Barbara and I were hitting it off, and all of a sudden... Oh, bloody hell. Guess I blew it, huh." He put the picture back down and started cleaning up the kitchen. As Jack worked, he reflected on everything that had happened tonight, trying to make sense of it.

The first thought that occurred to him was that Helen wouldn't have disapproved of his actions. She always used to tell him, if something happened to her, he must promise to find someone else to love. "Remember that?" he said, glancing back at his wife's picture.

That was a rhetorical question since Helen had not remembered anything for a long time now. Given the age difference, she and Jack had both anticipated she might be the one to go first. Such discussions between them took place a lifetime ago, before the dementia got bad.

Even though he had long been deprived of physical affection and emotional companionship, Jack had not contemplated being with another woman until recently. Over the course of this summer, as he got to know Barbara, he came to recognize he was ready for something else. But apparently, he and Barbara were not meant to be.

Nothing like an unwelcome pass from a pathetic geezer to get a woman racing for the exit, thought Jack. He said aloud in a self-mocking tone, "Barbara, you have a magnificent smile." He groaned at the embarrassing recollection, shaking his head in self-reproach. *Good God, is that the best I could do? I suppose that's what happens when you're out of practice. No wonder she ran out, clutching her stomach.*

Then, another more hopeful possibility crossed his mind. Maybe she hadn't invented the stomach trouble. Spicy Szechuan shrimp seemed in hindsight like a poor prelude to a romantic tryst.

Then his mind traveled back to another late July evening, forty-eight summers ago. Jack and Helen lived in New York City then—she with a female roommate in a stylish two-bedroom pre-war apartment building on the Upper West Side, Jack crammed into a small railroad flat in Brooklyn with two other young men his age. Jack was twenty-four, and Helen, about to turn thirty.

Helen and the older sister of one of Jack's roommates had become close friends in college. When Helen organized a birthday dinner for her friend in late May, Jack reluctantly accompanied his roommate to the party. This reluctance vanished on arrival upon receiving a warm welcome from a tall, slender, attractive woman with long ash-blond hair and startling green eyes. For the first half-hour, Jack assessed the small group, trying to determine if Helen had a boyfriend in tow or at least a date. To his pleasant surprise, she appeared to be alone.

Jack and Helen ended up talking at great length that evening. She held a good copywriting position at one of the fastest-growing midtown advertising agencies. As a "creative" herself, she took an immediate interest in Jack's career as a graphic design artist. Only two years out of design school, Jack had been working steadily, and they discussed the various career tracks he might follow.

He stayed until the end of the party. After thanking Helen, Jack turned to give her a small wave and said, "See you sometime." She responded with a smile that made his heart constrict.

Jack felt an immediate attraction to Helen but tried to put those feelings aside and think of her more as a mentor than potential girlfriend material. After all, what would this attractive, sophisticated older woman with a high-powered career want with a young kid still wet behind the ears? Jack feared Helen might dismiss him as the pesky roommate of her best friend's younger brother. But after about a week, he called to invite her out for coffee. She accepted at once, and they spent a pleasurable hour together.

Another couple of weeks passed, and he called to suggest getting together for lunch. This time, Jack had a professional issue to discuss with Helen. He had received a job offer from the in-house marketing group at a department store chain and wanted her feedback on the opportunity.

Though the new job involved a significant salary increase, Helen pointed out the negatives that would be associated with such a move. "You'll be doing one thing and one thing only—designing retail ads, flyers, that sort of thing. It won't leave you much room to grow, either from a creative standpoint or a professional one."

She had raised a good point. "Also, what if you can't stand the work or the people—or both?"

"Seems like that's a risk with any new job," said Jack.

"Well, yes. But when you work at an advertising agency

or design firm, the work is varied, and the clients come and go. It's a much more dynamic environment. I always say, if you don't like your agency job, wait a few months. Things will probably be different by then."

He trusted Helen's advice, and she convinced him not to take the job. As he got to know her better, Jack admitted to himself that the initial attraction had blossomed into a strong infatuation. Still, he continued to keep her at arm's length. What if he made a move and she rejected him out of hand? It would ruin the friendship, not to mention the already budding mentorship. Given the risks, the relationship stalled in neutral for several more weeks.

But then, he had an extra ticket to a chamber music performance on a weeknight evening in Central Park, and he invited her to join him. A magical New York summer night, the breeze stirred gently, and the sweet scent of night-blooming jasmine wafted toward them as they sat close together on the provided folding chairs. But as Jack tried to focus on the musical intricacies of the late Beethoven string quartets, he found himself distracted by Helen's physical proximity.

He remained uncertain of what to do, if anything. Jack knew he was attractive to women. Though not handsome in a conventional way, his face had character and appeal, with sapphire blue eyes that one immediately noticed. His curly dark hair and lithe build didn't exactly hurt him either. Normally Jack approached the opposite sex with a high degree of self-confidence, and normally he got what he wanted. But this woman was different. He pictured her with a mature man of thirty-five or forty, perhaps—someone successful and polished. Someone who was not Jack.

After the concert, as they walked toward Central Park West on an uneven and dimly lit pathway, Helen asked if Jack perhaps had a small flashlight.

"No, sorry, I'm afraid I forgot to bring one." He gripped her hand in his. "Hang onto me and take it easy in those heels."

Helen squeezed his hand in response. Emboldened by this, he started caressing her hand with his own. With the attentiveness of a skilled masseur, he stroked her palm, then rubbed his thumb up and down each of her fingers, then enclosed her hand more tightly.

Jack swore he could feel a powerful surge of attraction passing between them, right through their hands. Chemistry? It sounded like such a cliché, but he knew he didn't imagine it. When they emerged from the darkness of the park into the mellow light of a streetlamp at Central Park West, they paused, and Helen looked up at Jack. She was beaming at him.

Jack reached for Helen, and neither of them hesitated for a moment. Before he knew it, he started to kiss her without reserve, and to his great joy, she returned his kisses with equal passion. Once Jack understood they both wanted this, the rest flowed naturally.

After their first couple of weeks together, Jack and Helen forgot all about their difference in age and stature. They encountered some initial opposition from friends and family on both sides—people who feared that Helen might be using Jack as a boy-toy or that Jack might regard her as a meal ticket or a stepping-stone to a better job. But over time, it became obvious to all that these two people had fallen deeply in love, and the objections subsided.

Tonight, at Jack's home in Providence, the tables had turned. This time, he was the older one, wondering if this young woman (well, young to *him*) shared his feelings. It felt exciting and wonderful and terrifying all at the same time. It reminded him of his experience that night in Central Park with Helen all those years ago. Like history repeating itself. He'd read it as a sort of omen that he should take things to the next level with Barbara.

Evidently, this time he'd misread the signs. Big time.

Finished with the cleanup from dinner, Jack poured himself another glass of wine and sank down onto one of the banquettes. He could still imagine that Barbara sat close to him, that he could smell the light tropical scent of her shampoo. He took another sip of viognier.

Despite Barbara's sudden about-face and abrupt departure, the sweetness of the evening lingered with him, and he continued to float in a serene place somewhere above reality. He felt like a patient numbed by a soothing anesthetic that had not yet worn off. Tomorrow the pain would come, the crushing pain brought on by one loss atop another. First Helen, now Barbara. It seemed too unfair.

But for tonight, for a little while longer, he would allow himself to remember how natural and right it felt to have Barbara by his side sipping wine, enjoying dinner, laughing together. That soaring feeling reminded him so much of his first night with Helen decades ago.

Though this latest episode in his romantic life did not have a happy conclusion, Jack still thought: *To experience those same feelings over a woman, after almost fifty years . . . it was indescribable.*

21

MAKING THE LEAP

By three o'clock Sunday morning, I abandoned any hope of sleeping. The events of last night kept replaying in my head.

Over dessert, Jack kissed me sweetly—not in an aggressive or demanding way. But I reacted like a deer in the headlights, bolting in panic and running for cover.

When I'd driven about halfway home, I pulled the car over to the side of the road and sat there, puzzling over my own actions. What had I just done? All right, I knew *what* I'd done, but the real question was why? Did I flee the scene because I dreaded exposure to a sagging geriatric ass, à la Samantha and Ed in *Sex and the City*? But no, I doubted that. I think fear motivated me, pure and simple.

As much as I had felt compelled to run from Jack's place a short while ago, I now felt the urgent need to go *back*, though I didn't have a clear plan for what I would do once I got there. (*Soooo* unlike me.)

On the return drive to Jack's house, I composed a mental laundry list of possible negative outcomes.

(A)   I'll ring the bell, but Jack will have already retired upstairs to bed and won't hear me.

(B)   I'll ring the bell, and Jack will hear it but refuse to answer. *Oh, dear God, how humiliating. And if I am left standing at the front doorstep, I'll have no way to know whether the reason was "A" or "B."*

(C)   Jack will invite me back into the house but then blast me for behaving like such an idiot. *This is the worst of all the possible bad outcomes.*

(D)   Jack will invite me back in and engage in polite conversation, but he won't really want anything further to do with me, having judged me too neurotic and unreliable. *Which I evidently am.*

Given Jack's innate kindness, I couldn't believe he'd shut me out of the house ("B") or usher me in only to hurl a string of expletives ("C"). And could he have retired to bed in a few minutes' time ("A")? That left a polite invitation ("D") as the most plausible scenario. And this would be an unsatisfying outcome since another hour of aimless chitchat would only leave me wondering about Jack's true feelings. I'd find out sooner or later, but I hated uncertainty.

I rang the bell. Jack opened the door in short order—eliminating outcomes "A" and "B."

"Barbara." He looked baffled by my return, and who could blame him? He motioned for me to come inside. Since I encountered no screaming, cursing, or projectile vomiting, signs pointed in the direction of "D." The two of us stood in the foyer.

"Did you forget something?" he asked me.

"I forgot my manners, Jack. I lied about my stomach, and in the interest of full disclosure, I didn't want to leave things like that between us."

I knew I sounded nervous again as my words spilled

out, but I needed to speak my piece. "I don't know why I felt the need not only to lie to you but to lie so elaborately. The fact is, I never have stomach trouble. Vicky says, for someone who's such a bundle of nerves, it's unbelievable how strong my stomach is."

Jack pondered this for a moment. "Is that what she says?"

"To be accurate, she says it's un-*fucking*-believable. Pardon my French." I felt my cheeks grow hot.

"I didn't know this. Though it crossed my mind that a gastric disturbance might not be the real culprit. But since you're back and not in any apparent distress, will you join me in a glass of wine?"

"That depends." I had regained confidence, my manner somewhat coy now.

"On what?"

I paused for dramatic effect. "Do you have pretty American bar seating?"

He threw back his head and laughed. "Not just pretty. *Breathtaking.*"

"In that case . . . I accept."

He led me to a screened sun porch and gestured for me to take a seat on an upholstered rattan couch. I sat and concentrated on taking deep, steady breaths while I waited for Jack to return with two goblets of wine.

We clinked glasses for maybe the third time that evening. As the one who had interrupted the festivities with my rude departure, I felt it incumbent on me to say something.

"Jack, for some reason, I panicked before."

"Maybe you felt that we—no, never mind. It's not fair of

me to press you for an explanation."

In my opinion, it seemed totally fair of him, but I was happy to be relieved of the obligation. "I'm not sure I could explain it to myself, even."

"Then don't try. Let's both take a deep breath and dial it back," he said.

"Dial it back to . . . when, exactly?"

"Before tonight."

"Before tonight," I said. *Before we kissed.* I felt a sharp stab of disappointment at this idea.

"Oh. I thought you meant dial it back to right before I left."

"Right before you left," he said.

Why did we both keep repeating each other's phrases?

"Yes, after you . . . before I . . ?" I wanted us to dial it straight back to the kissing sequence but couldn't bring myself to tell him that. Instead, I said, "Oh, what the hell." I shrugged as he watched me with a puzzled expression. I took a big gulp of wine to fortify myself before reaching out to Jack and pulling him to me.

I kissed him with considerable enthusiasm on the lips, my arms circling the back of his neck. Only one teeny glitch: My aim fell a little off the mark, and when I first engaged Jack in the kiss, my nose kind of slammed against his, and for a moment, my nostrils tingled with that heavy fullness that sometimes preceded a major nosebleed. But the moment passed, and, to my immense relief, the gusher never materialized.

Jack seemed unfazed by the nose-bashing. Evidently, the angle of impact ensured that I bore the brunt of the trauma. He pulled back and smiled at me with a kind of happy, if dazed, expression.

"Oh, my," is all he said, putting his arms around me.

"Jack. Maybe I decided to cut and run because I felt scared."

"Of what?"

Truth be told, I didn't think I was a very good catch. I likened myself to a piece of real estate that'd been sitting on the market too long. But I simply said, "Scared I'd be bad at this, after all these years . . . that I wouldn't measure up . . . that you wouldn't like me."

"You were afraid I wouldn't like *you*?" Jack said, making sure he'd gotten it right.

I nodded.

"Oh, Barbara. You can cross that off your worry list. Right now."

And then we started kissing each other—I mean *crazy* kissing. We behaved like a couple of prizefighters in the ring, contending energetically to see who could rack up the most points. And though we seemed to be an even match, the judges might've given me a slight edge. Not to brag or anything.

Barbara, are you in there?

This wild woman sure as hell didn't feel like me, yet you couldn't describe it as an out-of-body experience either. I was very much *inside* my own body and could hardly wait for Jack to get in there too.

When I'd rehearsed the various outcomes during the return drive to Jack's, I had omitted one important scenario—the one where we fell into each other's arms. I guessed that would be scenario "E." For ecstasy, perhaps.

I wondered why I'd previously been wishy-washy about Jack. Nothing half-hearted about the way I was responding to him now. I had made the leap from befuddled to besotted in no time flat. It was a leap into unknown territory for me—a place of abandon, and passion, and risk.

Then, Jack drew back from me and rose from the couch, taking me by the hand. He led me up the stairs into a comfortable and well-appointed but unoccupied room—a guest room, I assumed. I felt relieved he did not bring me to the bed he'd shared with Helen for all those years.

Standing by the queen-sized guest bed, he turned to me and asked, "Do we need to be concerned about birth control?"

"Nope, no worries." Hooray for menopause.

He started removing my clothing and his own, stroking my skin with gentle fingertips as he slowly undressed me. When he unfastened my bra, I had an awkward moment when I felt myself blush. What if I looked fat to him?

But he gazed at my body with admiration and desire. "You're so beautiful."

Maybe he was only saying that to put me at ease, but I decided I didn't care and allowed myself to enjoy the compliment. He looked darned good himself. He had a lean and wiry build, still well-muscled and smooth-skinned for a man his age. I felt gratified to learn the shedding of outer garments had not revealed any unwelcome surprises.

He pulled me gently down onto the bed beside him. Where we had been frantic and untamed before, Jack now recalibrated the pace, which became slow and tender and deliberate. He traced a line of kisses down the front of my body with his lips, lightly brushing my throat, my breasts, my belly with feathery kisses. He lifted his head and gazed up at me.

God, those blue eyes.

"Everything okay?" he asked me.

Oh, yeah.

It occurred to me that "okay" might well be the under-statement of the month. But I simply whispered, "Yes, Jack."

He pulled himself back up to kiss my mouth again. I took in the faint musky scent of his body, the salty taste of his skin, the rough warmth of his cheek against mine. Everything about the man aroused desire in me, much to my astonished delight.

Finally, he slipped off my panties and lowered his body onto mine, devouring me with a long, deep kiss. I traced my fingers down his back, planting one hand on each of his buttocks—which, for the record, I found to be pleas-ingly firm.

Afterward, as we lay together with our bodies still entwined, I recalled the conversation last week when Vicky had harped on the age gap between Jack and me. At the time, I'd said in his defense, "There's nothing old about him."

As it turned out, I was right.

Back in my own bed after a sleepless night, I must have drifted off shortly before dawn, not awakening until nine-thirty. I smiled and awarded myself five minutes to day-dream about the most tender moments with Jack before jumping out of bed to shower and dress.

No sign of Sarah. Maybe she went to Starbucks to ren-dezvous with friends. But she'd promised to arrive early at Tropical Gardens to spend time with Ma before the Luau Sunday meal, and I knew she'd be true to her word.

I rummaged through the closet and found a multi-col-ored, floral print two-piece outfit—a clingy skirt and matching sleeveless V-neck top—that I'd purchased a couple of years ago for a Hawaiian theme party. I'd only worn it once since splashy tropical ensembles weren't my usual style.

I remembered, with embarrassment, that I had selected a boring cotton shell, navy slacks, and a strand of pearls to wear to my first Luau Sunday in July. To my chagrin, I'd been the only person in the room who had failed to rise to the occasion. Determined not to dress like a schoolmarm this time around, I donned the Hawaiian outfit, applied a touch of my one red lipstick, and put on a floppy yellow sunhat as the finishing touch. I examined my fashion efforts in the mirror, flashed a scarlet smile at myself, and went on my way.

After checking in at the front desk and selecting a plas-tic lei from a hanging rack—yellow to match the sunhat—I walked into the family lounge to find an unaccustomed sight. My mother and sister sat side-by-side with the

Scottie dog in Ma's lap. Everyone wore a different color lei, including the stuffed animal. I kissed them all in turn (even the dog—that's how euphoric I still felt). Ukulele music played through the PA system.

"Aloha," I said to the group, my voice a cheerful song.

Vicky skipped right over the pleasantries, greeting me instead with an irritable, "I thought you'd *never* get here. Nobody was here to help me, and I had to schlep Ma all the way from her room by myself."

"Welcome to my world," I said, grinning broadly.

She paused to check me out from head to toe. I could detect suspicion in her eyes, yet nothing right now could wipe that goofy smile off my face.

"Holy crap. You slept with him."

"Is it that obvious?"

"You said you weren't gonna go last night," she said, her lips in a pout.

"I changed my mind." Boy, did I ever change my mind.

Ma gave me her most endearing smile. "My girl Barbara. You look pretty in that lei."

"It's evidently not the only 'lei' Barbara got this week-end," Vicky said, ever the queen of the *double entendre*. I took off my sunhat and swatted her with it.

"You know, I said there was nothing old about Jack, and I gotta tell you . . . last night, from about nine o'clock until..." I didn't finish the sentence but started counting on my fingers one by one. Who knew it could be this much fun to bait my sister?

"*Please* stop," she said, rolling her eyes. "You can spare us the details of what a stud-muffin he is."

"You've heard the saying. Sixty is the new forty; eighty is the new sixty."

Ma held up the stuffed Scottie. "I love my doggie."

"Around here, eighty is the new *six*," Vicky said, gesturing toward Ma. Then she turned to me, shaking her head and assuming the Concerned Big Sister role. "I hope you know what you're getting into with Jack."

"For once, can't you let me have my day in the sun?" I asked, adjusting the brim of my hat as though trying to shield my eyes from the powerful summertime rays.

Vicky let out a long sigh. "Maybe you're right. Why not. God knows you could use a little..." She started to make a lewd pumping gesture, necessitating another swat with the sunhat.

"That's not the way it is with Jack and me. I don't see why you have to trivialize and—cheapen it. Also, promise you won't let on to Sarah about this. Jack and I agreed it's best not to share this with the kids, at least not for the time being."

"On that subject, we are agreed. Although when she sees you in that get-up, Sarah will suspect something's going on. You look like you're ready to go out and hustle Don Ho."

I couldn't help laughing at that. Seeing the two of us dissolved in giggles, Ma joined in with that loud, guttural laugh of hers.

"I don't think the concept of Mom having sex with a senior citizen is on Sarah's teenage radar screen," I said.

"I hope you're right."

Wayne walked into the lounge. He wore two leis over a birds-of-paradise print shirt that didn't look much different from his everyday garb. "It's nice that everyone's turned out for Luau Sunday. I just saw your daughter with Scott."

"You saw Sarah and Scott? Where?"

"Outside on the back patio. They seem to have become good friends." He walked over to Dolly and gave the stuffed dog a pat on the head. "Dolly, we have special dishes for the Luau buffet today. There's a nice pineapple salad, and baked ham with sweet rolls, and coconut pudding for dessert. Doesn't that sound good?"

Dolly listened to the menu description and said, "If you like eating puke. I would like a chocolate pudding . . . and a big scotch." She gave Wayne an impish grin.

"I'm afraid scotch is not on the menu, but I'm sure we can find you a chocolate pudding. You're one of our favorite guests, you know."

"That's nice. I love you," Dolly said. She seemed in a happy frame of mind today, the same as her younger daughter. Her mood brightened even more when she saw her granddaughter walk through the door.

"My girl Sarah."

"Hi, Grammy," Sarah said, kissing her grandmother on the cheek. Then she glanced over at me and did a double take.

"Whoa, you look festive today, Mom." I could sense she had to struggle not to burst out laughing at my overcooked outfit.

"I feel festive. It's a beautiful day."

"I heard you come in late last night. Where were you?"

"Dinner party," I said, perhaps a little too quickly.

"Yes, your mother was telling me how many, uh, courses the host served." Vicky started counting on her fingers in imitation of me.

"Vicky. What did I just say to you?" I said through gritted teeth.

"What's up with you two?" said Sarah with a shake of her head.

Vicky sprang up. "Sarah, sweetheart, your mother is abandoning herself to the aloha spirit." She broke into a sarcastic hula dance and said, in a singsong voice, "Tropical breezes . . . moonlight . . . Mai Tais . . . and you can hear the natives chanting 'kamanawanalea... kamanawanalea.'" She pronounced this last word "come-on-I-wanna-lay-ya."

I sat there, baffled for a few seconds, until I realized the not-so-hidden meaning of Vicky's chant.

"Vicky. You need to *stop* this," I said, still talking through gritted teeth. Glancing around, I observed that the entire exchange had gone over Ma's head, while Sarah gave us a stricken look that suggested she found us both too embarrassing for words.

"What's going on, Mom?" she asked. "This is getting so weird." Then she asked, "Can I go back out until lunch? I'm helping Scott rehearse for his play, *Instability*."

"Sure, honey." Go. Better she should leave before Vicky spilled all the beans.

"Scott is awesome in the role."

"My, I think everyone's a little lovesick today," Vicky said, giggling as she resumed her little hula dance. "Kamanawanalea, kamanawanalea . . . "

This time Sarah and I reacted at the same time, with

me shouting an angry "Victoria" as Sarah squealed an embarrassed "Aunt Vicky." My sister continued dancing to the ukulele music, oblivious, and we watched her in frustrated silence.

Then Jack came in. He had told me he wouldn't be here until lunchtime, so his early arrival took me by surprise. I didn't know how much he'd seen or heard, which threw me off balance.

"Jack. I—I didn't expect to see you till later." Then I noticed he appeared to be distracted and unsmiling. Had Vicky's crude little game upset him?

"I had a call from the nurse. Helen is running a high fever. They think it's an infection of some sort."

"Oh, dear. I hope it's nothing bad," I said.

On every other day, Jack was impeccably shaven, but this morning the stubble on his cheeks gave evidence he'd dropped everything to rush here. As if reading my mind, Jack reached one hand absently up to his face and rubbed his jaw with his palm, exploring the beard growth. I didn't favor the scruffy, unshaven look, but I had to say Jack wore it well.

"I need to check on her," he said.

"Yes, you should go right now. I'll see you at the luau lunch."

Jack paused before saying, "I don't think I'll make it to lunch. It'll depend on what's happening with Helen."

Sarah said, "I'll let Scott know what's going on. He's outside." She hurried out of the lounge, followed by Jack.

After a long pregnant silence, Vicky took her seat next to Ma. "Well, that didn't take long."

I feigned ignorance. "I don't know what you're talking about."

"I mean, it didn't take long for reality to get in the way of romance."

I glared at Vicky, who then added in a faux-sympathetic tone, "But don't worry. I'm not gonna say I told you so."

My sister had a funny way of *not* saying things.

"Now, that's a real comfort, Vicky," I said.

She'd been trying to deflate me ever since I had floated in earlier this morning, and with persistence, she'd succeeded.

As usual.

22

THE COVER-UP

The months leading up to Helen's retirement at the end of 2008 had been tumultuous. The economic slowdown and the October stock market crash left everyone shaken. Amid all this turmoil, Jack's career took an unusual turn due to circumstances unrelated to the financial crisis.

For many years, Jack and another graphic designer—a sole proprietor, like Jack—covered for each other during vacations and times of emergency or illness. Now Jack's colleague was fighting for his life. He faced surgery, chemo, and radiation treatments for cancer, and Jack agreed to take on his client load until his fellow designer could work again.

While many creative professionals had lost their jobs or found themselves more idle than normal, Jack's already solid workload increased by a substantial margin as he added several new clients to his roster.

The resulting schedule proved grueling. On weekday mornings, Jack set his alarm for six o'clock, downed a quick cup of coffee and a light breakfast, and headed out to his studio by seven, often before Helen had awakened. After an eleven or twelve-hour day in the studio, he came home, and they ate takeout from the East Side Market or a quick dinner at one of the casual restaurants nearby.

After dinner, Jack worked another couple of hours from home before climbing into bed, exhausted, next to his sleeping wife.

Weekends weren't much better. He promised Helen, "I'm going to take Saturday nights and Sundays off, no matter how busy I am." But it didn't always work out that way in practice.

In a conference call one day, his sick colleague said, "Why don't you hire a freelancer to carry some of the load? With all the layoffs everywhere, it shouldn't be hard to find skilled artists willing to do project work by the hour."

Jack couldn't argue with this logic, but if he had a professional flaw, it was his inability to delegate. Helen had always been brilliant at this sort of challenge, which explained her success as a creative director managing a large team. But Jack preferred to fly solo. After half-hearted attempts to subcontract a couple of design projects to local freelancers, he decided instead to bear the full workload on his own.

When Helen disclosed her intent to retire a few months into this madness, Jack felt both surprised and guilty. Retire? That didn't sound at all like Helen. Perhaps she thought that if she took the lead in retiring, he might follow suit before too long. She often fretted aloud about him working too hard.

Jack knew he'd be too busy to keep his wife company or plan any travel together for the foreseeable future, and he worried that she might become bored or resentful before long. Also, he knew he'd been neglecting not only Helen but the house, cars, children, grandchildren, and friends since taking on the extra work. Perhaps Helen felt she needed to be at home to prevent them both from falling hopelessly behind.

What if she'd decided to abandon the career she had always cherished to counterbalance his own excessive work schedule? That wouldn't be fair to her.

But in reality, Jack didn't have time to worry about it too much.

Tonight, he'd be accompanying his wife to her retirement party. He would confine himself to a single celebratory glass of champagne but then switch to water, knowing he would have to squeeze in a couple more hours of work back home after the event. He had hoped his schedule wouldn't be so crazy over the holidays, but the pace remained relentless.

At the reception organized by Marge Williams in honor of her boss's retirement, friends and colleagues agreed on one point. They couldn't believe Helen Winokur had decided to end her long and illustrious career.

Marge wished they would just get over it and accept Helen's decision.

"I thought she'd work till she was at least seventy-five," said a young copywriter.

"I expected her to work forever," said one of the account executives. "I can't even imagine the place without her."

Christopher Swain, a senior member of Helen's creative team, said, "I wonder what she'll do with herself. It wouldn't surprise me if she's back in six weeks, sitting at her old desk. Hey, Marge—you're closer to her than all of us put together. What's your prediction?"

Marge looked over at Helen, engaged in a separate conversation across the room, and then frowned at Chris. "You know, I'm not into predicting other people's futures. I think everybody should respect her choice and show some support."

Marge couldn't keep the edge out of her voice. But they were all testy these days, what with the dreadful economy and mounting talk of another Great Depression. Everyone agreed Obama's upcoming presidency cast a ray of sunshine on the otherwise dark horizon.

"Whoa, take it easy. We were only indulging in a little harmless office gossip," the copywriter said, raising one hand in a defensive posture. "Anyway, she told me she wanted to spend more time with Jack."

Marge knew from Helen that Jack had been working harder than ever and would not have time to laze around the house with his retired wife, but she nodded in feigned agreement. "I'm sure that must be the reason."

While her boss lamented to Marge that Jack was working nonstop during the last quarter of 2008, Helen, Marge, and the rest of the staff faced professional challenges of their own. The agency saw a drop-off in business as clients panicked over the financial markets and canceled or reduced their media advertising budgets for the following year.

The agency was better positioned than most. Much of their business came from public relations and publicity, and while clients were cutting back on expensive broadcast and print advertising buys, they maintained or even increased their PR efforts to keep a presence in the marketplace. As a result, the firm managed to stay afloat while many competitors closed their doors.

But due to the declines on the advertising side, Helen's creative staff suffered a worse fate than other departments within the firm. She had to let go of two people, including a young copywriter with a ten-month-old daughter. It took a tremendous emotional toll on the entire group.

Whether it was the stress of the layoffs, the uncertain economic climate, or Jack's pressure-cooker schedule (which Helen criticized with increasing frequency), Marge noticed that her boss acted a bit . . . *fuzzy*, of late. She became easily distracted, and she seemed off her game.

Instead of meeting once a week, every Monday morning, to review Helen's calendar for the upcoming week, they now held these reviews daily. Even then, Marge often had to nudge Helen and say, "Time for us to head over to the staff meeting," or "Shouldn't you be leaving now for your lunch with Karen Bergman? Traffic will be bad at this hour."

In the sixteen years Marge had worked with her, Helen had always been an incomparable multitasker. But nowadays, she relied on her assistant to prop her up. Marge was only too happy to do the propping. Revering Helen as both a dear friend and a mentor, she would do anything she could to help her boss.

When Helen worked on new business pitches, she often rehearsed in front of Marge, who enjoyed the challenge of appraising Helen's presentations and offering ideas on how to tweak the PowerPoints. During the first part of October, Helen had to head up a pitch to a major hotel chain. The company planned to open a luxurious oceanfront resort despite the failing economy—"the right place at the wrong time," as one of the writers said in a creative meeting. Amusing, though not exactly a slogan one would trot out to the client. Helen struggled with the strategic marketing challenge and with her portion of the presentation.

She walked through her PowerPoint with Marge. But instead of her usual smooth and forceful delivery, Helen stumbled. Sometimes she lost her train of thought and had to start over at the beginning of the slide. Once, she stopped mid-sentence and said, "I don't like that. Maybe I should change the whole thing." Marge offered suggestions, but Helen didn't scribble notes or react to Marge's ideas as she usually did in their one-on-one meetings.

After a frustrating hour in which they made little progress, Helen surprised Marge by saying, "You know, I think I'm going to hand this whole pitch over to Christopher. Give him a chance to shine."

Chris Swain played second chair to Helen in the creative department, but he specialized in business-to-business accounts. "Are you sure? Chris is a B2B guy," Marge said, using the agency lingo. "I didn't know he had any experience with consumer pitches."

"That's the whole point," said Helen. "He needs to spread his wings. Anyway, this account isn't limited to consumer marketing."

"How do you mean?"

"We'll also be promoting the new resort to trade groups, convention marketers, wedding planners . . . people like that."

"That's a valid point. You're right; involving Chris is a good idea." If Chris stepped in, at least no one would have to worry about Helen blowing the presentation—a genuine concern, if today's rehearsal had been any indication.

Helen's energy used to be unflagging, but nowadays, she looked exhausted most of the time. She admitted as much to her assistant.

"Maybe it wouldn't hurt to see the doctor. I can make an appointment for you."

"Oh, no, I had my annual checkup a couple of weeks ago, and I'm *fine*," Helen said with a wave of her hand.

As the keeper of Helen's calendar, Marge knew the checkup had occurred several months ago, not two weeks, but she said nothing. It had never been her style to issue orders to her boss, though she did offer a gentle suggestion. "Maybe you should take a few days off...you know, to catch up on your rest."

Helen furrowed her brow as she deliberated on this idea. "I don't know. Perhaps." She smiled at Marge, though her eyes were sad. "I'll think about it."

Then she said in a warning tone, "Don't say anything to Jack."

On a Wednesday during the last week of October, Marge was working at her desk when Helen's phone rang. "Helen Winokur's office," she answered.

"Marge, it's Jack. Do you know where Helen is?"

Marge was about to explain that Helen had gone out shopping and would return in about an hour.

Before she had a chance to say anything, Jack said, "I expected her to meet me fifteen minutes ago." He named a popular Federal Hill restaurant where he and Helen lunched together on occasion. "I tried calling and texting her cell, but she's not responding."

"Oh, Jack. Helen got called in on a client emergency. She's been over at Karen Bergman's office all morning," Marge lied. "She told me to cancel all the appointments on her calendar."

"But I don't see a message from you."

"Let me, uh, check the calendar again." Marge stalled for time. She knew there'd be no appointment on the calendar because Helen had failed to tell her about the lunch date. "Oh, dear. Here it is. My bad. I entered your lunch for tomorrow instead of today," she said, improvising. "I am so sorry."

"No problem. I was getting worried, but I'm relieved to know she's okay."

After the call, Marge walked into Helen's office and left a note on her chair.

—IMPORTANT. *Please see me right away. Marge.*

Marge noticed Helen's cellphone lying on top of her

desk. She'd forgotten both her lunch appointment and her phone, which explained why she hadn't responded to Jack herself.

When Helen returned toting two big shopping bags, she despaired to learn not only had she stood up her own husband, but she had also caused Marge to lie on her behalf.

"I feel terrible that you had to cover up for my foolishness. That went above and beyond the call of duty."

"No worries. It happens to all of us," Marge said.

But not to Helen. Not until now.

The next afternoon, as Marge slipped on her jacket and gathered up her purse to leave for the evening, Helen hurried over to her and grabbed her by the arm. "Don't go yet." Her green eyes darted in panic.

"What's wrong?"

"I can't find my keys. I've searched high and low for them."

"They must be in the cooler."

"The cooler?" Helen seemed uncertain.

"Yes, the little blue cooler where you always store them."

"Oh. Right."

Marge led Helen to the breakroom, opened the fridge, and pulled out the cooler, where they found the keys stowed in their customary spot.

"Oh, how funny," Helen said, starting to laugh.

Marge did not join in her laughter. Because an odd intermingling of pungent odors revealed that Helen's keys were not the only forgotten item in the cooler. Inside, Marge noticed an assortment of foods in various stages of spoilage: wedges of cheese, sliced cucumbers, wilted salad greens, a baked chicken leg, moldy peaches, stale triangles of pita bread. All told, maybe three days' worth of lunches—untouched.

The following Monday, when Marge went to Helen's office for the first calendar review of the week, Helen said, "I have some personal news, and I wanted you to be the first to know . . . apart from Jack, I mean."

Marge leaned forward in her seat, waiting to hear her boss's announcement.

"Remember when you suggested I take some time off? Well, I've decided that's what I'm going to do."

"Great. I'm glad to hear it. When? We can go over the calendar together and figure out who needs to cover what during the time you're out."

"Well, that's not what I meant. I'm talking about permanent time off."

"Permanent?"

"Retirement. I'm retiring at the end of the year."

Despite Helen's recent struggles, Marge did not expect such a drastic decision this soon. "May I ask why?"

Helen paused before answering. "It's . . . a lot of things. I've been feeling awfully distracted, like my mind is always wandering off someplace else. Maybe this damn economy has me frightened. I don't know. But the economy is another reason why this is a good time to retire."

"Don't we all fight to hang *on* to our jobs in an economic downturn?"

"Things are going to get worse before they get better. Maybe if I go, it will save someone else's job in the department. You know how much it pained me to let go of two capable people earlier this year."

"I know, but to sacrifice your own career over a hypothetical situation seems—"

"I wouldn't call it hypothetical. I'm almost certain we'll have another round of layoffs in a few months."

"What does Jack think of all this?"

"He seemed . . . surprised at first. I think he's a little worried about how I'll pass the time with him working day and night. But he supports my decision."

Marge nodded wordlessly.

Helen paused again, then said, "Another thing. I know I've been leaning on you too much these last few months, and I don't know what I would have done without you." Tears welled up in Helen's eyes. "It hasn't been fair to you. I'm sorry."

"Oh, Helen. Please tell me that's not one of the reasons you're retiring. You know I'll continue to do everything I can to help you as long as you choose to stay."

"I know you will, but this is best for everyone. I need you to promise me something."

"Whatever you want. You have my promise."

"I must ask you again never to discuss this with Jack. Anyway, once I stop working, my life will be simpler," Helen said. "I'll be able to get on top of my game again. I know I will. In the meantime, with him working this hard, I—I don't want to bother him with my own issues right now."

"Bother him? I'm sure your husband would want to help and support you. Jack adores you. It seems to me he's always held you on a pedestal and—"

"Yes. That's right, on a pedestal. It's a delicate balance, being perched up on a pedestal, and we don't want to upset that. I wouldn't want Jack to be . . . to be . . ."

"Alarmed?"

"Disappointed. I couldn't bear for him to be disappointed in me." She gave Marge a fierce look. "I have to be sure you're with me on this."

"Always, Helen. Always."

As the retirement party wound down, Marge stood together with Helen and Jack, Chris Swain, and a few of the other staff—Jack sipping from a water bottle, the rest of them nursing wine or beer.

"Helen, how do you plan to keep yourself busy?" Chris asked.

She responded with a bright smile. "Oh, I have lots of ideas. I think I'm going to make new pillows for the sunporch—I haven't done any sewing in years. I have a long list of books to catch up on and closets to clean out, and I'm planning to cook marvelous dinners for Jack every night."

"Sounds great to me," said Chris. "What are his favorite

dishes? Jack, maybe I should be asking you that question."

But as Jack was about to respond, Helen said, "I'm going to find new recipes and try experimenting with different cuisines. Out with the old."

"It will be a terrible economic blow for the local take-out restaurants," said Jack.

This ambitious and grandiose retirement scheme sounded very "Helen-esque" indeed. Everyone laughed in unison.

Everyone but Marge.

23

A POTENTIAL RIVAL

Browsing the internet today, I stumbled on an article containing guidelines on how to decide whether it's time to put your dog to sleep. The article advised pet owners to make a list of their dog's favorite activities, then review it every month or two to check off how many of the activities the dog could still do. If the animal failed to pass the test, i.e., if he or she could no longer manage most of the items on the list, the time had probably come to consider euthanasia.

I emailed the article link to Vicky with a message:

—*You might find this interesting. I bet if you wrote down all of Daisy's activities, you'd find that she's still getting along quite well. If you want to give me a list, I'll enter it into a spreadsheet, and you can use it to track how she's doing. XOX, Barbara.*

Vicky wrote back:

—*Hey, kiddo. You are the quintessential List Lady . . . me, not as much. You know me, I prefer to go with the flow. But I will keep this idea in mind. Thanks, V.*

I'd decided to send the article as a kind of peace offering. My sister and I had been bickering a lot, and I felt the time had arrived to steer us back into more pacific waters. It didn't escape my notice that I always had to extend the olive branch after our squabbles, even though Vicky played the role of instigator.

The dog article made me think back to the activity list I'd created for Ma soon after she moved into Tropical Gardens. I could now foresee the day when Dolly would no longer be able to participate in most of the activities on this list. How long would it be until she flunked *her* test, so to speak? Six months? Twelve? Helen had been flunking the test for a long time.

In the afternoon, Jack and I stood outdoors in the side garden. Ma and Helen were both in their rooms, napping. Jack asked me why I had arrived late.

"I went shopping this morning, and I procrastinated in the cleaning supplies aisle," I told him. "I needed laundry detergent and had trouble choosing the scent. I can never decide whether I want my clothes to smell like an ocean breeze, a lavender meadow, or spring rain."

"The shopper's dilemma."

"Then . . ." I sighed and informed him of my perennially bad checkout line karma. "I even went to the self-serve aisle, and I still had trouble." True to form, I'd managed to find the one kiosk with a malfunctioning scanner.

"After I got home, I did a quick load of laundry while I caught up on emails," I said.

"Well, what did you decide?"

"About what?"

"The laundry detergent scent."

"Oh." I laughed, having lost my train of thought, and extended my arm toward him. "See if you can guess."

Jack put one hand around my wrist to keep my arm extended and rested the other hand on my shoulder. He proceeded to sniff the sleeve of my cotton knit top from end to end, moving along a horizontal plane as one might when nibbling an ear of sweet corn. This set me off into a fit of giggles. Out of the corner of my eye, I saw Wayne standing in the doorway and peering at us with a delighted expression on his face. He turned away to leave us in privacy, pretending not to have seen.

"I haven't a clue which scent this is," Jack said.

"No matter. They offer something like fifty-eight different versions of Tide, and they all smell more or less the same."

Tonight, I would see Jack again. Earlier in the morning at home, as I waited for the clothes dryer to complete its cycle, I'd scribbled *Jack Winokur* over and over on a notepad, like an adolescent schoolgirl with a crush. I couldn't believe the extent of my infatuation.

I emailed my happy hour clique and learned, to my disappointment, that nobody could meet this Friday. I'd hoped to share my ebullient mood with my three best friends, but our group conversation would have to wait.

Carol did call, though, to ask me how our date had gone.

"Fantastic. I'm seeing him again tonight."

"Listen, Barbara, I—I'm sorry I sounded negative about Jack the other day. I still have issues with what you're doing. But it's nice to hear you sounding happy."

"Thanks. I'm glad you called."

"Tell me . . . did the two of you take things to the next level?"

"To the next level?" I started to snicker. "I'd say the elevator made it all the way to the top floor."

"Hah. You didn't waste any time, did you? But I gotta wonder . . . a man in his seventies . . . did everything go okay? Did he need Viagra?"

I hesitated before saying, "You know something, Carol? You didn't share any of the prurient details about Kinky Rabbi, and I'm not going to share the prurient details about Jack Winokur."

I felt certain the Cheshire-cat grin on my face spoke volumes. But Carol was not there to see me smiling.

The following Sunday, on my way to Ma's room, I saw Jack embracing a dark-haired woman who did not look familiar to me. When they moved apart and her face came into view, I knew I'd never seen her before. I guessed her to be around my age.

An ace at the game of snap judgment, I assumed the worst, fearing this woman was a potential rival. I hesitated, uncertain whether to approach them. Then Jack noticed me and waved me over.

"Barbara, this is Marge Williams. She and Helen were close friends at the ad agency where Helen used to work. Marge, this is Barbara Gordon. Her mother is a patient here."

I felt disappointed to be introduced in this impersonal manner, but I knew I was being unreasonable. What did I expect him to say to one of his wife's dearest friends? "This is Barbara, my girlfriend," or "This is Barbara, my lover," or simply, "This is Barbara. The two of us have been enjoying some outstanding sex."

"Nice to meet you," I said as I extended a hand in greeting, grateful Jack and Marge couldn't read my mind. "How long did you work with Helen?"

"More than sixteen years." Marge wiped a tear from her eye before reaching out to shake my hand. I realized they must have just come from Helen's room. "To quote the old saying . . . She taught me everything I know." She teared up again. "Forgive me, I—this is—"

"I know how it is," I said with a sympathetic nod. I excused myself and continued down the corridor toward Ma's room. I couldn't get away fast enough.

I felt ashamed of my own pettiness for yearning to be acknowledged as more than the mere daughter of a fellow patient. But even worse, I felt ashamed of the jealousy that raged inside me the moment I saw Jack and Marge hugging—an all-too-familiar feeling of wary distrust. You'd think only fifteen minutes had passed, not fifteen years, since I found the telltale lipstick stain on my husband's shirt. How quickly those old emotions resurfaced.

When I saw Jack embracing Marge, I assumed the worst of him. Did all men behave like this? Or only Barbara

Gordon's men, given that Barbara Gordon did not hold sufficient allure to keep a man's affection or fidelity for more than a short time?

Not only did it trouble me to have these old feelings bubble up, but I also felt disheartened to learn I remained as insecure and uncertain of myself as ever. Jack was not Richard. He had done nothing to hurt me; he had done nothing wrong at all. I needed to repeat this to myself, over and over, like a mantra.

24

AN EXPERTISE IN WORRYING

Jack bought two tickets for an early evening lecture at Brown University and met Barbara at the campus. The featured speaker had served as a senior official in the Department of Education. After retiring from her post, she set up sweeping literacy programs that had helped educate thousands of children in third-world countries throughout the past decade.

Over a cup of coffee and dessert at a little café across from the campus, they sat in the cozy booth and discussed the speaker.

"I wonder how it must feel to accomplish something that changes the world," Barbara said. "Sometimes I'm amazed at how much impact one person can make. Like Jimmy Carter. Remember how he almost single-handedly wiped out that horrible parasitic disease in Africa?"

"Guinea worm."

"Right. Anyway, I think about people who perform such grand and selfless deeds, and I feel like my own life has been so—so *small.*"

"We can't all be humanitarians playing on the global stage. Few people get to do that."

Barbara shrugged. "Granted. But even my own mother created cultural programs that made Rhode Island a better place to live. What have I ever done to distinguish myself other than developing expertise in worrying?"

"Don't be hard on yourself, Barbara. You've been a devoted mother to Sarah and now a devoted daughter to a mother who needs you a great deal. That's a job and a half."

Barbara said, "Okay, maybe you're right. But other people manage to juggle family with careers and volunteer work and all sorts of fulfilling activities."

"Your life is far from over. You still have plenty of time to figure out what you want to do . . . and go do it. Didn't you tell me you'd like to write children's books?"

"Yes, but that's more of a creative indulgence on my part. It doesn't count as something that helps others."

"Creativity isn't an indulgence—it's something we need for our survival, as much as food and water."

Barbara looked skeptical.

"Okay, maybe not as much as food and water," said Jack, waving a chocolate chip cookie at Barbara as he conceded the point. "But can you imagine a world without books, or music, or plays and movies? Eradicating poverty and hunger and disease are not the only forms of meaningful work. Art is important too."

"Ma would have enjoyed this discussion. It makes me sad to think of her diminished capacity." Shifting gears, she asked, "You know, Jack, I love the artwork in your house. Do you still paint and draw?"

Jack shook his head. "Not much since Helen got sick. But I know I'll get back to it. I'm lucky to have art in my life. It will always be there when I'm ready for it again."

"You *are* lucky. I don't even know how to get started."

"I remember you saying that you keep a journal for yourself and a binder for your mother."

Barbara nodded.

"Then maybe, someday when you sit down to write an entry in one of those, spend the time outlining ideas for a book instead. Or write a few paragraphs. Try to do that a couple of times a week to start. Don't put a lot of pressure on yourself. Baby steps."

"That's a good idea. It hadn't occurred to me to approach it that way. But suppose I hate what I've written?"

"Oh, you *will* hate it." He grinned at her. "That's a given. I can't tell you how many times I've painted over the same canvas, ditching the original to start all over again. It's part of the process."

Barbara smiled, encouraged by Jack's words. Then her cellphone rang, and the smile faded.

"Tropical Gardens," she mouthed to him as she answered the call. Clearly, this wouldn't be Dolly phoning for a pleasant bedtime chat. The worry lines deepened on Barbara's brow as she listened to the caller. "Okay, thank you, Wayne. I'll head over there right now." She pocketed the phone and jumped up.

"What's wrong?"

"Ma had a fall. The paramedics came, and they've taken her to the hospital." Her hands trembled a little as she fished out her keys.

"Oh, no. Is she unconscious?"

"No, Wayne said she's alert. To the extent that Ma is ever alert, I guess. But they have to do a thorough examination at the hospital."

"Let me pay the bill and join you there in a little while."

"Jack, you don't have to do that."

"I know I don't, but you shouldn't have to face this alone. I want to be there for you."

Barbara hesitated. "Thank you, but it's not necessary. I can handle it. I'll let you know what happens."

"If you need me to come, promise you'll call me."

"I promise," she said.

Jack stood as Barbara prepared to leave. They did not kiss in public, but he squeezed her hand in both of his before she hurried out. As he watched her go, Jack reflected with regret that Barbara probably wouldn't be starting that children's book any time soon.

25

WITH CLEAR EYES

"Look at this, Helen. We won. We won the Series."

Jack held up the morning paper to his wife and pointed at the front-page photo and headline. After an ignominious last-place finish in 2012, the Boston Red Sox had defeated the St. Louis Cardinals, four games to two, to win the 2013 World Series. Helen had slept through most of last night's broadcast, but Jack hoped in vain that the news of her favorite team's victory might ignite a rare spark of enthusiasm.

"Boston Strong" had been the rallying cry for the team throughout the 2013 season. When victory came, the city of Boston and the neighboring city of Providence went wild.

But Helen didn't celebrate much anymore. Not even Jack's birthday, since she no longer seemed to recognize her husband most of the time. More subdued these days and less prone to emotional outbursts, she now tolerated Jack as someone who lived in the same house and tended to her needs—a reliable yet annoying presence.

As her condition worsened, Helen also had less contact with old friends. Even Marge's visits had tapered off, although Helen's faithful former assistant stopped by every few months. On one visit, soon after the World Series win, Jack thanked her for remaining loyal.

"Are you kidding? Don't forget—she's the one who gave me my career break. She went out of her way to mentor me."

Jack knew the story well. Employed at a Boston publisher's office right out of college, Marge had found it hard to make ends meet on her entry-level salary and decided to try her hand at advertising and public relations. "I didn't have any experience, but Helen took me on anyway," Marge reminded him.

"Helen always said how capable you were. It wasn't long before you doubled as her professional assistant and office manager."

"I loved it. I loved the pace of advertising and the wit and creativity of the people in the profession. I still do."

Helen showed a gleam of recognition during Marge's visit. At least, she somehow still linked Marge with the concept of work. But the questions to her former colleague were now generalized in nature. "How's the job these days?" "Do you still see any of the old people?"

After Helen nodded off, Marge and Jack retired to the kitchen for a cup of tea. As they caught up on each other's work and the Red Sox victory, Jack asked her, "Do you remember the day at the mall? When Helen got lost and forgot to meet you."

"Yes, I remember."

"When you called later to tell me about it, you made a comment I never understood. You said something like, 'I thought I should let you know, in view of what's been going on.' Had Helen gotten lost before?"

Marge looked uncomfortable. "Well, no. I mean, not lost in a physical sense, but she had other issues at work."

"Tell me."

Marge summarized Helen's final months at the office—the difficulty focusing on work, the forgetfulness, the reliance on Marge to cover for her and keep track of the numerous tasks and responsibilities that Helen had managed flawlessly before then.

"Why didn't you tell me about this at the time?" asked Jack.

"I gave her my word I wouldn't discuss it with you. She—she didn't want to worry you. Though it occurred to me she must be showing the same tendencies at home."

Jack shook his head. "She wasn't. Although maybe I was too distracted to realize it. I had to work so damn hard that whole year. I couldn't see anything beyond my next project deadline." Then he asked, "Why do you think she retired?"

"I think she felt scared. She wouldn't admit it, but every day at the agency had become a struggle for her, and she wanted out."

He sat and digested this information. "That day at the mall . . . If you knew how forgetful she'd become, I don't understand how you let her go off on her own."

Marge shook her head. "I still haven't forgiven myself for that. But Helen insisted. She even designated the time and place where we would meet after doing our individual errands. Since she seemed fine that day, I went along with her plan. I guess she was still the boss to me."

Jack felt surprised and disturbed by what he had just learned. "I wish somebody had come to me about this earlier. You, or Helen, or . . . someone."

"Oh, Jack, I am so sorry. I assumed you knew."

After Marge left, Jack tried to calm down with a second cup of tea, but he found himself pacing the kitchen instead. Feelings of shame and self-reproach washed over him. How could he not have seen Helen deteriorating right in front of his eyes? Could he have been that self-absorbed? His wife had been struggling with memory issues for months before he acknowledged the problem.

Okay, that may not have been entirely true. He did notice Helen's growing forgetfulness on many occasions, but he remained in denial, finding excuses to dismiss her slip-ups as insignificant. Helen herself dismissed them as the result of fatigue, illness, or some other curable condition. Only Marge saw the problem with clear eyes.

He felt frustrated with Marge, too. Shouldn't she have come to him about this for Helen's sake, even if it went against her wishes? Maybe he could have done something sooner to help his wife. But he recognized that Marge's loyalty would always be to Helen, not to him. And though the two women had a close relationship, Helen—in Marge's words—remained the boss.

Doubts and questions about his wife and marriage also raced through his head about her refusal to confide in him. It seemed like a personal betrayal for her to hide something this important in her life. Hadn't they always agreed to share their burdens, big and small? For better or worse.

Jack became even more agitated as he wondered what other secrets she'd kept through their years together. But he would never know the answers to these questions. It was much too late to have that conversation with his wife.

Helen had begun to lose interest in food until Jack discovered, by accident, that music seemed to stimulate her appetite. One evening he turned on a classical station while giving Helen dinner, and he noticed she ate better than she had in a long time. He couldn't say if the two events were connected, so he tried experimenting. Classical music worked well, but Broadway show tunes and jazz-inspired pop songs were even better. Sometimes Helen sang along, still capable of remembering at least some of the lyrics.

One night, Jack played an old recording of Fred Astaire singing Gershwin songs. When "Shall We Dance?" started playing, in an impulsive moment, Jack said, "Why don't we dance?" He led Helen by the hand from the breakfast nook to the roomier portion of the kitchen, and they started to dance together.

He knew the risks involved. Helen sometimes reacted hysterically to anything out of the ordinary. But she seemed content enough to go along with the idea, not so much following the dance steps as rocking back and forth with a slow rhythm as she held onto Jack by the shoulders.

When the song ended, she kissed his cheek and said, "My darling Jack."

During the past few years, Jack had grown inured to a gamut of hurtful reactions from Helen: insults, slurs, accusations, hostility, indifference. Now and then, she treated him to an unexpected compliment or warm word. Jack had learned not to take her responses personally, whether good or bad, and he didn't think he could still be moved by anything she said or did. But this—this touched him to the depths of his soul.

26

WHEN CAN I GO HOME?

Ma's mind may have been disintegrating, but she maintained the body integrity of a Mack truck. I hoped I had inherited her bone density.

We spent many tedious hours in the ER. Several times, I found myself tempted to take Jack up on his offer to join me at the hospital. *Someone to buoy me up, to keep me afloat, to lighten the burden of responsibility.* Hadn't I'd been craving that? Still, I felt a reluctance to lean on him too heavily.

When the doctors saw that Ma had top-of-the-line supplemental insurance as well as Medicare, the hospital team had a field day ordering up every imaginable test. After checking her out from stem to stern, they couldn't find anything wrong. They said she had no breaks or sprains, no concussion, and no evidence of a stroke, heart attack, or subdural hematoma. No obvious injuries other than slight bruising on her right side.

"Can I go home now?" she asked, maybe thirty or forty times during her ordeal. When I grew tired of answering, she gave me an angry glare and shouted, "*Barbara*," to let me know she expected me to set things right. When the hour grew late, they admitted her for the night, though they discharged her this morning before lunch.

Nobody knew how or why she fell. Wayne explained upon our return to Tropical Gardens, "I was walking her back to her room, and without any warning, she went down like a ton of bricks."

"Did she black out?" I asked.

"At first, I thought that's why she fell. It happened very suddenly, and I didn't see her trip or lose her balance. But no, she stayed conscious the whole time. I've never seen anything like it."

Back at assisted living, Ma remained disoriented and continued to ask, "When can I go home?" She meant her old house. In her short time away at the hospital, she'd managed to forget all about Tropical Gardens. I walked her around her room, pointing out familiar objects. She froze in her tracks the way she often did when something caught her attention.

Though Ma had emerged physically unscathed from her inexplicable fall, I couldn't help feeling the last twenty-four hours had been a setback for her. But I could see one saving grace. She still recognized me.

"Barbara."

"Yes, Ma."

"What's this?" She pointed to a framed certificate on the wall.

"That's the diploma for your honorary doctorate degree. Remember?"

But she shook her head and turned away.

During her next nap, I started a new entry:

Memories of Dolly: 1993

I scribbled on the back of the Tropical Gardens weekly

newsletter. Later I would transcribe it onto the cloud paper to match the other handwritten recollections.

Dolly Gordon rises from her seat and walks to the podium at the local college, where she is about to receive an honorary doctorate degree for her years of outstanding community service. The audience applauds as she mounts the short staircase to the stage. Dolly turns to face the commencement crowd, squinting into the bright May sunlight, and smiles warmly.

"Thank you all. As thrilled as I am to receive this honor, the real honoree today is theatre. Theatre opens us up to new worlds. It expands our minds and our emotions. It makes us better than who we were before. And it's never too early to begin immersing ourselves and our children in theatre.

"That's why Providence Players has reached out to bring the incomparable experience of live performance to young students from across the state of Rhode Island. This school program is now in its fifth year. Originally for sixth graders, it has expanded to grades four through six, and the results have been rewarding beyond measure. On behalf of everyone who has been part of this wonderful program, I'd like to extend our gratitude."

As Doctor Dolores Gordon holds up her diploma to a cheering crowd, she concludes, "I will never forget this day."

I recalled that the carton in my study contained a newspaper photo caption story of Ma on the podium receiving the degree. Later, I would insert the photo in her binder with the new write-up.

How pleased I'd been with myself the first time I completed this exercise. But today, I took little solace in it. It depressed me to realize I could compile enough lists to stock a library and enough memories to fill a museum, but to what end?

Ma would only continue to get worse.

27

CELL TROUBLE

Sarah leaned in toward the bathroom mirror, carefully applying a slender stripe of eyeliner to her left lid when Barbara poked her head in the doorway. A scowl creased the older woman's forehead.

"Mom, I'm not twelve years old anymore," said the teenager.

"What?"

"I thought you were going to get on my case about the makeup."

But her mother didn't even mention the eye makeup. Instead, she thrust her cellphone in Sarah's face and said, "There's something the matter with my phone. It doesn't ring when people call, and I don't realize until later that the messages have come in."

Her mother always fretted about one thing or other— although these past couple of weeks, Sarah had noticed, Mom seemed abnormally light-hearted and upbeat. But now, she'd reverted to full worry mode, talking in that nervous, trembling high voice she reserved for catastrophes. Sarah didn't think a non-ringing phone qualified as panic-worthy.

She grabbed her mother's cell, and as she started to examine it, Barbara continued, "I'm composing a group text to everyone in my Favorites list. I think I should tell friends and family that my cell is out of order, and if they're calling about something important, please send a backup email. I'll check the phone and email as often as I can until the phone is repaired. Can you think of anything else I should put in the text?"

"Mom, you need to chill out. I know what's wrong with your phone."

"Oh, no. How bad is it?"

Sarah pointed to a tiny crescent moon icon in the upper right corner of the screen. "You see that little moon symbol? It means your phone is in the Do Not Disturb mode. The phone won't ring or vibrate or light up when it's set that way."

"But I don't know how that could happen. I didn't turn on that setting. I wouldn't even know *how* to."

Sarah didn't doubt that for a moment. Old people were hopeless with electronics. They always swiped screens the wrong way and hit buttons by accident, triggering problems they didn't know how to fix and freaking out like the end of the world had arrived.

Sarah swiped her finger down to the bottom of the screen and gave a light tap on the crescent icon, turning off Do Not Disturb. She held up the phone to show her mother what she'd done.

"Oh, thank you," Barbara said, heaving a sigh of relief. "Are you ready? Your father should be here in around ten minutes."

"I know, Mom. My overnight bag is packed, and I'm almost ready. I have to finish my eyes and decide what shoes I'm wearing."

Sarah would be spending the next two nights with Richard at his place. He planned to take a couple of days off and had organized some activities with her. Tonight, he informed Sarah, he'd reserved his regular table at his favorite downtown steakhouse. Sarah knew they would bring him his preferred brand of bourbon without asking, that he would order ribeye so rare it was "still mooing," that he liked the Brussels sprouts and the asparagus but never the spinach as a side dish.

Sarah screwed the cap back on the eyeliner and started out of the bathroom when her mother said, "One more thing. Will you delete that group text I started to write?"

Sarah grabbed the phone again. "Sure." She swiped the message and punched the "delete" button. Then, by accident, Sarah hit an adjacent message with her finger, causing another text thread to open. (Such errors, she had to acknowledge, were not entirely confined to old people.) She read the text messages.

—*Are we still on for tomorrow night?*

—*(Barbara): Yep. I'll get back to you tmo with a time.*

—*Looking forward.*

—*(Barbara): Me too* 🎱🎱🎱

The other person on the thread was not identified by name, only a phone number that began with the Rhode Island "401" area code. He or she must not be in the address book that Barbara maintained in her usual meticulous fashion, meaning it couldn't be an old friend or relative.

"What are you up to while I'm with Dad?" Sarah asked with mock innocence.

Barbara shrugged her shoulders. "Oh, um . . . no plans."

Did Sarah imagine it, or did her mother seem flustered?

Barbara had never been one for secrets, and her schedule had remained predictable and unvarying for as long as Sarah could remember. But her mother would be spending tomorrow evening with some unknown person and had chosen not to divulge the details to Sarah. And judging from the friendly informality of the text exchange and the accompanying wine glass emojis, this would not be a business appointment.

Very interesting.

28

TOXIC FISH

Sarah had gone to visit her father for a couple of days, and I decided to take advantage of her absence by inviting Jack to dinner. I had turned into a bit of a wreck over it.

For starters, what if he didn't like my house? I had a nice house, spacious and well-built. But picturing it through Jack's eyes, my place seemed flat-out boring compared to his. It had a professionally decorated, cookie-cutter look that could be described as tasteful but not personal. Funny, it had never bothered me before now.

And whatever would I wear? I tried on half a dozen outfits, which remained piled in a chaotic heap on the bed. Four of them were a little baggy. I'd dropped a few pounds, and my old clothes had started to hang on me. Must be all that exercise I'd been getting . . . *hah.* The new items were a perfect fit, but one seemed too informal and the other too fussy. I needed to strike the exact right note with Jack. Oh, God, I've forgotten how to do this.

I also kept stressing over the menu. My original plan had been to serve an ahi salad with fresh greens, sliced mango, and avocado. I'd already seared the ahi, washed the greens, and prepared the dressing. It was the perfect summer entertaining dish, or that's what I thought at first—until it occurred to me, this afternoon, that some people diligently avoided raw seafood or dishes with high levels of mercury. Great. Earlier this week, Jack treated me to a lovely Italian dinner, and now I was about to repay the man by serving him toxic fish?

I rummaged around in the fridge and found some leftover baked chicken. I could slice it up and use that in place of the ahi, I supposed. But seriously, chicken salad for dinner? Could I possibly bore him more?

Getting dinner on the table without incident also gave me cause for concern. Suppose I let my nerves get the better of me and I broke a dish, or a wine glass, or an ankle?

I knew I had to stop panicking and focus on preparations. I'd promised to text Jack with the desired arrival hour. I considered scheduling dinner in "Barbara time"—i.e., specifying a 6:50 p.m. or even 6:52 p.m. start—but he would think I'd become unhinged.

I told him seven o'clock.

29

WOULD FLOWERS BE APPROPRIATE?

Jack noticed that the two women in his life were both losing weight and with very different effects.

Helen had been painfully thin for a year or two, but now her body looked almost ready to cave in on itself. Jack didn't see how she could lose any more weight without imploding into a pile of wizened skin and bones.

Barbara, on the other hand, had been a few pounds to the north of ideal weight when he first met her. She had been slimming down, and the effect pleased him. The curves of her breasts and hips seemed more sculpted and better defined these days. She also had some new outfits that were less conservative than her older wardrobe. Yesterday, he admired her in a form-fitting, coral-colored sundress with big buttons down the front. The dress clung in a tasteful but tantalizing way to those newly chiseled curves. The mental image of Barbara in that sundress instilled in him a sweet ache of desire. And that, in turn, caused him substantial amusement. *You're a horny old bastard, Winokur.* He laughed out loud.

This afternoon, the task at hand was to use every persuasive trick he knew to get Helen to eat at least a little vanilla pudding. She had hardly touched her lunch. Jack acknowledged that he would not be scarfing down meals either if everything on offer looked like sludge.

For a long time, all Helen's solid foods had been pureed, giving them the quality of mush. Liquids had to be mixed with a thickening agent that made them resemble the slushy drinks that came from those big metal machines at 7-Eleven, except that the thickener added a distasteful gritty texture to the beverages. The nurse had mandated these precautions for safety reasons, to prevent fluids from entering Helen's lungs by accident.

Helen and Jack had first learned of thickened liquids at an art class she took soon after the Alzheimer's diagnosis. One of the men in the class boasted about his nightly cocktail hour when he would sip on a thickened martini or gin and tonic. Helen found this hilarious at the time.

Jack dipped the spoon into the pudding and launched into an enthusiastic rendition of Gershwin's "'S Wonderful" as he attempted to feed his wife. The cheerful up-tempo tune that celebrated the joy of newfound love had always been one of Helen's favorites, but today even Jack's world-class baritone couldn't seem to jump-start her appetite.

His phone buzzed with an incoming text. Barbara. Tonight, he would dine at her house for the first time. Sarah would be spending the night at her father's, and Barbara had informed him that the coast was clear. Now she was writing to confirm the seven o'clock start time. Jack texted back his affirmation, and he inquired about the menu so he could select an appropriate wine.

He resumed feeding Helen, announcing in his best cheerleader voice, "Okay, my dear. Let's try this once more." This time he sang, "They Can't Take That Away from Me." Even after a romance ended, the bittersweet song proclaimed, you could find solace in happy memories of your beloved. But this time, Jack was sure the Gershwin brothers had it wrong. There was to be no such solace for Helen. Her memories had been taken away, erased forever.

"Well, that song is plain depressing," Jack said, more to himself than his wife. "No wonder she's gone off her food."

He sighed, defeated, and let the spoon drop onto Helen's tray. He removed the bib from around her neck, draped her sweater across her shoulders, and wheeled her out of the family lounge toward Cindy's office. The door was closed, and nobody answered his knock, but as Jack turned the wheelchair around to head back to Helen's room, he saw the nurse approaching from the other end of the hall.

"Looking for me?" Cindy asked.

"Yes. Remember I told you last week that Helen wasn't eating well? The problem seems to be getting worse."

"Sorry to hear that, Jack. Is she dribbling the food out like she can't manage it, or is she refusing to eat in the first place?"

"A bit of both," Jack said. "I couldn't even tempt her today with pudding or yogurt. I'm wondering if this could be related to the infection she had a couple of weeks ago."

"I doubt it. We re-checked her, and the antibiotics knocked that infection right out of her system."

"I see."

"Let me order a few tests for her. It may take a week or so."

Jack nodded and thanked the nurse for her help. As he

wheeled Helen back to her room, he reviewed his plans for the upcoming evening. He tried to compartmentalize his life, keeping Helen and Barbara as separate as possible. But that was easier said than done, given how much time he and Barbara spent together under the same roof as Helen and Dolly.

Barbara planned to serve a chilled ahi salad, which would pair well with either a dry rosé or a light red burgundy. He'd find a nice bottle at the wine shop. Then he pondered the question of a hostess gift. Should he bring flowers, or would it look like he was trying too hard?

He remembered back to a conversation with their son Michael after his divorce. Michael had re-entered the dating circuit with apprehension and had asked his parents, would flowers be appropriate? At the time, Helen had responded by saying, "You know, you can't go wrong giving flowers to a woman."

Did Jack qualify as a complete son of a bitch, a monster even, for following his own wife's counsel on whether to present flowers to his lover? To most observers, it might seem that way. But Jack didn't feel like a monster. He and Helen had been close enough for him to know that she would've approved and even encouraged this liaison.

He would bring flowers to Barbara, but nothing too sentimental.

It hadn't been long since that first roller-coaster evening together, the night of the Indian dinner fiasco when Jack felt certain he'd scared Barbara away forever. Since then, in addition to the daytime visits at Tropical Gardens, they had seen each other every second or third night—for drinks, a foreign film screening, dinner at a popular Italian place, a lecture at Brown.

He had not intended for sex to be on the agenda with every nighttime encounter, not wanting Barbara to think his interest in her was purely carnal. However, except for the recent evening when an emergency with Dolly intervened, they always ended up at Jack's house making love. But Barbara had been careful not to stay out too late or do anything that might arouse Sarah's curiosity.

It was hard to fathom that he only met Barbara at the beginning of the summer, and he'd never kissed her or held her in his arms until a few short weeks ago. Jack marveled at the warmth and intimacy that had already blossomed, causing this woman to become such an important part of his world. It astonished him to note how his life had turned around, how he found himself pleasurably immersed in both physical and emotional sensations he'd never expected to experience again.

30

A DANGEROUS GAME

Twenty minutes before Jack was due to arrive, I still couldn't decide what to wear. Then I remembered, when he saw me in my new sundress, I caught him giving me a kind of—hungry look, I guess I'd call it. I wouldn't want to say he was ogling me because that would make him sound like a lecherous creep, which didn't do him justice. But I figured, what the heck, and I put the dress on and applied my new matching coral lipstick.

It turned out to be a good call. Jack arrived right at seven o'clock with wine and sunflowers (could any woman ask for more?). And after all my worrying about whether he would be bored to tears by me, my house, or my culinary choices, my fears vanished as I realized how relaxed he seemed to be there with me.

Before I knew it, we were kissing feverishly on the living room couch, and he whispered in a husky voice, "I want you."

I stood and took him by the hand to lead him upstairs, but he shook his head and said, "No, let's stay here," pressing me back down onto the sofa and covering my body with his own. Then, when I reached for the top button on my sundress to undo it, he said, "Leave it on."

"Leave it on" sounded to me like a line from a porno

film. But this film must've been the softcore—no, make that the PG—version. After all, the apparel item being "left on" was a mere sundress, not thigh-high spike-heeled boots or leather dominatrix lingerie. Still, the old Barbara would have demurred, pointing out the impracticalities associated with having sex in a brand-new garment that might become wrinkled, torn, and/or stained.

I left it on.

The next afternoon, I called Vicky and made the mistake of boasting about the previous night's escapade with Jack. I expected she'd find it amusing, that she might even applaud this departure from my customary tight-ass behavior. Instead, she launched into one of her "are-you-fucking-kidding-me" rants.

"Listen up, kiddo. I don't know what's gotten into you with this sex kitten act, but you're playing a dangerous game with this man."

"Oh, come on, Vicky. You sound like me," I said before realizing I'd just insulted myself.

"Suppose Sarah had walked in on you two going at it on the living room couch."

"That wasn't about to happen. She's at Richard's for a couple of days."

"Maybe she is, but it's not impossible. What if she forgot something at home or stopped by to get more clothes?"

I shuddered a little as this idea took root. It's true; Sarah often left the workbook for her SAT prep class someplace or other and had to go retrieve it. All the "what ifs" started to percolate in my head. I started worrying retroactively about a catastrophe that had not occurred (thank God) but unequivocally *might* have happened had the planets been aligned against me.

What if Sarah *had* walked in on Jack and me fornicating? (That horrid word seemed apropos here.) She could have been scarred for life. Worse yet, what if she and Richard had walked in together? Maybe he would have sued for sole custody and tried to take my daughter away from me. Okay, that seemed a bit extreme. Still, I felt overwhelmed by the enormity of my recklessness.

Perhaps things with Jack were moving too fast. It hadn't even been three weeks, after all. I must make a conscientious effort to rein it in.

31

THE LAST FRAGILE THREAD

At four o'clock in the morning, Helen called out from her bed. *Again.* Jack counted this as the third time she had awakened him since he'd tucked her into bed last night.

It was the fall of 2014, five years since Helen's diagnosis.

"Where's my breakfast? I want breakfast," she demanded, confused and disoriented.

A weary Jack padded into her bedroom. "Helen, it's not morning yet. Look how dark it is outside," he said in a futile attempt to reason with her.

"But I'm hungry."

"Here—drink this." He handed her a mug half-filled with warm milk. When Jack first heard her calling, he stopped in the kitchen to warm up the milk in the microwave, an emergency response he had perfected after his wife's nocturnal disturbances became a regular event.

He propped her up in the bed with a stack of pillows. Helen sipped the warm beverage as Jack searched the bedside table for something to read. He knew she wouldn't care if he read her the phone book if he did it in a soothing voice. Selecting a book of Shakespearean sonnets from the lower shelf, Jack leafed through it for a few minutes, choosing Sonnet 116.

"Let me not to the marriage of true minds

Admit impediments. Love is not love
Which alters when it alteration finds
Or bends with the remover to remove.
O no! It is an ever-fixed mark
That looks on tempests and is never shaken.
It is the star to every wand'ring bark,
Whose worth's unknown, although his height be taken..."

By the time Jack finished the poem, Helen had settled back into the pile of down pillows, snoring lightly, the empty mug still clutched in her hand. Jack loosened her fingers to remove them from the mug handle and tiptoed out to the kitchen. He knew sleep would elude him for what remained of the dark hours before dawn.

As he fixed himself a pot of coffee, Jack reflected on the meaning of the sonnet he'd just read. Shakespeare claimed that love remained steadfast, immutable, and true, that it never altered even if circumstances around it changed drastically. Though he commended the romanticism of Shakespeare's notion, Jack didn't feel like he could buy into it anymore. Had the bard contemplated what happened when one's *beloved* changed beyond recognition?

He glanced at the clock. Four-thirty. Three more hours until the daytime caregiver arrived. He hoped Helen would sleep in so he could have some time to himself in the interim.

Jack knew he had reached a crossroads. If he wanted to preserve his own health and sanity, he must hire a live-in caregiver or move Helen into a memory care facility—both deplorable options.

He thought back on the various stages of Helen's care

from the time of her diagnosis in 2009. For a few years, she retained enough independence for him to juggle his work schedule with his wife's needs. As she worsened over time, he hired a woman to come in three mornings a week to help with personal hygiene and miscellaneous chores. Then he increased her schedule to five mornings a week.

When he knew he needed help in the afternoons as well, he had to find a new caregiver who could work full-time. Helen became agitated by the personnel change, not liking the new hire, and they went through three different people before finding the current aide, a cheerful young woman who lent a calming presence to the household.

For the next several months, the new schedule seemed manageable. As he gradually dialed back his professional commitments to a part-time workload, Jack even had a little free time to himself on weekdays. But nights and weekends, he remained on duty a grueling "24/7." Still, he felt fortunate to have the financial means to hire professional aides who could take part of the burden off his shoulders.

Helen had become increasingly wakeful of late, making her care more challenging. For Jack, it felt like having responsibility for a young child who needed to be helped with every task and kept on a short leash for her own safety. A child who no longer seemed to know who or where she was.

Working through a local home health agency, Jack engaged a live-in caregiver who would sleep on a foldaway bed in the room Helen now occupied in the former den on the ground floor. Under the new schedule, she would live with them five days on and two days off, with a replacement aide coming in to relieve her on weekends.

But after three nights, the caregiver came to Jack, wearily shaking her head. "Is no good," she pronounced.

"What's no good?"

"She wake up too much. No sleep. Very, very tired." She yawned and stretched to illustrate that she was speaking about herself, not Helen.

The next thing he knew, she got on the phone to the agency, speaking in rapid-fire Spanish before handing the phone over to Jack. The manager of the agency greeted him brusquely from the other end of the line.

"Mr. Winokur, it seems that we have a situation."

"Ah, a situation."

"Yes. I just learned that your wife wakes up three or four times every night and wants food, or milk, or attention."

"I guess that's true. Helen hasn't been sleeping well, even with some of the medications we've tried."

"Well, you know, there are strict rules about overnight care. Not our rules, mind you. Any agency you hire, you'll find the same guidelines. Our people need a reasonable night's sleep to be functional and effective. If Helen is demanding attention every hour or two, that falls outside the guidelines for a live-in caregiver."

"What do we do?" Jack asked, knowing he would not like the answer.

"We'll have to send two aides a day, in twelve-hour shifts. The late-shift person will stay awake by Helen's bedside to minister to her needs during the night." Jack choked a little when she went on to quote the cost for double-shift caregivers—more than twice the price he had budgeted for a live-in.

It had only been a few days, and Jack already found himself at a crossroads yet again. Should he agree to the exorbitant two-shift-per-day schedule or consider the move to a facility?

Jack had always felt a moral obligation to keep Helen in her own home at all costs. He arranged a Skype call with Michael in Maryland and Paul in California.

"Why keep Mom at home if she no longer knows where she is?" Michael said.

"She doesn't recognize you, and she doesn't even recognize herself," said Paul. "Does it matter to her where she is?"

"To be honest, I can't say whether it matters to her anymore. But it matters to *me*, and my position is that your mother stays here in the house."

"And that's your position because of—what?" said Paul. "Some misguided sense of honor, or duty, or whatever you insist on calling it."

"It's too much for you to handle, Dad, even with paid help," Michael said. "Especially when you have no family nearby to support you."

"Kids, you need to respect what I'm trying to—" said Jack, but Michael interrupted him, angry now.

"If Mom is at a memory care place, maybe you can start to live a normal life again." Then he said something Jack would never forget. "She's already lost her battle with this

246

disease. She's surrendered, Dad. And now you need to give up the fight before it kills you too."

"If you won't do it for yourself, do it for us," said Paul. His younger son's comment sealed the deal.

Jack still had one final hurdle to cross—finding a suitable facility for Helen. He wait-listed her at Tropical Gardens, which appeared to be the nicest of all the places he researched over the next several weeks as private caregivers came and went twice a day, supervising Helen for her remaining days in their home. Not only did Tropical Gardens have the best reputation, but it also sat on a beautiful healthcare campus a short drive from their house. But the director could not predict when a bed might become available, and now that the decision had been made, Jack felt antsy to move ahead with it.

He found another reputable memory care facility over in East Providence, about a twenty-minute trip from home. They could take Helen right away. But he didn't feel comfortable with it, for reasons unclear even to himself, and he procrastinated for several days on signing the paperwork.

Then, when at last he steeled himself to email back the signed contract, the director of Tropical Gardens called to say a private room had become available, a spacious room on the sunny side of the building. Fate had intervened. Jack felt it was meant to be, and he moved Helen in the following week.

One person disagreed with the decision—Scott. Upon receiving the news, he sent a bitter and accusatory email to his grandfather, copying his father:

—I cannot comprehend how you can lock up your wife in some dismal old people's home. I don't know if I can bring myself to visit you or Nana in that place.

After reading the email, Michael called Jack with apologies and reassurances. "I'll explain things to Scott and try to help him understand how we all reached this decision together as a family. Don't worry, Dad. He'll come around."

When Jack moved Helen into Tropical Gardens in the first days of 2015, he didn't expect to see a change in her. But he'd been mistaken in that. The move into the memory care unit somehow severed that last thread connecting her to Jack—that last fragile thread of memory.

In Helen's case, the tropical décor worked its magic. She believed herself to be on vacation at a luxury resort. And in her mind, she elevated Jack from a home invasion criminal into a kindly personal butler who tended to her needs. She even referred to him in front of Wayne, the aide, as "that nice man who takes me to my meals."

The day after she moved in, as she and Jack strolled through the foyer, Helen paused to look around. She used a cane at that time, which she lifted and waved at a large fake potted palm to the side of the foyer. She sauntered over to the palm tree, took one of the fronds in her hand, and stroked it with curiosity.

"I wonder how much they get for this place?" she asked Jack. "It's not bad. Not bad. I hope it's not too expensive."

Jack didn't reply. Then Helen said to him, "I want to go

to the—the place with sand. And—you know—water with waves." She searched for the word.

"The beach?" asked Jack.

"Yes, the beach. They must have a beach here. Can you take me? You work here; you must know where it is."

This is what Helen failed to comprehend about her desire for a beach excursion: It was a cold January day in New England, and a dusting of snow covered the frozen ground outside. After the first week, she stopped asking about the beach. But whenever Helen walked through the foyer, she would make a detour over to the potted palm and affectionately touch one of the fronds, like an animal lover stooping down to scratch the ears of a favorite pet.

Jack couldn't describe Helen as *happy* living at Tropical Gardens, but from the day she arrived, she seemed more peaceful, at least. In the daytime, Jack worked for a couple of hours each morning before going over to the facility to help his wife settle in. But evenings had become his own to enjoy.

During his first week in the house without his wife, Jack behaved like a boy who'd been let out of school. On Monday night, he Uber-ed to his favorite wine bar downtown and sat at the counter, enjoying an animated discussion about wine with the barman and a couple of other customers as he sampled a variety of Italian reds. His immersion in one of his favorite hobbies left him no time to dwell on worries about Helen in her new living situation.

On Tuesday, a group of friends organized a poker

game in Jack's honor. The six men played cards and drank whiskey until midnight. The camaraderie felt excellent, inspiring Jack to invite them to his house the following night—until he realized these men would be expected to stay home with their wives.

The one exception was a friend named Victor, who had been somewhat adrift since his divorce the year before. Victor jumped at the invitation, and on Wednesday night, Jack served a purchased pasta dish with salad. After dinner, they debated what genre of movie to watch on TV, settling on "guy cry" over action, then drilling down to *Saving Private Ryan* over *Braveheart*. Through the course of the evening, they finished off three bottles of wine and a glass each of cognac.

By Thursday, Jack needed a night to himself. He considered dining out alone, but it had begun to snow heavily by the time he left Tropical Gardens just after dusk. He stopped at the market for provisions and went home to fix himself a couple of broiled lamb chops, a baked potato, and asparagus. Helen had always disliked both lamb and asparagus, and it felt better somehow to choose a menu they would not have shared. Concerned that he may be on the path to full-blown alcoholism if he repeated his behavior of the last three nights, he confined himself to a single six-ounce pour of a California cabernet with his food.

After dinner, Jack donned an overcoat but no hat and walked outside to watch the falling snow. He stood in silence on the front stoop for several minutes, not thinking about anything, mindlessly letting the large wet snowflakes land on his head, his eyebrows, his lashes. The snow came down so hard now that he found it impossible to make out the normal demarcations between sidewalk and lawn, curb and roadway. All the different surfaces that made up a neighborhood had merged into a single, seamless white expanse.

Jack didn't even realize he was crying until he noticed the sensation of hot tears mingling with the icy snowflakes. He did not cry these tears for Helen . . . at least, he didn't believe that was the case. No, Jack cried at the unexpected revelation that here he stood, alone outside his beautiful but solitary house, with absolutely no path ahead to follow. His entire future now appeared before him as a stark white canvas, a roadless span that bore a chilling resemblance to the thick covering of fresh snow that blanketed his property that night.

True to his word, Michael reached out to Scott to explain how Jack— together with his own two sons—had jointly agreed to move Helen into Tropical Gardens. And sure enough, Scott relented. Now a sophomore in the acting program at Tisch, he took a bus from New York to Providence over spring break and went with Jack to visit his grandmother.

Although Helen didn't recognize her grandson, she seemed pleased enough to have this handsome young man calling on her. Jack watched from the sidelines as an emotional Scott embraced his grandmother and launched into an upbeat monologue about the excitement of life in New York City and the trials and tribulations of drama school. It had the quality of a rehearsed scene.

This boy will do fine as an actor, Jack said to himself as he observed Scott's little performance with a combination of amusement, relief, and melancholy.

32

THE COMMON CHARACTERISTICS
OF DECLINE

Jack and I arrived at Tropical Gardens at the same time. As we walked in, he pulled me through a doorway into a deserted stairwell and pressed me against the wall, burrowing his face into my neck and brushing his lips against my hair.

I took it up a notch, pulling his head down to plant a fierce kiss on his mouth, which still had the pleasant taste of morning coffee. I pressed myself against him with a suggestive thrust of my hips. I heard the sharp intake of his breath followed by a soft moan as he exhaled, and I marveled that a simple moan could be that sexy.

So much for my resolve to rein it in—a resolve I maintained for a full ninety seconds upon seeing Jack this morning. I reminded myself of an overweight woman who kept postponing the launch of her diet. *Starting tomorrow, I'm only going to eat broiled fish and salad. But right now, there's this hot fudge sundae in front of me, and I intend to devour every bite.*

Later, we all sat in the family lounge together—Jack and Helen, Ma, and me. He'd been trying to feed Helen chocolate pudding, singing to her the way he always did. But he could barely get her to stay awake, let alone manage a spoonful or two of dessert.

"Off her food again, huh," I said to Jack. "Is she still sick with that infection?"

"I asked Cindy the same question, but she said no. They're running a few tests to see if they can figure it out."

Dolly eyed Helen's pudding and said, "I want to feed her."

"Jack, what do you think? I asked.

He shrugged in response. "Can't hurt to try." He handed the pudding cup and plastic spoon to Dolly.

She leaned toward Helen, holding the spoon up to the other woman's mouth. "Open up," Ma said bossily.

No response from Helen.

"Here's how you eat it." Ma demonstrated by popping the utensil into her own mouth and swallowing a generous spoonful of the chocolate dessert.

"Oh, Ma, no. Let me get a clean spoon." But while I went to grab one, Ma downed another three bites of pudding. Poor Helen.

Thinking back to the activities I'd itemized in Ma's binder to stimulate her brain, I made a mental note to cross *Feeding Helen* off the list. The only things getting stimulated here were Ma's salivary glands.

"One to a customer. You already had dessert," I said, though I knew she couldn't remember what she'd eaten five minutes earlier. "Also, you've got physical therapy today. We don't want your tummy so full you can't move." I was about to mention that Helen's pudding contained sugar, which might aggravate Ma's diabetes, but I realized this would be too much information.

Dolly glanced again at Helen, who sat with her eyes

closed, and said, "What's the matter, honey? You're no fun. You need to join the party."

"Ma, Helen can't help it." But Ma's words reminded me: "Jack, speaking of parties, it's Ma's birthday on Sunday, and after the evening meal, we're going to have a little celebration in her room with cake and ice cream. Sugar-free, natch, but I promise it will be edible. You're all invited."

"Count us in. I'll mention it to Scott as well. Dolly, what birthday is this?"

Ma didn't answer him, gazing down at her stuffed Scottie dog instead.

"Glad you can come," I said to him.

"I'm happy to be there." He gave my shoulder a quick squeeze, and I smiled up at him.

We took care to keep the touching to a minimum when we were in the same room with Helen and my mother. But somehow, some way, Ma picked up a vibe from us. She sat straight up in her chair and addressed Helen again, in a louder voice this time.

"You need to get with it, lady. If you don't watch out, this guy's gonna find someone else."

I couldn't get over it, the way Ma looked meaningfully back and forth between Jack and me and laughed in this kind of wicked way.

Ma said to Jack, "Better tell your wife, you're gonna step out with some other woman if she's not careful." She glanced back and forth between us again as if she knew a secret that we didn't want her to know.

"*Stop talking like that,*" I screamed at my mother. "I *mean it.*"

Ma looked stricken and started to weep like a young child after a severe scolding. I felt mystified by her insight yet consumed with guilt by my reaction.

"I'm sorry, Ma, I'm sorry," I said, hugging her to me. "Oh, God. I didn't mean to yell at you like that. I know you can't help it either."

But she shied away from my embrace, reluctant to trust me after my harsh outburst.

Wayne popped his head through the door and cast an inquisitive look toward Ma, who had quieted down but still sniveled a little. "Dolly, is everything okay?" he said in a soothing drawl.

"Oh, we had a little meltdown," I said, ashamed of myself. "I think it's all right now."

"Good." With his flawless bedside manner, Wayne knew when not to pry. "Why don't I take Dolly to her therapy session?"

"I'll walk with you," I said, eager to try and make things up with Ma.

Jack resumed trying to feed Helen her pudding. Glancing at them as we exited, I noticed that Helen's limbs curled up in an unnatural way, and she flinched when he touched her arm. I had a feeling there was more going on here than a woman who'd forgotten how to feed herself. It looked like it pained her to use her hands and arms for the everyday tasks that most of us took for granted.

Certainly, Jack must be aware of this. Then again, men didn't always notice the same details as women. However, I stopped myself from speaking out. I needed to focus on Ma's care and not intervene in Helen's. Besides, I still smarted with embarrassment over my temper tantrum, and I felt impatient to make an escape, leaving Jack and Helen alone in the lounge.

Back home in my study, I consulted my AD literature for more detailed information on Stage Seven and its various substages. I would familiarize myself with what to watch for as the disease continued to progress with Ma.

Under *Common Characteristics of Decline*, I read that speech would become limited to a half-dozen words, then a single word at most, then no speech at all. Ma's vocabulary might be shrinking, but she wasn't even close to single digits yet.

I went on to read that the loss of ability to walk independently came after the loss of speech. Next came the loss of ability to sit up and, later, to hold one's head up without assistance. Worse still, a patient would often exhibit grimacing expressions in place of smiles.

It went downhill from there, if possible. *Major joints such as elbows become increasingly rigid*, I read. *The patient experiences contractures of joints and extremities (elbows, hands, fingers). It becomes extremely painful to use a full range of motion.*

I shuddered and thought back to Helen's unnatural posture earlier today and her pained reaction to Jack's touch.

The patient exhibits infantile reflexes such as sucking and grasping.

Oh, no.

I tried to maintain a clinical distance as I made my notes, but I found it hard not to worry. Would all these unspeakable things happen to Ma? Many of them had already happened to Helen. I read on and learned that most patients didn't make it to the final endgame. The mean point of death occurred when patients lost their ability to ambulate and sit up independently, about half-way through the various substages of Stage Seven.

I took some small comfort in that statistic.

To distract myself, I watched the *Sex and the City* installments in which Carrie became entangled in an affair with Mr. Big, who had married someone else. I envisioned myself as Carrie, the morally indefensible mistress, and Helen as the wronged wife. I didn't feel proud of being caught up in an illicit triangle. Yet, I was too swept up in the excitement to say no to the man.

33

THE ROMANCE DEPARTMENT

The way Jack saw it, dinner at Barbara's on Monday had been their best evening yet. They'd reached that stage in a new relationship when familiarity bred comfort and confidence but decidedly *not* contempt, while mutual ardor remained undiminished.

That had been one of the most pleasant revelations about Barbara from their first night together. Jack perceived she had a caring and gentle nature but had not expected her to be such an uninhibited lover. This morning, her passionate response in the Tropical Gardens stairwell became the latest in a series of delightful surprises.

As they broke apart from their embrace in the stairwell, he said, "You know, I nearly moved Helen into a different facility. If I had, we never would have met."

"Oh, good God, I can't believe it. My worst habits are rubbing off on you," Barbara said with a throaty laugh.

"What do you mean?"

"Remember what I explained to you about retroactive worrying? It's when you get upset about something that *might* have happened in theory, even though it never did. Well, you're doing it."

Jack considered this. "I guess I am."

They laughed and embraced again. Another surprise:

Barbara's often serious and worried demeanor might suggest a humorless disposition, but the opposite held true. She evinced a witty and nuanced sense of humor—sometimes self-deprecating, to be sure, but amusing nonetheless—and it gave him great joy. Vicky and even Dolly got more laughs with their profane language and vulgar jokes, but Barbara reigned as the true comedian of the family. She simply didn't know it.

Scott had a rare night off from the theatre, and Jack treated him to dinner at a downtown gastropub. After a couple of craft ales, Jack's grandson discoursed at length on his favorite subject: Scott.

First, he talked about his responsibilities at Providence Players, which he acknowledged to be a good learning experience and a strong resume item. But the grueling schedule had taken its toll.

"I've never worked such long hours in an internship, and that's saying a lot in the theatre. It hasn't left me any time for women. To tell you the truth, there's been no action at all my whole time in Providence. That's, like, a record for me. Not a record I'm proud of."

Jack gave a sympathetic nod and reflected on the irony of enjoying such a fruitful summer in the romance department while his handsome, twenty-year-old grandson complained about his dry spell.

Part of the problem, Scott went on to say, had been the lack of suitable candidates. "I've been spending time with that girl Sarah at Tropical Gardens, and she's cute, but she's only in high school."

"Barbara's daughter. She's sixteen, I think."

"Yeah, she's way too young."

"What about the women in your program?"

"There is another intern named Rachel who's a senior at Brandeis. She's always coming onto me, wanting to get together after work."

"But?"

"But I don't know. I haven't felt like acting on it. Now that I think about it, maybe I should have a couple of drinks with Rachel and give things a chance."

"If you feel the need for female companionship, might as well—"

"Companionship? No offense, Grandpop, but I'm not eighty."

Jack laughed to himself as he thought about the nature of his own "companionship." He and Barbara weren't exactly behaving like a pair of doddering old geezers consigned to shuffleboard and canasta.

This reminded him he'd promised Barbara to invite Scott to the birthday party for Dolly. "It will be early Sunday evening, and I'm sure it won't take long if you're able to stop by," he told his grandson.

"Oh, yeah, Sarah already texted me about it. Sure, I'll come. I haven't seen Nana in a while anyway. I'll hang out with Sarah afterward."

Jack cast a doubtful glance at Scott, who said in a defensive tone, "She's only gonna help me rehearse for the fall play."

"Why not rehearse with this other girl Rachel instead?"

Scott scowled at his grandfather. "Rehearsing with Sarah is harmless, okay? Anyhow, you don't need to make such a big deal out of it. In a couple of weeks, I'll be in New York and back in school."

34

TOUCHING HOT COALS

Twilight had descended over Tropical Gardens, and despite the early hour, most of the residents had retired to their rooms for the night. After the little party in Dolly's room, Scott had taken Sarah outside to the back patio to rehearse a scene. But a few minutes later, three coyotes loped out from the adjacent woods onto the back lawn, not far from the patio, and Sarah sprang up from her seat.

"Coyotes give me the creeps. Let's go inside."

They retreated to the foyer, deciding what to do next.

"Do you think we'll disturb people if we rehearse inside?" Sarah asked.

"Nah. They've all got their hearing aids out by now."

"It's amazing all the old people have gone to bed already. The sun just went down five minutes ago."

"Yeah, I know. I hope I'm not like that when I'm eighty."

"When Beryl Markham was eighty, she was still writing and doing interviews," Sarah said.

"Let's hope we can both be like Beryl, then." Scott raked one hand through his thick black hair.

Sarah's cellphone rang. She turned away from Scott and spoke *sotto voce*. "Hey, Dory. I'm busy with Scott right now."

He heard her giggle at her friend's response and say, "No, *you're* the bad girl."

Sarah pocketed her phone and turned back to Scott. "It's nice that you and your grandpa came for Grammy's birthday party."

"The timing worked out okay for me. We're dark tonight."

"Huh?"

"It's a theatre expression. That's what we say when there's no performance."

"I wonder if Grammy remembers the party."

Scott gave this some consideration. "Well, she remembered it while it was happening."

Sarah shook her head. "I'm not sure that counts as remembering. Scott, she didn't know how to blow out the candles. Even when my mom showed her, she still couldn't do it. And when Jack asked about her age, she said, 'I think I'm fifty.' She seems more and more confused all the time."

"At least she talks and cracks jokes and stuff. I can't remember the last time Nana recognized me or spoke to me. Tonight, I didn't even get to see her awake. She'd already gone to sleep by six o'clock."

"Grammy talks, but it's like the words are coming from a different person. It's her, but it's not."

Scott nodded. "Yeah, I felt that way about Nana when she started getting angry a lot. She never used to act that way."

"It's horrible to see them like this," Sarah said, and tears started streaming down her face. She swiped at her eyes with one fist and said, "Oh, God, I'm as bad as my mother."

Acting on instinct, Scott put his arms around Sarah. Her enormous tear-filled eyes looked warm and vulnerable.

"It's okay," he said, knowing that it wasn't. With those sexy eyes, she could have passed for nineteen or twenty, easy.

"Let's go into the lounge. Take your mind off your grandma."

She gave him an unhappy nod.

Someone had closed the blinds in the lounge, making the room nearly dark. Scott flipped on the light switch adjacent to the door. Nothing could have prepared the two young people for what they saw next—Barbara and Jack, together on the sofa.

She was perched *on his lap*, entwined in an embrace, and they were kissing in a way that old people shouldn't be allowed to kiss, if only out of respect for simple decency. Worse yet, Scott caught a brief glimpse of Jack's hand cupping Barbara's left breast over her blouse.

The moment the light came on and everyone realized what had happened, chaos ensued. Jack pulled his hand back as if it had been touching hot coals, and he and Barbara jumped up from the sofa, shocked and embarrassed. Scott dropped Sarah's hand and gaped at the older couple, even more astonished. Then everybody spoke—or, more accurately, screamed—at the same time.

Scott: "*Jesus, Grandpop.*"

Jack: "*Oh, God.*"

Barbara: "*Oh, no.*"

Sarah: "*Ew ew ew ew.*"

After the *ew*-ing subsided, Sarah dissolved into hysterics, capturing the attention of the group. An awkward silence followed. They all stood frozen in place, uncertain what to do or say next.

Barbara smoothed down her dress, attempted to compose herself, and said, "Sarah, come with me."

"Where?" Sarah asked in a challenging tone.

"Home." Barbara led her daughter out of the room.

Left alone inside the lounge with his grandfather, a seething Scott confronted the older man. "I don't fucking believe this."

"You forgot to request permission to swear," Jack said with a small salute, hoping this familiar catchphrase from Scott's childhood might defuse the tension.

It had the opposite effect. "Not funny." Scott's voice rose in anger.

"Let's try to calm down and discuss this rationally."

"Rationally? The whole thing seems pretty *irrational* to me. You're fooling around with Sarah's mother in front of your own wife."

"I don't think that describes the situation," Jack said. "And on that subject, you haven't forgotten Sarah is sixteen? I hope things haven't gone too far with her."

Once again, Jack had said the wrong thing.

Scott bristled at the idea of his grandfather turning the conversation back against him. "Oh, don't worry about that. I wouldn't dream of doing anything *inappropriate* like Grandpop. Sarah's cool. But she's not my girlfriend or anything."

"Good. Scott, I realize that seeing Barbara and me like that must have been a shock to you, but—"

"Can we please, please, *please* not discuss this?"

"It's important that we discuss it. You know I've been married to your grandmother for forty-five years."

"I know, Grandpop. That's the whole point." Scott raised both hands in a gesture of frustration.

"Will you hear me out? Forty-five years. And for most of that time, I've been blessed. I don't have to tell you that Nana was a talented, dynamic woman. Not to mention the best wife I could ever hope for. Our life together was fulfilling on every level. Do you think I've forgotten that? Not a day goes by that I don't miss what we had and who she used to be. I want you to know that nothing—and no one—will ever replace your grandmother."

Scott replied, "If that's how you feel, I don't know how you can ignore all that and pretend the past never existed."

"I'm not ignoring anything or pretending anything. But 'all that' happened a lifetime ago. I'm trying to move on with a new life now. I had hoped for your understanding. But to be frank, I don't require your approval. We both need to be clear on that point. These last years have been incredibly hard, but I want you to know that until recently, I've been true to your grandmother's memory."

"Her memory? In case you hadn't noticed, Nana is still alive."

"In case you hadn't noticed, Nana has left the building."

Scott took a deep breath, drawing himself up to his full height, and informed his grandfather, "Which is exactly what I'm gonna do. Right now."

After leaving Tropical Gardens with a dramatic flourish, Scott headed back to the friend's house where he'd been living all summer. He heaved a sigh of relief to find the place empty. He sure as hell didn't feel like making conversation right now. All Scott wanted was to get spectacularly wasted. Which he proceeded to accomplish, utilizing a combination of tequila shots and beer.

A hundred different questions raced through Scott's head as he tried to work out the involvement between Grandpop and Barbara. Had he interrupted a spontaneous, unplanned encounter, like the sort of thing that happened to Scott himself when he'd get drunk at a party and hit on some random girl? Or had Grandpop entered a real relationship? And if the latter, was it only a kissing relationship, or?

But then, he remembered the way his grandfather's hand had rested on Barbara's breast with the proprietary assurance of a man who knew he had groping rights. And when Scott made the wisecrack about "not doing anything inappropriate like Grandpop," Jack didn't attempt to deny that he and Barbara were lovers.

What else had Grandpop said? "Until recently, I've been true to your grandmother's memory." Meaning that now, he'd stopped being true to her.

That about summed it up.

"Shit, I can't think about this," Scott said aloud. He wished fervently he could hit a delete button to erase that disturbing image of Barbara and Grandpop on the sofa together.

Well, he'd keep his distance from Tropical Gardens for a while. He had no desire to see his grandfather after this incident, and Nana wouldn't know the difference. He had to concede that she *was* getting a lot worse.

At least one good thing came out of discovering Grandpop with Barbara. It knocked some sense back into him. He'd been about to kiss Sarah when he led her into the lounge. The irony of the situation did not escape him. Scott had reached the age of his sexual peak, but Grandpop was the one who couldn't even keep it in his pants. It would have been a huge mistake to get involved with Sarah, even if he'd been careful not to let things go too far.

Scott had a practical as well as an ethical motivation to exercise self-restraint. Last semester, his girlfriend at the time had dragged him to a feminist lecture at Tisch about something called the "Me Too" movement that supported victims of sexual harassment or abuse. The movement had been founded ten years earlier, in 2006, and until now, not much had happened, but the speaker predicted it was only a matter of time.

Professionals in the entertainment world were vulnerable, the lecturer said, because the widespread stories that had long been told about the infamous "casting couch" held true in many cases. People in positions of power in the industry often preyed on women and sometimes on men as well. But in time, the predators would get their just desserts. Proper behavior was no longer only the moral thing to do, but it also would someday be necessary for professional self-preservation.

Suppose Scott became a famous actor, and Sarah went

public with a story that he had molested her or taken advantage of her as a minor? Women sometimes did these things to attract attention or to extort money. Sarah didn't strike him as that kind of girl, but you never could tell.

This seemed like a lot to process when hammered. Scott went to the bathroom and peed like a racehorse, eyeing himself in the mirror as he washed his hands afterward. He studied his puffy face and his bloodshot eyes.

"Fuck," he muttered. He needed to be more cautious about drinking. If he wanted to be a leading man, he must take greater care to safeguard his appearance.

Life wasn't fair. He wouldn't turn twenty-one until next month, yet he already had to concern himself with the risks of getting shit-faced *and* the risks of getting laid.

Then again, maybe a little "female companionship," to use his grandfather's genteel term, could be within Scott's reach after all. He felt horny thinking about Sarah's warm brown eyes and the way she felt when he'd hugged her. Also, that image of Grandpop with Barbara . . . sure, it was repugnant, yet at the same time, witnessing his grandfather as an active sexual being was kind of a turn-on, in a pervy sort of way.

No way could he contact Sarah, but maybe he should send a text over to Rachel, the girl from Brandeis. Scott extracted the cellphone from his pocket but then felt overcome by a wave of fatigue. He'd sit and relax for just a moment before texting Rachel.

Scott sank into a comfortable armchair, spilling half a bottle of beer all over himself and the upholstery in the process. No worries—he'd clean up the trail of sticky foam later. Within two minutes, he fell fast asleep.

35

CHICKEN LITTLE

One time when I was acting particularly anxious (even for me), Vicky told me my last name must be "Little."

"What are you talking about?" I asked.

"You know how I like to call you Chicken. Well, you're Chicken *Little* because the sky is always falling where you're concerned." Her shoulders shook with laughter.

Last night, the sky did fall.

The birthday party in Ma's room went all right, though it was disappointing that Vicky and Martin didn't come. My sister had texted me a couple of hours earlier, saying:

—*Can't make it, something came up.*

A string of emojis followed this cryptic message: birthday cake, party hat, balloons, kiss mark.

Ma was quiet and withdrawn at her own party. I'm not certain she even understood it was her birthday. She seemed tired, though not too tired to eat a large helping of cake and ice cream. At least Jack and Scott tried to make things more festive.

It wasn't until afterward that the trouble began.

Sarah and Scott walked in on Jack and me making out like a couple of teenagers in the lounge, and it's difficult to say who freaked out more, the kids or Jack and me. I knew the four of us wouldn't be engaging in a cerebral panel discussion about what had occurred, so I decided to get away as fast as possible and take my daughter with me.

I pulled Sarah out to the foyer, and she proceeded toward the exit. But I stopped her, saying, "I want to run to Grammy's room to give her a quick kiss goodnight."

"Haven't you had enough kissing for one evening? Seriously, Mom. What the hell?"

"Sarah, please—"

"I don't know why you couldn't have been dating like a *normal* person all this time."

"What is that supposed to mean?"

"I mean—I don't know—like, maybe it might have occurred to you to go out on e-dates like Carol and every other divorced woman. But no, you had to hook up with an old guy in a nursing home."

"Jack is not *in* a nursing home. He's not, like, a *patient*."

"No, right. His *wife* is the patient. Scott's grandmother. Did you see the look on Scott's face?"

I sighed and nodded. Scott had worn an expression of shock, but it was more than that. I recalled how his eyes had sizzled with fury as he stared at Jack.

"I've never seen such a hateful look . . . at least, not in real life," Sarah said.

I turned away from my daughter. "Let's go say goodnight to Grammy."

"You go. I'll wait in the car."

I fished the car keys from my purse and tossed them to Sarah, who hurried out the door, anxious to escape me as fast as she could.

But I never made it to Ma's room.

After Sarah left, I overheard Jack and Scott speaking in raised voices in the lounge. Though I wasn't proud of it, I remained in the foyer to eavesdrop on their conversation.

Jack spoke to Scott about how he and Helen had been married for forty-five years and how, for most of that time, he'd been blessed.

"The best wife I could ever hope for."

"Fulfilling on every level."

"Not a day goes by that I don't miss what we had."

"Nothing—and no one—will ever replace your grandmother."

After this last comment, I bolted for the car, unable to listen a moment longer.

As I slid into the driver's seat and fastened my seatbelt, I turned to Sarah and said, "Honey, emotions are running high right now. Maybe we should wait until tomorrow to discuss this."

Sarah hissed, "Sure. Whatever."

We drove the rest of the way home in silence. She ran to her room and I to mine. I couldn't stop imagining how Sarah must have felt discovering the two of us together. It was mortifying to recall the expressions of disbelief in her eyes and Scott's.

Then I kept replaying Jack's comments to his grandson about how brilliant his marriage had been.

"Nothing—and no one—will ever replace your grandmother."

These past weeks I'd tried to forget about Jack and Helen being a married couple. I pretended she was only some unfortunate relative he'd been tasked with taking care of, not a beloved spouse. Who was I kidding? It dawned on me: Jack had been married to Helen for most of my life.

Forty-five years.

"Nothing—and no one—will ever replace your grand-mother."

What did that make me?

Since he'd ruled me out as a Helen replacement, I wondered if that made me a younger trophy girlfriend. Perhaps the term "trophy" sounded immodest, but next to Helen, in her current state, I was the epitome of glamour. I worried I'd behaved like a shameless sex kitten, to use Vicky's characterization. An erotic plaything for Jack's pleasure . . .

Most of all, I wondered, *where do we go from here?*

I started an email to my happy hour group to ask if they could meet tomorrow for an emergency session. I composed the message and rewrote it twice before hitting the "delete" button. I couldn't bear to talk about what had happened. The entire event seemed too painful and embarrassing to discuss, even among old friends.

After a restless night, I moved gingerly around the kitchen. I could feel a dull but persistent throb behind my tired eyes, like a woman with a bad hangover. Cheerful sunlight streamed in through the window above the sink, mocking my exhaustion and unhappiness. I wanted to crawl back into bed and pull the covers over my head, but I knew sleep wouldn't come.

When Sarah came in to fix herself breakfast, I attempted to initiate a conversation. I still didn't know what I would say to her, though I figured I'd try to explain in a generic way that relationships are complicated, and circumstances can sometimes bring two people together when they least expect it. I hoped she would not press for details.

But as it happened, we never got that far. She cut me off at the pass with, "Mom, it's okay. Please don't say anything. There's no need to discuss this."

Her tone of voice implied it was *not* okay. But being a coward at heart, I took her at her word and backed off.

I drove over to Tropical Gardens and stayed with Ma in her room for the rest of the day. We remained in seclusion to avoid Jack, but my excuse to myself was that Ma seemed unwell.

This happened to be true. Once again, she appeared lethargic and confused, and the cold symptoms had also worsened. She blew her nose nonstop, building a Mount Everest of used tissues on the floor next to her favorite chair. Dr. Sam had tried telling Ma that constant nose-blowing made things worse by propelling mucus up into the sinuses, but such technicalities went way beyond her.

She even seemed perplexed by my presence. One time, she looked at me in puzzlement and started to say, "Are you my—?" She stopped in mid-sentence, and I couldn't coax her to complete the question. She slept so much that I thought I'd wear out the nib of a pencil recording her nap schedule.

A text from Jack arrived.

—Where are you? We need to talk.

I arrived ahead of him most mornings, and he must have seen my car and known I was somewhere inside the building. I didn't respond to his text.

Thus far today, I had managed to hide from my daughter and from my lover. Not a highly dignified performance.

36

PERMANENT DAMAGE

Sarah had been a jumble of emotions ever since the surreal discovery of her mother on Jack's lap, the two of them going at it. For maybe the first time ever, she comprehended the meaning of *hysterical*. She see-sawed between laughter and tears, not even sure which emotion dominated at a given moment.

As Sarah thought back on it, the pieces of the puzzle all fell into place. She now understood that Jack had been the mystery man in that recent text exchange with her mother, and Barbara must have been seeing him on those other evenings when she'd been vague about her whereabouts. Also, this new romance most likely accounted for Mom's sunny demeanor of late.

That all boded well for Barbara—but not so well for Sarah. She fumed at her mother over the timing of what had occurred. After Scott's comforting hug last night, when he suggested they go into the lounge, she felt confident he was going to kiss her. Sarah had limited experience with the opposite sex, but she knew enough to recognize when a spark of attraction ignited between two people. Something had been on the verge of happening with Scott. But that spark had fizzled at the sight of Jack and Barbara in each other's arms. The whole thing was unspeakably bizarre.

It ruined her evening, for sure. But worse still, what if it'd done permanent damage? In a few years, the age difference between Scott and Sarah wouldn't matter as much, but could they ever turn the friendship into something more without recalling that mental image of her mother and his grandfather in a lip-lock?

Sarah's anger and uncertainty had boiled over when Barbara attempted to talk to her in the kitchen. Although she could tell her mother looked upset and uncomfortable, Sarah couldn't handle one of their little talks about "feelings" right now. Barbara would give her some bullshit explanation to try and make it all better. Sarah didn't feel like playing along. How could she forgive her mother? She might have ruined Sarah's chances with Scott for good.

Well, at least Aunt Vicky had it right about one thing. Barbara was not gay.

But the whole situation was much too weird.

37

CIRCLE OF LIFE

Yesterday I spent another day hiding in Ma's room. She remained unusually subdued. At my insistence, the nurse gave her a thorough checkup. Apart from the nasal congestion, she had no fever, no stomach issues as far as anyone could tell, and no UTI. I'd learned that urinary tract infections were the bane of the elderly and could manifest in many forms of erratic behavior among patients with dementia.

Cindy and I tried to get Ma to articulate how she felt, but that was an exercise in futility. If you pointed to a body part and asked if it hurt—her head, her knee, whatever—Ma would say "yes" but would then reverse herself. She was an unreliable witness at best. After examining her, Cindy gave Ma a dose of decongestant and a couple of Tylenol capsules for good measure, figuring it couldn't hurt.

Jack texted again yesterday, several times, and tried to call as well. He left a voicemail message, but I lacked the courage to listen to it.

Vicky also called, but I didn't pick up because she phoned in the middle of Ma's examination by the nurse. I played back her message later and learned she expected to stop by around ten o'clock the next morning to give Ma a belated birthday present. My sister always had a knack for making Ma laugh. Maybe a visit from Vicky would be what the doctor ordered.

Wayne collected Ma at around quarter to ten the next day for occupational therapy, and that's when I remembered Vicky was due to arrive soon. Good, it would give my sister and me some time to talk before Ma returned. Then I realized Vicky would expect me to be in the family lounge, and I could feel my chest constrict in a surge of panic. What if I ran into Jack?

I grabbed the phone and shot her a text.

—*Meet me in Ma's room. Important!*

But by ten minutes past ten, still no sign of Vicky. She must not have seen my text. With great reluctance, I left the safety of my mother's room to intercept my sister. Insanely, I put on sunglasses for the terrifying trek to the lounge, as though this crafty disguise would conceal me from possible discovery by Jack.

Sure enough, I found Vicky sitting in the lounge—alone, thank God. No sign of Jack on my way there. A row of pills lay on the table in front of my sister, and she swallowed them one at a time with a bottle of water. Next to the pills, I noticed a gift-wrapped box that must've contained candies. Even in my anguish, I worried about whether they were sugar-free.

I scooped up the pills and said, "Not here. We need to go to Ma's room right away."

"What are you, a lunatic?" But recognizing the urgency

in my voice, she shrugged, picked up the gift, and followed me back to Ma's room. I slammed the door shut behind us.

"May I have those back now? Pretty please," she said, indicating the fistful of pills in my hand.

"Yes, sorry. Whatever it is you're popping today, I think I could use one."

"Don't get into a lather. They're only calcium supplements."

"Why so many?" I asked.

"I'm cramming for a bone density test."

"Be careful. You know, there's a new study out that says too much calcium can increase your risk of a heart attack."

"Oh, for fuck's sake. You and your damn studies," said Vicky, groaning.

At that point, I removed my sunglasses.

"Jesus Christ, what happened to you?" she said. "You look like Krapp's last tape."

I gave her a blank look. "I don't get what tape has to do with crap."

She groaned again. "No, it's the name of a play by—forget it. I meant you look like hell."

I guess three days of anxiety and three nights of sleeplessness had taken a toll on my appearance. I sank into a chair and sighed.

"I've barely slept since the night before Ma's birthday."

Her lips curled into a little smirk. "Been rolling around in the sack with that old steed of yours?"

"Funny, but no. I've been lying awake trying to decide what to do about that old—" I caught myself. "About Jack. Something happened the night of Ma's party. Where were you, by the way?"

Vicky shrugged. "Martin and I had to take some air conditioning contractors to a Red Sox game."

"Your customers were more important than Ma's birthday?" I ended this query in a whiny upward inflection that Vicky referred to as my Jewish-mother voice. She credited me with mastering the voice to a level of proficiency that few actual Jews have been able to achieve.

"Oh, don't lay on one of your guilt trips," she said with her signature dismissive wave. "You know Ma can't remember for thirty seconds whether I've been here or not. Anyway, I want to know what the hell happened with Jack." She gave me another smirk, impatient for me to brief her.

When I told Vicky about the encounter with Sarah and Scott in the lounge, she slapped her thighs in hilarity, relishing this juicy morsel of gossip.

"That is too fucking funny."

"No, Vicky," I said in a somber tone. "Not funny. *Awful.*"

Then I let everything pour out. I told my sister about my humiliation over Sarah walking in on Jack and me. I told her about my shock over realizing Jack had been in another relationship for almost as long as I'd been alive, a cherished relationship that would never again be equaled in his life. I told her about my inadequacy in confronting the situation head-on with Sarah. I told her my doubts and fears about Jack's feelings for me and my confusion over my own feelings for him. I told her that even Ma, as loopy as she is, detected something sort of, I don't know— *improper?*—between Jack and me.

"He's been trying to call and text me since the other

night. I've managed to avoid him for three days by keeping Ma in her room, but that can't go on forever. I need to decide what to do."

To her credit, Vicky checked her sarcasm at the door for once and gave my problem thoughtful consideration. "Barbara, honey," she said, "I've made no secret of my misgivings about you and Jack. But don't listen to me. Listen to yourself."

I shook my head, not sure where my sister was going with this.

She said, "You've just mentioned several important reasons why things aren't working between the two of you. It's turning you into a wreck, and you can't go on this way. You know you'll have to confront it sooner or later. Wouldn't sooner be better?"

"Maybe I could use some of your pills."

After countless failed attempts to ply me with offerings from her arsenal of feel-good medications, Vicky broke into a triumphant smile. At long last, I'd shown the good sense to embrace pharmaceutical relief. She reached for her bag and pulled out four little pale green pills, which she transferred into a baggie and handed to me.

"Xanax. Don't take more than half a tablet at a time."

I gave a grateful nod and stashed them in my purse.

"Maybe it wouldn't hurt to have a little right now?"

"No thanks. But I promise to think about it. Maybe it will help. I feel like everything is spinning out of control."

"Everything? What else?"

"It's Ma, too. She hasn't been herself the last few days. I thought she was sick, but they can't find anything wrong except a stuffy nose. Something is different about her, and it scares me."

"Tell me what you're afraid of with Ma."

"I worry that she'll die soon, and I worry that she won't." I surprised even myself with this answer. "God, Vicky, I feel like such a weak, indecisive coward."

My phone started to buzz. I checked the caller ID and dropped the phone on the table as if it were radioactive. "It's Jack again."

"You're not going to answer."

I shook my head.

Vicky reached for my cell. For one scary moment, I feared she'd answer and speak to Jack herself. But she handed me the phone and said, "Barb, you can't keep hiding from him."

I took the call.

"Jack. Hello."

"Barbara, I'm glad I finally reached you. Have you gotten my messages?"

"Yes, yes, I got the messages. I'm sorry I've been keeping to myself. Ma's not so hot this week and—well, I needed time to think." I looked over at Vicky, who stared at me with intent concentration.

"We should talk," Jack said. I could detect the urgency in his voice. "I mean, in person. Maybe later today? After we leave Tropical Gardens."

"You want to meet and talk in person later," I said, repeating for Vicky's benefit. I gave her a questioning look, and she shook her head, wagging a finger to emphasize the point.

"I—I don't think that's a good idea," I said.

This time, Vicky gave an encouraging nod.

"But there are some things I need to explain about what happened with Scott, and—well, other things too."

He had no way to know I'd overheard his argument with Scott, and I already had a fairly good idea of where he and his grandson stood. But I only said, "There isn't much to discuss."

Vicky nodded again.

And then I did it. I said, "Jack, it's best if we stop seeing each other. It doesn't feel right on a lot of different levels."

"Barbara, that's not what I want—and if we could just talk this through, I think you might see things in a different light."

"No," I said. "No. I don't think there's anything you can do to change my mind."

This time, I heard only silence at the other end of the line—a silence more deafening than the loudest din.

I said in a mere whisper, "Please try to understand. I—I'm so sorry." I put down the phone.

Vicky fawned all over me. "Well done, sweetie," she said, rewarding me with a rare hug. "And not cowardly at all. Very courageous, if you want to know. Now you can both get on with your lives. It's better this way."

"Oh, God. I didn't know it would be this hard. This is terrible."

"Honey, you're gonna be fine. I promise. You'll feel like your old self again in no time."

"But I don't want to feel like my old self. I want to feel the way I felt with Jack."

"Let's think of something to get your mind off this."

Nodding in assent, I picked up Ma's present and asked, "Is this candy?"

"Yes, chocolates. Ma's favorite."

"But are they—"

"Relax, honey. Sugar-free." My sister knew me well.

Then I heard a noise—the sound of the door latch opening. Suppose it was Jack, bursting in to confront me face to face?

"Who is it?" I asked, my heart pounding.

"Cindy and Dolly. We're back from occupational therapy," said the nurse as they entered the room. I noticed Ma's shuffle was slower than usual, and she seemed to have trouble manipulating her walker.

"How'd it go?" I asked.

The nurse helped Ma into a chair and said, "It's getting harder for your mother to navigate basic tasks like using the walker or climbing steps. It's not physical weakness. Her brain isn't connecting to her legs, her hands, et cetera. We'll keep working with her in the therapy sessions to try and retain those skills as much as possible."

"Hi, Ma," I said, summoning up my most cheerful voice. "Are you feeling okay? How lucky is this? You've got both your girls today." I gestured toward Vicky, who gave Ma a wave.

I expected Ma to smile and say, "My girls"—her stock greeting—but she gave us a strange look and didn't speak.

"It's a little chilly in here. Let's put your sweater on," I said, retrieving her beige sweater from the basket of her walker. I tried to drape it over her shoulders, but she shook it off with a defiant shrug.

"No. That's not mine."

"Ma, this is your favorite sweater," Vicky said.

"I told you, it's not mine. I won't wear it."

"Christ on a crutch. My happy-go-lucky mother is turning bitchy, and my straight little sister is begging for sedatives," Vicky said, pulling a face. "The whole damn family is running amok."

Ma said, "What family? I don't see any families in here."

"Ma, it's us. Your girls. Barbara and Vicky." I pointed to myself and to Vicky as I spoke our names. But Ma only shook her head, her expression vacant.

I picked up the Scottie dog from the walker basket and placed it in her lap. "Remember your dog's name?"

Ma squirmed a little in her chair before replying. "Umm . . . Blackie."

"That's a terrific name for him," Vicky said, "but his name is Scottie."

I tried in desperation to jog my mother's memory. "Let's sing that tune you like," I said, breaking into song.

"*How much is that doggie in the window?*

"*The one with the waggly tail . . .*"

Vicky joined in on the next line.

"*How much is that doggie in the window?*"

Dolly threw the Scottie dog to the floor and said in a cranky voice, "I want a scotch."

Vicky cast a sardonic look at Ma. "Evidently, some memories remain more firmly entrenched than others."

I guided the nurse away from my mother toward the window for a talk. My attempt to maintain secrecy was irrelevant, with Ma so out of it.

"Has she been like this all day?" I asked Cindy.

"Yes. A lot of confusion," the nurse said.

"What if . . . I've been wondering about increasing her Aricept and Namenda. Maybe a higher dosage of the AD drugs will help with her memory."

"You'd have to discuss any medication changes with her doctor." The words rolled off her tongue so readily that I suspected the nurse often delivered this stock response to family members. "But to be honest, I'm pretty sure he'll say that Dolly wouldn't tolerate a higher dose—and at this stage of the disease, it isn't helpful."

This stage of the disease. "Are we talking Stage Seven?" I asked, dreading her reply.

Cindy dodged the question. "Like I said before, we prefer not to pigeonhole anyone. But there has been a change."

"Oh, God."

"Barbara, I realize this is difficult," she said.

"I—I want to make sure we're doing everything possible for her. There must be something you can do." I had another idea. "What if something happened when she fell a couple of weeks ago . . . like, I don't know . . . a brain bleed? That could account for the changes in her behavior, couldn't it?"

Cindy shook her head. "The CAT scan was clean. No sign of bleeding on the brain."

"But maybe—"

"This is the way it goes with Alzheimer's," Cindy said, her tone a little less gentle this time. "Unless something else takes her—and that can often happen at this age—the process is inevitable." She turned her gaze toward Vicky to make sure my sister was listening too.

"Think about what happens after a baby is born," said the nurse. "She learns to lift her head, and eat solid food, and recognize her family. She forms memories. Little by little, she becomes self-sufficient."

"What does that have to do with Ma?" I asked.

"With Alzheimer's, it's the same process, but in reverse. Everything that's been learned is unlearned."

"Is this supposed to be making us feel better somehow? Because if so, it's not working," Vicky said, her voice edgy.

The nurse frowned a little. "Barbara, you've been recording the changes in your mother's behavior for a long time now. In fact, you're much more knowledgeable about the progression of this disease than most of our patients' relatives. None of this should come as a huge surprise." I sensed she was growing impatient with the two of us. I almost expected her to say, "Don't waste my time. You should know all this by now."

Then Dolly, who had been nodding off, pointed at the gift box and said, "What's that?"

"A birthday present for you, Ma," said Vicky. "I'll help you open it." Vicky tore off the balloon-print wrapping paper, opened the lid, and displayed the candies to Ma.

"Isn't that nice," said Cindy. "I'm afraid I've got to get to a meeting. You three enjoy your visit." She made a hasty retreat. Sometimes I suspected Cindy had graduated with an advanced degree from the same School of Excuses as my sister.

"Which one would you like, Ma?" Vicky asked, holding the candy box above Ma's lap. Our mother surveyed the collection of assorted chocolates but only shook her head, incapable of decision-making.

"Why don't we pick one for you?" I said.

Ma wrinkled her nose and waved an indifferent hand at the box as if to say, "Take it away."

I moved the candy to the table and kissed my mother's wrinkled cheek. "How're you doing? Do you remember who I am now?"

I could tell she wanted to figure it out, eager to please me. "You're—you're my mother."

"No, Ma. I'm your daughter. Barbara."

"Where's my mother?" Ma asked, looking from me to Vicky. "I want to see her."

"Oh, Ma. She isn't here," I said, beginning to cry. "Can anything else possibly go wrong?" Never before had Ma failed to recognize Vicky and me.

Vicky shook her head and wagged a finger at me, much the way she did while coaching me through that ghastly break-up call with Jack. "Try not to act upset in front of Ma."

But I remained inconsolable. "As long as she knew us, I felt like I could handle it. But this—this is the day I've been dreading for the longest time." I started to cry harder.

"Holy crap, Barbara. After all these years, I think I get why you worry all the time. You're never at peace. You're always trying to change reality, instead of accepting it. Instead of letting things happen. Going with the flow."

"Please don't get on my case now, of all days."

A knock at the door interrupted us. Ma's room had become a beehive of activity, a veritable Grand Central Station. Again, I felt a sharp stab of fear that it might be Jack.

Instead, Wayne popped in. "Will Dolly be having lunch in here again today, or are you taking her to the dining room?"

Vicky replied, "Dining room" at the same moment that I declared "here." My sister shot me a look. I knew I couldn't hide in Ma's room forever. Helen never ate in the dining room anyway, so we wouldn't run into Jack there at lunch.

"We'll take her to the dining room," I said.

"Okay, good," said Wayne. Noticing my tear-stained face, he approached me with sympathetic concern. "Barbara, what's wrong?"

I bemoaned to Wayne the difficulty of accepting that Ma had lost her memories and the faculties she'd developed as an adult—physical, mental, social, *everything*— and I could do nothing about it. "It seems so . . . so cruel." I sniffled.

Wayne nodded in understanding. "I know it may seem cruel to you. But in Bali, where I come from, Hindu people regard it in a different light, as a natural human condition. There's a belief about the life cycle of memories. The idea is that when an elderly person returns to a state of infancy, it wipes the slate clean and prepares him to be reborn. It's like . . . the circle of life."

"Circle of life?" Vicky looked skeptical. "This is our mother, not the fucking *Lion King*."

"I don't mean to suggest you start believing in reincarnation," Wayne said to us. "But it might be helpful if I can give you a different perspective on the situation. A different way of looking at your mom's circumstance."

The idea intrigued me, and I had to admit it sounded

less bleak than the interpretation Cindy had offered. "I'm going to make some notes on this in my binder. Thank you, Wayne. I appreciate it." Later, I would Google "Hindu circle of life" for more information as well.

"No problem. Any time you need to talk, I'm here for you," he said and left the room.

Ma now sat snoring in her chair. Dejected, I picked up the Scottie dog from the floor and placed him back in her lap.

Vicky fixed her gaze on me and said, "You know, I have a thought. Rather than increase Ma's medications, maybe we should ask the nurse to wean her *off* the meds."

"I'm not sure I understand."

She addressed me in a conspiratorial tone. "It's only that—well, we don't want to prolong her suffering, do we? And I think if they pull back on the meds, it might help to—you know—hasten things."

I couldn't believe my ears. "*Hasten* things? What exactly did you have in mind?"

"Chicken, I'm just sayin', you tend to hang onto things when you should be letting go. And maybe now is the time to let go."

"Does letting go mean we stop her blood pressure drugs so she can stroke out? Or maybe we take away the heart pills, so she can drop dead of a heart attack?" I shouted. "Pick your poison, Vick. Wait, *there's* an idea. You could slip a little arsenic into her pudding for even faster results."

"Terrific." Vicky rolled her eyes. "I'm trying to have a rational discussion, and you go into total drama queen mode. Do you want her to linger in this final stage for months, or maybe even years? Does that help anyone? And by the time it's over, neither of us will have a pot to piss in."

I guess we must have been raising our voices because Ma was awake again, turning her head to and fro between us like a spectator at a tennis match.

"Ah, that's what this is about, the money." I pointed an accusing finger at my sister.

"Someone in this family needs to have a practical bone in her body," she said.

"Every bone in *your* body is a selfish bone. You're always ready to cast aside anyone or anything that's inconvenient. If it interferes with your precious agenda, out it goes with the garbage."

"Stop with the drama," said Vicky. "That is completely unfair—"

"Is it? Jack and I were an inconvenience too, admit it. You figured if I became serious about a man, maybe I wouldn't be on call '24/7' for Ma anymore. Then *you* might have to step up to the plate. God forbid."

"*Drama, drama, drama,*" Vicky said, shaking her fist for emphasis. And she dared to call *me* the drama queen.

The nurse popped her head in. "Barbara, Vicky—what's going on? We can hear you halfway down the hall."

My sister and I ignored Cindy and continued sparring.

Cindy said, "Ladies, please. You need to take this conversation somewhere else." But we kept right on exchanging barbs.

"You're preaching about how I need to let go. But where Jack's concerned, maybe I should have been hanging on—not letting go," I said.

"This isn't about your goddamn gentleman friend."

"I don't know why I ever came to you for relationship guidance."

"It's time you faced reality about what's happening with Ma."

But Ma didn't occupy my thoughts at that moment. I started saying over and over, "Oh, God, what have I done? Jack . . . *Jack*."

The intensity of this argument had exacted a toll on our mother, who now rocked back and forth in her seat, disconcerted. In a monotone, she said, "I want . . . I want . . . I want . . . I want . . ."

The nurse grabbed the candy box from the table and ran over to Ma. As she did this, she commanded us, "Ladies, please stop." Then she placed a comforting hand on Ma's shoulder and said in a softer voice, "Dolly, dear, have a piece of this nice chocolate."

Our mother rose from her seat, and the rest of us fell silent as she yelled, "I don't want the damn chocolate. I *want those crazy girls to shut up*."

38

A HUGE VOID

Jack felt resigned yet also perplexed over what had happened with Barbara. He knew she must feel embarrassed and shaken by the kids' discovery of their physical involvement, as did he. But had that been the real reason for the breakup? It seemed to Jack that something else was afoot, but he couldn't manage to puzzle it out.

Not too long after their painfully tense and awkward phone conversation, he looked out the window of Helen's room and noticed the older sister, Vicky, walking in the direction of the parking lot. Had she been complicit in this somehow? He knew from discussions with Barbara that Vicky could manipulate her with cold calculation.

In the few days since Dolly's party, he had not run into Barbara once. Jack knew their schedule and tried to keep his distance, avoiding the lounge above all. He calculated that perhaps Barbara needed time to get over the shock of Sunday night and work things out in her own head. But now that she'd broken things off, he would have to continue this strategy of avoidance going forward. The prospect of doing this made the current bleak landscape appear even more desolate.

Barbara's absence left a huge void. He already missed their easy conversations during the long days at Tropical

Gardens, the same way he missed the feel of her soft curves on those evenings when they had clung together— evenings that had been too few and too brief.

But it was not in his power to reverse this course of events. As Jack walked Helen around Tropical Gardens later that day, judiciously avoiding the lounge, he tried to formulate a plan—not an alcohol-infused evening with the guys, but something to look forward to in the future. Maybe when the time came, he'd go to California to visit Paul and his family. It had been much too long.

"When the time came" meant "after Helen died," and Jack found it strange that he should choose to speak in euphemisms of this inevitable day, even to himself.

Walking through the foyer, he wheeled Helen up to the potted palm in the corner and pointed it out to her. No reaction. He touched one of the leaves himself, but she couldn't even focus her eyes on this once favorite object. It occurred to Jack that weeks—no, months—had passed since Helen had taken any notice of it.

Distracted by all the recent drama with Barbara and the kids, he'd forgotten about the tests Cindy had promised to order for Helen. Hadn't it been more than a week now? He must inquire about it right away.

The following morning, Jack rode his bike to Tropical Gardens for a ten-thirty meeting in the nurse's office to go over Helen's test results. After a brief exchange of pleasantries, Cindy handed a clipboard across the desk to him.

"Helen's down eight pounds since we last weighed her. That's a rapid loss. Here's her weight chart from the last six months."

Jack perused the sheet on the clipboard, which included a line graph with a distinct downward trajectory. "Wow. What did the tests show?"

"No sign of infection and her vital signs are fine. No change with the heart or organs." At least some of the news was good. Then, shifting to a less upbeat tone, she said, "But we also did a swallow test, which came back with a diagnosis of dysphagia. This tells us that Helen's swallowing reflex is impaired."

"That explains why she's eating very little . . . and losing weight," said Jack.

"Correct."

"What do we do?"

"She's already eating pureed foods and thickened fluids only, so there isn't much we can change about her diet."

"I see. Is this part of the Alzheimer's, or do you think something else is going on?"

"We think it's the Alzheimer's. Patients forget how to chew and swallow, the same way they lose their memories. It's not at all uncommon."

Jack nodded in understanding.

Then she said, "Jack, I haven't had a chance to pull Helen's advance directive from our files. What were her wishes for end of life?"

Jack raised his eyebrows, not expecting the question.

"Helen didn't want to be kept alive with ventilators or feeding tubes or any other interventions. When she could still make those decisions, she was adamant about that."

"Good. In that case, if medical complications arise, we'll do everything we can to keep Helen comfortable, but we won't treat her aggressively."

"What sort of complications?"

"Well, this kind of weight loss isn't good because it leads to general weakening, which can hurt the immune system. Dehydration is another problem in these situations. And aspiration pneumonia is always a risk when a patient can't swallow correctly because food or liquid can travel into the lungs. Going forward, I recommend that we treat Helen as a hospice patient."

"Hospice," he repeated, startled by this recommendation. "Do you have any idea . . . how long?"

"No one has a crystal ball around here. Helen's a fighter, and she's hung in there a long time. It's unusual to see a patient continue this long in the advanced stage of the disease," she said. "A hospice patient, by definition, is within six months of end of life. But given the risks we talked about, and Helen's current condition, something could happen sooner than that. In other words, we may be talking weeks or even days, not months."

Jack sat there, trying to absorb this. On the one hand, it felt as though Helen had been sick forever; but on the other hand, everything seemed to be moving at lightning speed now. "I don't know why I should feel shocked by what you've told me, but I do."

"We think we've prepared ourselves, but when someone

turns a corner like this, it's always a shock," Cindy said.

"Yes. It seems like we lose them twice with this illness—first, when they stop being who they used to be—and second, when they finally die."

"I know, Jack. I see way too much of that here."

They spoke for a few minutes longer before Cindy took her leave. Jack ambled down the hallway, still trying to digest what she'd told him. He knew this day would come. But he and his wife had not expected their golden years to end like this. He wished he could've done something more for her.

In the hall, Jack ran into Dolly and Sarah headed toward the family lounge. He noticed that Dolly did not hold the walker in her usual manner. Instead, she sat on the bench seat with her feet dangling in the air as Sarah pushed her along. He greeted them both.

"Hi, Jack," Sarah said, but Dolly was silent.

"Grammy, say hello to Jack."

But Dolly closed her eyes and shook her head as if to say, "Don't bother me."

Sarah gave Jack an apologetic smile, but his mind was elsewhere.

"I need to go see Helen now." He turned and walked away, quickening his pace.

Sarah settled her grandmother in the lounge and tried to think how best to perk up Grammy's spirits. It occurred to the girl that all three women in the

Gordon-Allinson family were unhappy these days. Sarah had been trying to contact Scott ever since the infamous night of Dolly's party, with no response. Maybe she'd been right about Barbara and Jack ruining her chances with the young actor.

But try as she might to stay mad at her mother, Sarah couldn't help feeling sorry for her. Barbara had been moping around the house all week and hadn't been out a single night. Sarah even caught Barbara crying a couple of times. When she asked her mother about it, Barbara answered, "I'm sad about Grammy."

Sarah didn't buy it. "Are you sure that's all?"

Barbara paused for a moment and gave a solemn nod. But Sarah knew the naked pain in her eyes did not only reflect sorrow over Grammy. She could see her mother's heart had been broken, and Sarah suspected Jack had called off the relationship. She remembered that look of ice-cold fury on Scott's face after the initial moment of shock that night. Maybe Scott had gotten to his grandfather and convinced him to break up with Barbara.

Dolly didn't seem to be faring any better than her daughter or granddaughter. The old woman no longer recognized family members, and her usual bawdy sense of humor had taken flight. She showed no enthusiasm for anything but sleeping.

Sarah took the stuffed dog from the walker basket and addressed it.

"What are we gonna do, little pooch?" she said to the dog, imitating that high-pitched voice she'd heard people use when manipulating hand puppets. "Grammy's not acting herself. Mom totally warned me, but I hoped things might be different. Can you cheer her up, Mr. Scottie?" She waved the dog close to Dolly's face.

"Woof, woof. Look, Grammy, Scottie wants to play."

But Dolly refused to open her eyes.

Sarah heard a familiar voice behind her.

"Are you talking about the dog or me?"

Scott. Sarah turned to face him, thrown off guard by his unanticipated arrival. But even the entrance of "Mr. Pretty" couldn't shake Dolly from her torpor today. She snored loudly.

"Oh, hi," Sarah said to Scott. "You haven't been answering my texts." She tried to keep her tone friendly, so it wouldn't sound as if she was chastising him.

"I've been super busy at my internship. We just finished the last summer production at the theatre."

They both stood for a moment in awkward silence. Then Sarah asked, "Scott, why did Jack break up with my mother? I hope it wasn't because of what happened with us that night."

Scott seemed surprised. "I didn't know they broke up. Grandpop and I haven't talked since then."

Sarah described Barbara's mopey behavior and lonely evenings at home. "From the way she's acting, I assumed *he* broke up with her."

"I doubt that," said Scott. "The other night after you left, Grandpop made it real clear he planned to move ahead with his life, and he had no apologies about what happened in the lounge with your mom. I could tell he meant to keep seeing her. Anyway, whoever ended it . . . it's for the best."

Sarah shook her head. "I don't know about that. I mean—sure, it's kinda gross—but it's their lives. And I'd rather see her smiling than acting, like, miserable the way she is now."

Scott said, "But you seemed upset too when we found them together."

"I did feel upset, sort of. More shocked than upset, I guess. Mom with Jack... That was so not like my mother. But looking back on it, she seemed happy—really happy—until that night."

"I guess . . . Grandpop acted happier too," said Scott. But he abruptly stiffened. "Your mother isn't married to someone else. It's different for Grandpop. He cheated on my grandmother."

"Did he? I don't know."

"How can you not know? You saw your mother in his lap, same as I did."

"That's not what I meant. Like, it would be cheating if your grandmother was still a *real* wife to him. But she isn't, Scott." Sarah searched for a way to characterize Helen that would not be unkind. "This may sound kinda mean, but it's like she's . . . she's . . ." She paused, uncertain how to continue.

"She's left the building," Scott said. His tone was dull, matter of fact. Suddenly he became perturbed. "Shit."

"Huh?" Sarah didn't understand Scott's agitation.

"Have you seen him today?"

"Jack? Yeah, we passed him just before you got here . . . on his way to Helen's room."

"I have to go to them. I—I think I've been wrong about

something, and I need to straighten it out with Grandpop before I leave."

"You're leaving?"

"Gotta head down to NYC to start rehearsals. It's almost September, you know." He gestured toward the whiteboard on the side of the lounge. Under today's date, it said in big lettering, NINE DAYS TILL SEPTEMBER LUAU SUNDAY.

"I'm taking a train tonight."

"Tonight. Jeez." Sarah did not anticipate this. "You—you'll keep in touch from New York, huh."

"We'll see, Sarah. I'm gonna be crazy-busy." His tone was noncommittal.

"Do you think you'll come back to Providence for school vacation?" she asked, trying to appear nonchalant as well.

"That's not in the plans right now," he said, fidgeting. "Hey, I have to run now. Have a good year at school and everything."

"Uh, thanks. You too. Good luck with the play."

Scott's mouth puckered as if he'd bitten into a lemon. "Didn't you know, you never say 'good luck' to an actor. You're supposed to say, 'break a leg' instead."

Sarah felt her cheeks redden. "Oh, I didn't know. In that case, break a leg."

"Bye, Sarah." He paused for a second and looked down at her as if deciding whether to kiss her goodbye. He settled on a brotherly kiss planted on the top of her head—the epitome of humiliation—and rushed off.

Sarah sank down into a chair, angry with herself for bungling the farewell scene.

"Dammit. *Dammit.*" She slammed one hand down on

the coffee table. The noise woke up Dolly, whose eyes sprang open with a startled gaze.

"Sorry, Grammy."

She handed Dolly a water glass and coaxed her to take a couple of sips. Then Sarah started to talk about Scott—more to herself than to her grandmother, who sat there uncomprehending.

"Why did I have to act all pathetic, begging him to keep in touch with me? I don't see why a guy like Scott would care about being friends with a stupid high school girl anyway. I don't even know the right way to talk to an actor. *Good luck.* Jeez."

She took a seat next to her grandmother, sniffling a little.

"Why are you sad? Are you lost?" Dolly asked, examining her granddaughter with a concerned frown.

"No, Grammy. Oh, God, I'm acting like Mom again. This is really dumb. I need to . . . I need to think what Beryl Markham would do. Beryl never hung around feeling bad for herself. She always jumped into her airplane—or whatever—and flew off to the next adventure. That's how I'm gonna be, too."

Sarah got up and hugged Dolly, who did not respond.

"That's how I need to act from now on, Grammy. Beryl—not Barbara."

Dolly gave her a blank look and asked, "Who's Barbara?" Within a few seconds, she resumed her snoozing.

Determined not to obsess over her unrequited crush on Scott and his imminent departure, Sarah focused on what she'd just learned about her mother and Jack. Barbara seemed so desolate that Sarah had been certain Jack must've broken things off. Scott insisted that hadn't been the case. But if Barbara had ended it herself, with apparent reluctance judging from her current demeanor, then *why*?

Then Sarah remembered the morning after Grammy's party, when Barbara had tried to talk about it, and Sarah had cut her off, saying, "We don't need to discuss this." Sarah had made a big scene when she discovered Barbara with Jack, what with the screaming and the hysterics and the cutting words to her mother in the foyer afterward. The next day, she rebuffed her mother's attempt to talk things through. It dawned on the girl that Barbara might've broken up with Jack because she felt Sarah couldn't handle the relationship.

Sarah did not want to be the cause of her mother's profound unhappiness, and the possibility she had triggered the breakup upset the girl. She'd talk to her mother and let her know it was okay with her if Barbara and Jack got back together.

There must be a way to set things right. Sarah vowed to find a solution.

39

GO BREAK A LEG

When Scott arrived at Helen's room, he found his grand-mother stretched out on the bed, sound asleep. Jack was by her side in the bedside chair but not reading or watching TV as he usually did. He sat there, unmoving, with a pensive look on his face.

"Hey, Grandpop," said Scott. "I'm going back to New York tonight, and I wanted to say goodbye to Nana before I left. Also, I—I hoped maybe you and I could talk."

Jack looked up. "I'm glad you want to talk, Scott. We left too many things unsaid the other night."

He suggested a walk outside. Even though they both knew their conversation wouldn't wake Helen and that she wouldn't comprehend it even if she did awaken, it somehow felt wrong to discuss the "unsaid" topics in front of her.

They strolled the manicured grounds lined with col-orful summer blooms, the smell of fresh-cut grass filling their nostrils.

Scott conceded, "I—I shouldn't have run out like that on Sunday night."

"You were obviously shocked and upset."

"I used to admire you and Nana so much. You always seemed to enjoy each other and respect each other.

Remember the bad ad campaigns the three of us wrote in Narragansett? Those summers with you made life with my parents bearable."

"Oh, Scott. That means a lot to me."

"You and Nana were always like my rock. But seeing her in such bad shape . . . and you with someone else . . . it felt like the ground was crumbling under my feet. No more rock. I couldn't stay another minute at—at Tropical Gardens." Scott spat out the name with distaste.

"I remember you opposed moving Nana in here at first. I've never told you this, but the move turned out to be a blessing," said Jack.

Scott was surprised by this.

"Once she came here, she stopped fighting the disease; she stopped fighting me." Jack described to Scott how Helen's mood became more tranquil and accepting in those days. How she believed she was vacationing in the tropics. How she liked to stroke the palm tree every time she walked through the foyer, and how he would later wheel her over to that tree, believing she somehow took comfort in the artificial palm fronds. How she no longer acknowledged Jack as a husband but mistook him for a personal servant.

"That must have been tough," Scott said.

"Yes and no. I will admit to feeling an overwhelming sense of relief."

"Relief?"

Jack stopped walking to face Scott. "You have no idea how heartbreaking it is to take care of the woman you love and to see confusion and fear and even hatred in her eyes. You can't imagine how I felt when she blamed me for her condition and treated me like . . . like a mortal enemy."

"But she couldn't help it."

"That's true. The same way she couldn't help losing her grip on reality. A few months after arriving here, she stopped talking. Not long after that, she stopped walking. And now.. . . . well, you know how she is now."

Scott nodded. "And what about Sarah's mom?" He was ready to hear everything.

"I wasn't actively looking for someone. It kind of happened on its own, and when it did, I decided to pursue it. Barbara is a sweet, caring person, and from the beginning, I felt a strong connection to her. In a short time, I grew to care about her a great deal."

Scott paused, trying to rein in his emotions. "I felt so bad for Nana all this time that I didn't think about how lonely you were. I shouldn't have given you such a hard time about Barbara. I'm sorry."

"It doesn't matter now," Jack said, his voice flat. "We're no longer seeing each other."

Well, then, they *had* broken up. "Yeah, Sarah told me."

Scott started to walk again, but Jack caught his arm. "There's something else you need to know."

His grandfather's foreboding tone sent a shiver through Scott. "I spoke with the nurse today, and Nana's not doing well. We think she's—nearing the end."

"Oh, God, Grandpop." Scott threw his arms around his grandfather, which brought tears to the older man's eyes.

"Shhh, I know." Jack gave Scott a rhythmic series of gentle pats on the back, as one might do to comfort a small child.

"I'm supposed to go back to New York for rehearsals. I'll call the director and see if they can work without me for a few days," Scott said, thinking on his feet.

Jack smiled a little at this. "That's wonderful of you to offer, but you shouldn't stay. We have no idea how long this may go on."

"But I can't leave at a time like this."

"You can, and you must. You're the star of the show. Nana wouldn't have it any other way."

Scott looked reluctant. "Grandpop, are you sure?"

"I'm positive," Jack said, and they hugged again.

"Now, you get back to New York and go break a leg," Jack Winokur said to his grandson. And they turned on the newly mown lawn and walked back to Helen's room so that Scott could say goodbye to his grandmother.

40

PITY PARTY

I sipped my morning coffee while my daughter nibbled her cereal with about as much enthusiasm as Helen Winokur gumming one of her purees. Suddenly, Sarah slammed her spoon down into the bowl, spraying milk across the tabletop.

"Did you break up with Jack because of me?"

"What? Where did you get that idea?"

She took a deep inhale. "I talked to Scott yesterday, and I asked him why Jack broke it off with you, but he told me—"

"Whoa," I said, holding up one hand. "Let's back up and take this one step at a time."

"Okay. You guys did break up, didn't you?"

I nodded.

"Do you mind telling me who broke it off?" my daughter asked.

"I did."

"Wow. Scott was right."

I didn't reply.

She asked, "Did you do it because of me?"

How could I best explain the complexities of my involvement with Jack to a teenage girl? "Oh, Sarah. Being caught by you and Scott may have been the catalyst, but it wasn't the cause."

She knitted her brow into a perplexed frown. "I'm not sure I get the difference."

"What I mean is, that whole unfortunate scene in the lounge generated a series of reactions and events that all led to my breaking up with Jack a few days later. I can't assign a single cause, honey. A lot of factors contributed."

"But Mom—if I was one of those factors, I want you to know I can handle it. I admit I kind of went crazy when it happened, and I realize I acted mean to you when you tried to talk to me about it later. But now that I've thought about it more, I want you and Jack to be happy again. It's okay, really."

"Darling, that's sweet of you and mature as well." Mature in one sense yet naïve in another, for my daughter to believe a vote of approval from her would make it all better. I wished it could be that simple.

"This isn't only about Jack and me," I tried to explain. "There are too many people involved . . . you, Scott, Helen, Grammy, Jack's children, Aunt Vicky—"

"I don't see what Aunt Vicky has to do with it."

"Oh, God, it's too complicated. Let's leave it at this: I had to plug a lot of things into the equation, and I couldn't find a happy solution. The one I came up with was to stop seeing Jack."

"But you seem sad all the time," said Sarah.

"Remember in *Sex and the City*, where the girls talked about breakups?" I said, referring to an episode we'd watched together. "Charlotte said it takes half the total time you went out with a man to get over him. I only dated Jack for around a month, so I shouldn't be sad for more than a couple of weeks. I'm gonna be fine, I promise," I said, echoing Vicky's empty platitude from the day of our breakup.

Though my daughter and I found it entertaining to watch *Sex and the City* together, I knew she'd disapprove of my extracting a serious personal life lesson from the show. Sure enough, she groaned and rolled her eyes at my comment. But I'd been hoping for that exact reaction.

Anything to bring an end to this pity party.

Ma didn't recognize me that day or the next, though she mistook me for her older sister Estelle, who died over ten years ago. She also asked twice for Daddy, who'd been gone nearly as long. She may have been confused, but at least she was back in the right family.

I caught a glimpse of the old Dolly when I asked if she wanted eggs over easy at lunch, and she said, "No, I want eggs over sleazy," and chuckled at her own rhyme.

At this point, I knew I'd take whatever crumbs she could hand out.

During one of Ma's nap marathons, I did some online research about the whole "circle of life" concept that Wayne spoke of the other day in his attempt to provide us with a more sanguine view of Ma's decline. Vicky had dismissed the notion with her usual sarcasm, but I held out hope there might be something to it.

According to what I learned, the Balinese believed in a continuous cycle of life, death, and rebirth. Each life represented a single step in the process of achieving eternal release when the soul became one with the universe. This state was known as "Moksha," the liberation from all sorrow and attainment of enlightenment. Followers of this belief system observed a series of important rituals through the different stages of life, to help ensure that the soul would someday be freed from the chains of incarnation.

I recalled Wayne showing me the picture of his brother growing his hair out during his wife's pregnancy. Perhaps his brother's act had been linked to this complex system of life rituals.

I found the whole idea intriguing and—strange as it seemed—even a bit comforting.

Mercifully, I hadn't seen much of Jack and Helen. I knew Ma and I would be safe from chance encounters in the dining room, and he seemed to be avoiding the lounge. In return, I steered clear of the back patio since I knew he liked to feed Helen out there when the weather cooperated. Yesterday afternoon, we passed each other in the hallway and nodded solemnly, like a couple of polite strangers.

I didn't expect to miss him this much.

41

ENDING THE DECEPTION

"Dory!"

The end-of-summer party was in full swing when Sarah caught sight of her friend walking across the pool deck. As they embraced, Dory's flushed cheek felt warm against Sarah's own face, still cool from a dive into the refreshing turquoise water just minutes before.

Sarah noted that her friend wore a broomstick skirt in multiple shades of purple and a loose-fitting, raglan-sleeved heavy cotton top.

"Hey, Dory, why don't you join us in the pool? The water feels great," said another girl from the shallow end of the swimming pool.

"No, I'm good," Dory replied, but she swiped the back of one hand across her hairline, which glistened with perspiration from the humid afternoon heat.

It dismayed Sarah to see her friend still covering up in public. A summer away and even the loss of virginity had not improved Dory's body image.

Forty or fifty kids were jammed together around the pool area. To escape the rising noise level of the crowd, the two friends walked across the wide adjacent lawn and found a shady spot under a tree.

"Is Scott here?" Dory asked. "I can't wait to meet him."

"Oh, no. He's gone back to college." Sarah didn't bother mentioning that she couldn't imagine Scott at a high school pool party.

"Will you see him during the school year?"

Sarah knew she'd misled Dory about the true nature of her relationship with Scott, ever anxious to impress her friend as the summer progressed. But the time had come for ending the deception. "I doubt it. I had fun hanging out with him, but I knew it would never go anywhere. Like, I mean, he lives in New York. Anyway, I'm kinda *over* him."

"Why? Did something happen?"

"He always gave me a hard time about my age, and sometimes he could be kind of condescending about it. But when his grandfather and my mother—" Sarah stopped in mid-sentence. Someday she would share the recent events with her good friend. But not here, not now. "Something happened with his grandfather, and Scott acted totally immature about it. I felt like I was the grownup giving advice to some mixed-up teenager."

"Guys can be such jerks. I mean, most guys. Not Nick."

"And listen to this. Did you know it's bad form to say 'good luck' to an actor?" asked Sarah.

Dory shook her head.

"Yeah, who knew? But Scott treated me like I was a pathetic loser cuz I wished him luck with his next play. It seemed stupid to make such a big deal about it. And mean, too."

"If he's such an asshole, why were you that into him?"

Sarah smiled ruefully and let out a long sigh. "Because . . . he is the best-looking guy I've ever met."

A dark-haired girl, someone she'd never seen before, glanced shyly in their direction. Sarah motioned for the girl to join them.

"Hi—I'm Emily," said the stranger, extending her hand to both Sarah and Dory. "I just moved here from Chicago. I'm about to start Classical as a junior."

"Cool. Sarah here is a junior too, and I'm a senior," said Dory. Her phone buzzed, and she walked away to take the call, leaving Emily and Sarah to chat.

It turned out Emily had acting experience and planned to try out for plays this year at school. Sarah couldn't claim that a few afternoons of patio rehearsals with Scott qualified her as an experienced actor, but she said to the new girl, "I've been thinking of getting involved in drama myself. Maybe something behind the scenes."

Then a cute guy walked over to them, punched Emily in the arm, and said, "Hey. Introduce me to your friend."

She punched him back, and Sarah wondered if this could be some sort of new girlfriend-boyfriend dynamic Emily had exported with her from Chicago. Then she introduced him to Sarah as her twin brother, Jacob.

Sarah wouldn't have even guessed them to be siblings, let alone twins. Jacob had blond, curly hair, a fit but stocky build, and endearing dimples—while Emily was thin with more delicate features and long straight hair like Sarah's, except darker. They both seemed smart, funny, and easy to talk to.

"When we were born, our brilliant parents came up with the most popular girl's name in America for Em, and the most popular boy's name for me. You can't exactly give them an 'A' for creativity," said Jacob. They all laughed at this.

"Yes, I'm sure everyone at Classical will be thrilled to have another Emily and Jacob on campus," Emily said. "They might have to assign numbers."

"Oh, I wouldn't worry about it. It's not like 'Sarah' is a whole lot more original."

Sarah introduced the twins around to several of her friends and made plans to meet up with them for lunch at school the day after Labor Day, the first day of the fall semester. In the meantime, she had one more end-of-summer party and a lot of back-to-school preparations to keep her busy. She felt grateful to be occupied most of the time.

Things were looking up. Being a high school junior might involve a lot of work and a lot of stress at a competitive place like Classical, but Sarah looked forward to the new challenges and friendships. She had to admit she'd gotten into a bit of a rut this summer, daydreaming about Scott and hanging around Tropical Gardens too much, hoping to run into him. Time to jump into the new school year.

Sarah remained sad about one thing—her mother. She still didn't fully understand why her mom had broken up with Jack. But whatever the reason, she could see it had been torturous for Barbara. It wouldn't be easy for her mother to hold herself together going forward.

Ending her marriage to Sarah's father to raise an infant daughter as a single parent had been a much more wrenching decision, but Barbara had done that too. And even though something awful must have happened for Barbara to take such a drastic step with a young child to care for, she followed the high road and behaved with dignity, never throwing it back in Richard's face.

While Sarah's father always seemed to have a woman in tow—it didn't matter who, he wasn't all that discriminating—Barbara continued to go it alone all these years, not willing to compromise herself as women sometimes do to settle into the security of marriage again. She had even changed back to her maiden name, Gordon, in an admirable display of feminism.

Sarah had always viewed Barbara as a frail, over-emotional person who cried too often, worried too strenuously, and balked at taking risks. But now, she understood she had always focused on her mother's weaknesses without giving her enough credit for her strengths. True, despite sharing her name with a superhero, Mom was still no Batgirl—but she was no coward either. All through her childhood, Sarah had relied on books and movies for heroic women to look up to when a perfectly good role model lived right in the same house.

42

LOST AND FOUND

"Mom, let's order pizza and watch a movie at home."

"Sarah, honey, that's a great idea," I said with fake cheer. I smiled like someone forced to pose for a group photo in the middle of a family altercation. "No parties tonight?"

"No, not until tomorrow."

"Are you coming to Luau Sunday?"

She looked uncomfortable. "Mom, do you mind if I miss it this time? I've got a lot to do before school starts."

"Oh, sure, no problem," I said.

Sarah seemed excited about the end-of-summer parties and the start of the new school year. Thank heavens I no longer had to worry about her and Scott spending time together. Her cheery demeanor informed me that Sarah had moved on—unlike me. Sadly, I continued to grieve over another Winokur gentleman.

Oh, to be a teenager again, with the ability to bounce back in a heartbeat.

And yet. To be honest, whether at fifteen or fifty, I'd never been as well-grounded or resilient as my daughter. How did she turn out this way, with an anxiety-ridden train wreck for a mother and a self-absorbed heel for a father? I could only attribute it to a bizarre scrambling of flawed DNA that somehow came out right, like when an unattractive couple gave birth to a beautiful child.

It touched me to think Sarah would spend the evening at home to cheer me up. It must've been depressing for her to hang around the house with me in this dejected state. I would stage a rally tonight, I promised myself. My daughter and I would talk and laugh and have a wonderful evening.

After sharing a wild mushroom pizza and arugula salad, we agreed to revisit a favorite old movie, *Love Actually*. The heart-warming film had us both smiling until we reached the scene where Laura Linney hooked up with the man on whom she'd had a mad crush throughout the movie. This sexy heartthrob was about to bed her with great tenderness when she tore herself away from him, fleeing to tend to her needy, troubled brother who was confined to a mental care facility.

That's all it took to get the waterworks going again. I shut myself in the bathroom, undone by this poignant reminder of precious love lost. Several minutes passed before I returned to the couch with red-rimmed eyes, clutching a wad of soggy tissues.

(Note to self: Until I snapped out of this, no *Downton Abbey*, no stories involving lost or dying dogs, and absolutely no more rom-coms.)

Sarah did not comment on my outburst. But she did say, "You know, I changed my mind. I *will* come to Luau Sunday to visit with you and Grammy for a little while."

Ah. So, it had come to this. I'd descended to such a pitiable state that my daughter would sacrifice the final Sunday of her summer to placate me. How much lower could I sink?

But when I arrived at Tropical Gardens for Luau Sunday, I was in for a rude shock.

Ma was missing.

I went straight to her room as usual but did not find her there. No sign of her walker in the room either. I checked the dining room to see if she'd lingered late at breakfast, then poked my head into the family lounge. Nothing.

I knew she wouldn't be in therapy on a Sunday morning, so her absence had become alarming. I hurried to the front desk. "Dolly Gordon—my mother. I can't find her anywhere." I couldn't mistake the look of panic on the receptionist's face as she radioed security and followed with a message to the nursing station. The hunt was on.

After I'd searched for about ten minutes, I stopped to fire off a text to Vicky and Sarah.

—*Come to TG asap. Important!*

I continued my frenetic hunt for Ma with no real strategy. Maybe fifteen minutes after I'd texted her, Vicky walked in and found me in the lounge.

"I didn't see your text until I pulled into the parking lot." Vicky saw the worry on my face. "You seem completely unglued. Are you still upset about the other day?"

"It's not that." Tears sprang to my eyes. "Oh, Vicky—Ma's gone."

Her mouth dropped open in shock. "Jesus Christ. She died?"

"No, she didn't *die*; she's *gone* gone. As in missing." I explained the sequence of events to Vicky. "She's been

MIA for nearly half an hour since the time I arrived, and who knows how long before that."

Vicky looked incredulous. "But the nurse always brags about how safe it is here because of the monitors and sensors and alarms and shit. I don't get how this could happen."

"NOCDAR."

"Can you please talk in words instead of initials?"

I'd forgotten my sister didn't know the acronym.

"No One Can Do Anything Right," I said.

She ignored this and cranked up the volume of her rant. "This is supposed to be the Ritz-fucking-Carlton of dementia wards."

"I know, I don't get it either. Wayne told me he's certain she'll turn up, but I don't know. Oh, Vicky, what can we do?"

She put her hands on my shoulders with unaccustomed tenderness and eased me down into a chair. "Okay, honey, here's what's going to happen. You stay right here and don't budge in case Ma shows up. After all, the lounge is one of her favorite spots. The staff is probably covering the obvious places, so I'm going to focus on areas like the stairwells and the back of the building."

One thing about my big sister: She excelled in an emergency. Though her day-to-day responsiveness was subpar, to say the least, you could count on her to come through in times of crisis.

I had a brief flashback to a time, years ago, when we'd managed to lose a young Sarah at the beach. Vicky had taken charge and succeeded in calming my hysterics until we found Sarah at the lifeguard stand, contented as she chomped on a handful of gummi bears the lifeguards had provided to distract her. Perhaps Ma, too, was safe and being placated somewhere with candies—preferably sugar-free.

"All right," I said. "I'll stay here, and you go search for her."

"*On it.*" She rushed out of the room faster than I'd seen her move in years.

Left alone in the family lounge, I started to pace. Though I knew Vicky's game plan made sense, it would drive me insane to stay there and do nothing. I checked my text messages, but nothing from Sarah yet. I called her.

"Sarah, honey. Where are you?"

"I'm on my way to Tropical Gardens."

"Well, you shouldn't be talking on the phone if you're driving," I chided, though I continued to speak to her on the forbidden device. "You know, they just published a study about distracted drivers, and—"

"Mom, I'm at a red light. About to turn off Waterman Street."

"Oh, good. Then you'll be here soon. There's something going on. I'll explain everything when you get here. I love you. And Sarah, don't talk on the phone anymore."

I paced for another half a minute, tops. Time to check in with my sister.

"Vick, it's me. Anything yet?"

"For fuck's sake. I only started looking like a minute ago."

"I know, sorry, but this waiting is making me crazy. Sarah will be here soon. I didn't tell her yet what's going on, but she can help try to find Ma. I'm worried that—"

"Chicken, let's hang up so I can concentrate on searching."

Okay, now I had succeeded in distracting my sister as well. I didn't feel guilty about it, given the way she had just addressed me. But this was not the optimum time to raise a stink about her calling me "Chicken" again. I ended the call.

I put the phone down on the coffee table and forced myself to sit again.

Deep yoga breaths, that's what I needed. If I remembered it right, I should count to five on the inhale and seven on the exhale...

I took a deep breath and counted on my fingers, trying out the relaxation method for the next few minutes. But this breathing pattern felt unnatural to the point of making me more tense, and I even gasped a little for air.

Maybe I should try counting to *seven* on the inhale and five on the exhale.

I experimented with that for a while without success. Then I said aloud, "Does anyone find this helpful? I'm better off worrying."

No sooner had the words come out of my mouth than who should walk into the lounge but Ma, Wayne . . . and Jack Winokur.

Ma trudged along on the walker with Jack holding her arm, and Wayne followed a few feet behind them. I couldn't contain my enormous relief.

"Ma. You're back," I said, running to intercept her. "We've been looking everywhere for you. I was so scared. Are you okay?"

As I closed in on Ma, Jack stepped away, averting my gaze as he did this. The way he recoiled from me, you'd think I was Typhoid Mary.

"I'm wonderful," Ma said in a cheerier tone than I'd heard her use for many days. Then she smiled at me. "My girl. Barbara."

I couldn't believe my ears.

"You know me."

Ma gave me a look of mild annoyance that implied the question was absurd. "Why shouldn't I know my daughter?"

"Ma, this is amazing. You're *back* back."

"Of course, I'm back." Peering around the room, she asked, "Where was I?"

Wayne settled Ma into a chair and said, "Dolly had gone out to the side garden, and she was sitting on a bench behind a tree in the shade. You couldn't see her from inside the building, but Jack found her."

"I don't know how to thank you," I said to Jack.

"I can't take all the credit. Wayne and I spotted her about the same time," he said, focusing on Wayne like he was desperate to avoid eye contact with me.

Wayne glanced from Jack to me and said with great concern, "I am terribly sorry. This is highly unusual. Another patient fell out of his wheelchair, and the staff got distracted by that. Someone left the door to the unit open for a few moments while they were tending to him, and Dolly must have slipped out then. With people arriving for Luau Sunday, that just added to the confusion."

"The important thing is, Ma's safe."

"Yes," Wayne said, giving me a grateful look for being such a good sport. "I'll have to excuse myself now to see to the man who fell. I'll check in with you again later." He made a hasty retreat, leaving me alone with Ma and Jack.

I leaned over to hug my mother. "Please don't scare us like that again."

"How did I scare you? Like a Halloween monster?" Ma made a mock-scary face. She and I laughed together.

Jack said in a formal tone I'd rarely heard him use, "Since everything seems to be under control now, I'll leave you ladies to yourselves."

He turned to go, still avoiding eye contact. As he headed toward the door, Ma pointed at him and said, "You're pretty. Isn't he pretty?"

I wanted to kiss Ma for feeding me that line because, at that moment, I recognized I must keep Jack from leaving at all costs, and she had given me a way to do that.

Turning in Jack's direction, I said, "Not just pretty—breathtaking." I borrowed that line from our first date when we'd joked together about pretty American bar seating. I prayed he would understand the reference.

Jack stopped walking and turned to stare back at me. At least he wasn't leaving. I knew I had to continue down this path.

"Jack, please don't leave." I didn't care what happened. I knew I had to go for it. Okay, that's a lie. I cared desperately, but I recognized this might be my only chance.

"I . . . I seem to keep running away from you, and I don't even know why. But I do know this. Almost from the moment I broke it off with you, I realized what a terrible mistake I'd made. I don't want to keep running, but I haven't been able to find my way back to you. I mean—that is—if you even want me back. I know I'm a neurotic mess, and if it were me, I'm not even sure I would want me back. But I . . . I'd like us to try again. If it's not too late."

There. I'd said it.

Jack stood still, meeting my gaze but not speaking for what seemed like half an hour. In real-time, it was probably six or seven seconds. Then he said, "No."

Jesus, I had no clue what that meant. "No, it's not too late? Or no, you don't want to try again?" The question regrettably came out in that squeaky mouse voice that always sounded pathetic to my own ears.

But Jack smiled and said, "Hush. Come here." Before I knew it, he had reached for me and encircled me in his arms.

"Thank God." I sighed deeply and hugged him back so hard it was a miracle all his ribs survived intact. We were locked in this rapturous embrace when my sister entered the room and took in the scene.

She dealt with our mother first, as was appropriate. "Ma. You're back safe and sound."

"My Vicky," Ma said.

"Vick, she knows us again. She's *back* back."

"Back back," echoed Ma, cackling.

"Yes, I see." Vicky smiled at our mother and turned to Jack, who now grasped my hand in one of his.

"From the look of things, I gather you're '*back* back' too."

"Yes, you could call it that," Jack said.

I cocked my head toward him, a foolish grin on my

face. Then, like some cheesy scene out of the movie *Blue Hawaii*, ukulele music started playing in the background. I half-expected Elvis to slink into the lounge.

"It sounds like Luau Sunday has officially begun," my sister said, and right on cue, she went into her sarcastic little hula routine. I waited for her to embarrass us both with the "kamanawanalea" chant, but she spared us that indignity. Jack seemed amused by the sight of her little comic dance with its undulating hand movements, as did Ma.

Vicky ended the dance and guided me away from Jack so we could speak out of Ma's earshot. "I hate to interrupt this euphoric display," she said, "but I hope you realize that Ma's remembering is apt to be temporary."

Not even Vicky could dampen my spirits. "Holy crap, Vick, do you think I don't know that? But let's relax and enjoy it for however long it lasts. You know, let it happen. Go with the flow."

She shook her head in disbelief. "*Barbara? Are you in there?*"

I smiled. "I've been thinking a lot. I mean, really *thinking* instead of fretting. I keep remembering what you said about—well, accepting reality instead of always trying to change it."

She nodded, encouraging me to continue.

"I've also given a lot of thought to what Wayne said to us. I've even done some research. You know, that business about how regressing to childhood and infancy doesn't have to be an unnatural course of events."

"The circle of life thing."

"Yes," I said. "If we can try to hang on to that idea, maybe this whole ordeal won't be quite as much of a nightmare. If we can consider what's happening to Ma and feel a little less horrified and a little less frightened for her, perhaps it'll be better for everyone."

I anticipated another sardonic *Lion King* remark, but to my gratification, Vicky said, "Maybe you're right, kiddo. Maybe you're right."

We all sat, Jack at my side again, and talked to Ma about the upcoming Luau Sunday meal. Then Sarah arrived and broke into a smile, surprised to find Jack and me in a posture of cozy but respectable closeness.

"Hi. Mom, is this what you wanted to tell me?" she said, looking from me to Jack.

"What?" I asked. It took me a moment to process that Sarah knew nothing about Ma's disappearance. She must have interpreted the "something going on" I'd mentioned on the phone as this latest turn of events with Jack.

"Oh, no, honey. Grammy went missing for a while, and I wanted you to help find her. But as you can see, that's no longer necessary."

"My girl. Sarah," said Dolly.

Sarah kissed her grandmother's cheek and said, "Hi, Grammy." Only then did the realization sink in. "Wow, you know me again."

Vicky and I said in unison, "She's *back* back."

"That's fantastic." Sarah beamed. "But what do you mean, she went missing?"

"She slipped out of the building, and no one could find her. Your grammy still has a few tricks up her sleeve."

"Listen, I have news too," Sarah said. "Scott texted me this morning. His play opens the first weekend of November, and he'll get us tickets if we want to go to New York to see it."

This surprised me. I didn't think she and Scott had stayed in touch.

"Do you want to go?"

Sarah paused before answering. "Nah, I don't think so. There's a big football game at school that weekend and a lot of parties and stuff. Better for me to stay here with my friends."

Then she looked straight at Jack and me. "But you two could go." My daughter was channeling Yente the Matchmaker.

"Maybe we could," Jack said.

Without thinking before I spoke, I said, "I don't think Scott would like that too much."

Jack gave me a curious look before replying, "Leave Scott to me. He'll be all right."

I pulled Jack up by the hand and led him away from the others. Sarah occupied herself with Ma and the Scottie dog, but Vicky stared at us unabashedly during our little "private" chat.

"But what about—" I started to ask him.

"Helen."

I nodded.

"There are some things I need to explain to you," he said. "But not now." He had a poker game with friends that night, he told me, but why didn't I come over for a glass of wine before he had to leave?

I accepted his invitation but couldn't stop myself from asking, "Should I worry?"

"No, you shouldn't." But then he reconsidered and said, "Now that I think about it, maybe you *should*. I'm reaching the conclusion that worry, to you, is like a meddlesome old friend who manages to be infuriating yet somehow comforting at the same time. It doesn't seem right for me to separate you from your old familiar friend."

We both smiled.

"All right, then. If you insist, I'll force myself to worry. There have been changes with Ma that I want to tell you about, too."

"Six o'clock?"

"Six is perfect."

"Ahem," said my sister. "At the risk of being a wet blanket again, let's get Ma to the dining room. I don't have all day." She latched on to the walker and started rolling it in Ma's direction.

"A moment," I said, holding up one hand. Adopting a rare tone of authority, I said to her, "Vicky. The first Sunday of November is Luau Sunday, and Ma needs a family member to take her. I expect to be in New York that weekend, and Sarah will be busy with friends. Put it on your calendar."

"But I'm not sure if I'll be available," she said, sidestepping my request.

"I don't care if you and Martin are planning to entertain a client, or if Daisy is getting her nails clipped, or if you have eighty-five other critical agenda items on your packed schedule. I need you to handle this."

She fidgeted with the handles on Ma's walker.

"And I'm not talking one of your usual ten-minute drop-ins. You need to stay through the meal," I said.

"I'll do what I can," said Vicky, with a little less bluster this time.

"Better still, plan to spend the afternoon. You and Ma need more time together."

"Fucking hell. All right. I'll do it, Chicken, if only to put an end to this rant," she said with a snort. She started toward Ma again, and once more, I held up my hand.

"Oh, and one other thing. From now on, you're to stop calling me by that stupid name. I've asked you a hundred times. But I am no longer asking, I'm *telling*."

"Maybe I should call you Bossy Barbie instead." Now she was sulking.

"How about plain old *Barbara*. I know lifelong habits die hard, but I'm sure you can manage this small adjustment."

Then I smiled at Ma and said, "Time for the Luau lunch." I reached for the walker and helped my mother out of her seat. Jack walked along on Ma's other side, and Vicky and Sarah fell into line behind us. As our little entourage headed to the dining room, I listened as my daughter conversed with my sister.

"Aunt Vick, there are two super cool new kids in my class. Twins—a boy and a girl. They moved from Chicago this summer."

Vicky replied with a wicked laugh, "It's nice to make new friends. Is he—you know—a love interest? 'Kamanawanalea.'"

"Hah. Is that all you ever think about?"

"Most of the time, baby," said my sister.

As we continued along, I addressed my mother. "Ma, tell me what you'd like to eat today." I read from a menu posted on the wall. "They have pulled pork on a bun—"

"Crap on a bun," she said.

"Fried rice with chicken—"

"Fried rice with crap."

"And coconut pie."

"Coconut crap."

Dolly was definitely "*back* back." At least, for today.

After Luau Sunday ended, I plummeted down from cloud nine and re-entered Full Worry Mode. I once more resumed my negative list-making, cataloging all the reasons why Jack might change his mind about getting back together with me. At the top of the list: Why would any man want to be involved with a woman so phobic she kept coming up with these outrageous lists?

On the way to Jack's, I tried to reassure myself that all would be well. Perhaps I could look forward to an interlude of emotionally charged makeup sex. But when I arrived at his house, Jack greeted me at the door with a European-style kiss on either cheek.

What did this mean? It looked like he was *dialing it back*— an expression Jack had used on our first evening together at his house. Maybe I'd been right to worry after all. He led me to the kitchen, gestured for me to sit on one of the island stools, and poured us each a glass of chardonnay.

I perched both elbows on the gleaming granite countertop and tried to find a comfortable position on the wooden barstool. Everything I touched felt hard and unyielding. I grew more and more nervous about the impersonal nature of this encounter, but I understood Jack's reserve when he delivered the news.

"Helen is dying."

I took a deep breath. "Oh, Jack, I'm sorry. Tell me what's happening."

"She's hardly eating at all, and she sleeps most of the time. She's a hospice patient now." He recapped a grim report from Cindy about Helen's test results, which showed that her swallowing reflex had stopped functioning. He must have learned about this a short time after I broke up with him. This made me feel even worse about having added to his pain.

"Ma's gone downhill too. It's been kind of a precipitous decline. She has almost no energy now, and she's lost her sense of humor. The worst part is, she doesn't know us a lot of the time. Her turnaround today was almost miraculous, but I'm afraid Vicky is right. It's probably temporary at best."

"We knew they'd get worse," Jack said.

"We did. Then why is it still such a shock?"

"Cindy said that's the way it is."

We sipped our wine in silence for a few moments.

"Barbara. Why did you break things off with me? I mean, I have an idea, but it would help if you explained in your own words."

I paused before responding. "That night after the kids found us in the lounge, I accidentally overheard you and Scott arguing."

He looked taken aback by this. "You did?"

"Yes—I didn't mean to, but your voices were so loud I couldn't help hearing." Okay, I admit I fudged on the details a bit to present myself in a more favorable light. I didn't want to come across as a modern-day Polonius hiding behind the arras to eavesdrop. Or whatever you called an arras in the twenty-first century.

"And something we said disturbed you."

I nodded. "When I heard you talking about how much you loved Helen and how nobody could ever replace her, I kind of lost it."

"Lost it how?"

"Lost my confidence, I guess. I felt like I'd never be able to measure up to her."

He gave me a piercing glance with those impossibly blue eyes. "Barbara, that's the same thing you said before."

"Before?"

"That first night together at my house, when you ran out on me but then came back later. You said you ran because you were afraid you wouldn't *measure up*—that I wouldn't like you."

Oh, dear God. I couldn't deny it. I kept claiming that "multiple factors" contributed to the decision: my mortification in front of Scott and Sarah, my guilt over Helen, my powerlessness in the face of Vicky's manipulation. And while those factors did carry weight, my own self-doubt and insecurity were the ultimate culprits.

"If you hadn't fled the scene when you did, you would have heard me tell Scott that I intended to go ahead with my new life—with or without his approval."

"How did he react?"

"Well, at that point, Scott fled the scene as well. But if he'd stayed, I would have told him how much you mean to me."

Exactly how much is that, on a scale of one to ten? I badly wanted to ask. But I exercised self-restraint for once, allowing myself to enjoy the little flutter of excitement his words stirred in me.

"Later that week, I finally did have the opportunity to tell Scott how I felt about you. I told him everything about his grandmother's condition as well. This happened the same day as my meeting with Cindy. Anyway, the two of us reconciled. He apologized for behaving the way he did."

Jack also made it clear he had never shared my view of himself, Helen, and me as some sort of illicit love triangle. "I like to think of us more like three separate points. You could draw connecting lines between all the points—but there is no clash, no collision," he said.

I liked that image. We sounded like stars in a constellation.

Jack and I filled each other in on the other less consequential events of the past several days. I had the impression he had missed me as much as I'd missed him.

We made plans. Tomorrow, I would be cooking Sarah's favorite dishes for the two of us the night before her classes began, but I agreed to have a drink with him at the wine bar on Thayer Street the following evening. We would once again be together in the daytime as well. I also sensed a tacit understanding that Jack and I would refrain from sleeping together for whatever time remained in

Helen's life. It seemed like the respectful thing to do.

Jack peered up at the kitchen wall clock and said, "Will you look at the time?" like a therapist tactfully announcing the end of a session to his patient. "Sorry, but I'm off to my poker game."

He walked me to the door, and this time it was my turn to initiate the discreet double-cheek-kissing maneuver. But halfway between the left and the right cheeks, he intercepted me. He followed with a lingering kiss in four distinct parts. I liked to think of them as movements in a symphony. First, he gave my upper lip a playful nibble; then he pressed his mouth against mine and explored my teeth with his tongue; after that, he dug in deeply and expertly; and finally, he pulled back to nibble my lips once again, reprising the main theme of the first movement. By the time he played the final notes, I was in a sort of pleasurable daze.

It was one for the memory books, that kiss. I knew I could live on it for however long I needed to.

43

GOOD FOR YOU

Jack got the call early one morning in late September. The torrential rain pounding on the roof and skylights almost drowned out his ringing cellphone.

"Mr. Winokur, this is Angie over at Tropical Gardens."

Both the name and the voice were unfamiliar to Jack. She must've been temporary staff, subbing for a regular out sick or on vacation.

"I'm afraid I have bad news. Mrs. Winokur passed away."

Jack grimaced at the news, squeezing his eyes shut. "How did you—what happened?"

"She went in her sleep. It was very peaceful."

"I see."

"She's still in her room. We won't move her until after you've had a chance to visit with her, sir."

"All right. I'll be over in a few minutes."

Jack jumped in the car to make the short drive to the facility. Water splashed across the windshield as he navigated through deep puddles. The teeming rain, dark skies, and unseasonably cold, gusty winds sent a chill into Jack's bones.

Helen had been cheated of so many things during the last seven years of her life. As he drove to Tropical Gardens to see his wife for the last time, it struck Jack as a cruel, final injustice that she should die on such a gloomy day.

Michael came up from Baltimore to help his father with the arrangements. He remained with Jack for several days. During this time, Jack felt sad, then relieved, then guilty about feeling relieved, then sad again in an alternating pattern.

One day he excused himself from Michael's company to go on a bike ride, and he pedaled as fast as he could in the direction of Barbara's house. She was such a consummate planner—might she object to him showing up unannounced on her doorstep?

But when Barbara opened the door, she flung her arms around his neck without hesitation, and they stood in the doorway, locked in a wordless embrace. When they broke apart, Sarah poked her head out from the kitchen—looking uncertain at first, but then hurrying across the room to give Jack a hug herself.

The girl assessed the situation and said, "I have to go to Dory's." She grabbed her purse from the front hall table and headed out the door, car keys jingling in her hand.

"Will you be back for dinner?" Barbara called after her.

"Not sure. I'll text and let you know."

After Sarah's obliging departure, Barbara took charge. She enfolded Jack in another embrace, this time showering him with sweet, generous kisses. Then she led him to her bed, where she demonstrated in no uncertain terms that she held the power to break his relentless cycle of sadness, relief, and remorse.

Jack and Michael arranged a small private service for immediate family only, per Helen's wishes. Paul and Elise flew in from California with their two young children, Willy and Becca. They also invited Michael's ex-wife, Anne, who begged off citing a commitment to attend a business conference the day of the service. The family breathed a collective sigh of relief at this news. Relations with Anne remained strained, and she and Helen had never been close. Scott, immersed in rehearsals for his upcoming play at Tisch, could only manage a day trip from New York, but he took a train up for Helen's service and gave a beautiful reading.

Barbara maintained an appropriate distance from this family affair. But she sent a donation to the Alzheimer's Association in Helen's memory and baked double batches of cookies and lemon bars for the Winokurs to enjoy, discreetly parking the treats in a covered basket at Jack's front door when she knew the family would be out attending the private service.

"Wow, these are delicious. Who left the goodies?" Paul asked later, smacking his lips as he finished his second lemon bar.

"A very dear friend," said Jack.

Before the California contingent departed for their flight to LAX, Elise said to her father-in-law, "Why don't you come to visit us over Halloween and take the kids trick-or-treating? They would adore it." She touched his arm. "I wish you'd at least think about it."

Jack's blue eyes twinkled. "Be careful what you wish for, Elise. Maybe you expected me to decline, saying it's too soon—but I'd love to come. Thank you."

In late October, Jack traveled to Los Angeles for a five-day visit. He had a wonderful time getting to know his two delightful grandchildren. On Halloween night, he surprised them by dressing up in a Los Angeles Dodgers costume.

"Grandpop, I thought you were a Red Sox fan," said Willy.

"I am. But this is enemy turf, and I didn't care to get arrested or maybe cause rioting on the streets." Jack winked at the boy.

They spent the first hour walking around the immediate neighborhood. After the children emptied their bulging bags of candy into a large ceramic bowl in the kitchen, all five Winokurs—Paul, Elise, Jack, and the children—piled into the car to head to a special neighborhood for another round of trick-or-treating.

"Where are we going?" asked Willy.

"It's a place called Sleepy Hollow."

"Will we have to sleep when we get there?" asked little Becca.

"No, sweetheart," Jack said, laughing. "It's a special neighborhood in Torrance."

They arrived at Sleepy Hollow about twenty minutes later. Becca had dozed off in the car, but she sprang back to life when she saw the bright orange and yellow lights that illuminated every home.

This residential section of south Torrance had been transformed into a Halloween fairyland. Front lawns were elaborately festooned with cobweb-covered grave-yards, goblins, ghosts, and every other imaginable form of holiday décor, complete with spooky sound effects. Hundreds of families strolled the sidewalks, and children of all ages bounded up front walks to fill their trick-or-treat bags. The whole neighborhood pulsed with energy and excitement.

Jack had read about Sleepy Hollow online and sug-gested the excursion there.

"How did we not even know about this place? It's fan-tastic," said Elise as they drove away later, inching along in the heavy traffic.

Jack said, "It's supposed to be even more fantastic at Christmas. I saw pictures of unbelievable decorations. Not to mention carolers, hot chocolate stands, people sitting around firepits eating fresh-baked cookies..."

"I wanna go. You have to come with us, Grandpop," said Willy.

Jack's online research to find appropriate activities for young children led them to other adventures as well—a local whaling museum along the rugged coastline of the Palos Verdes Peninsula, an excursion to a locally-spon-sored haunted house. But Jack and the children seemed just as content pursuing simpler pleasures like reading books together or visiting the playground on the next block.

By the end of the five days, Jack was ready to go home.

He missed Barbara. On the drive to the airport, alone in the car with his son, Jack finally told Paul about the relationship.

"I hope it's not too distressing for you to learn about this when your mother's been gone only a short time."

"Wrong, Dad. Mom's been gone a very long time."

Jack nodded.

"I assume Michael knows?"

"Yes. As you'll recall, Scott spent the summer in Providence, so he knew about it before anyone else in the family. Although that's a whole other story." Jack shook his head at the memory of that night. "Anyway, Scott told his father, and I discussed it with Michael myself later on."

After he pulled over to the curb in front of the terminal, Paul turned to Jack and asked, "The lemon bars after the funeral. Were they . . . did Barbara . . . ?"

"Yes."

Paul nodded slowly. "Good for you, Dad. Good for you."

Jack returned to Providence a couple of days before the scheduled trip to New York to see Scott's play, *Instability*. Scott crushed it, as expected. And to Jack's great relief, his grandson treated Barbara warmly at the show and their subsequent late dinner together.

Jack and Barbara enjoyed a magical weekend in New York. At last, they could be together for more than a couple of hours at a time, away from Tropical Gardens and all the complicated family dynamics that had characterized the previous summer. As he held Barbara in his arms in the decadent comfort of the Midtown hotel bed with its pillow-top king mattress, Jack pondered the strangeness of feeling like a widower and a honeymooner all at once.

44

BAD OMENS

Vicky's informative text message came to me on Sunday evening as my train from New York pulled into the Providence station.

—*I spent the whole fucking afternoon with Ma, even though we're behind in our end-of-month billing and Martin BEGGED me to come into the office to help him. BTW, she slept three-quarters of the time.*

My sister always knew how to get my goat, but I found this especially masterful. In a single statement, she managed to showcase her own selflessness while invoking guilt over my thoughtless imposition to both her livelihood and her marriage. And although Vicky's final "by the way" appeared offhand on the surface, it added another dimension of blame by implying that she could have been accomplishing important work instead of wasting her time watching Ma sleep.

Reluctant to engage, I replied only with a double-thumbs-up emoji. She responded, absurdly:

—*If you don't believe how long I stayed, ask Ma.*

We both knew Dolly to be incapable of corroborating anything.

But lucky for me, I had a trusted spy on the premises. My buddy Wayne kept tabs on the situation and confirmed the details of Vicky's Luau Sunday attendance as soon as

I returned to Tropical Gardens the next morning. He told me her visit lasted four hours—a record-shattering total, by any measure.

Sarah returned home Monday afternoon after staying with her father in my absence. Richard had promised her some "special surprises" for the weekend that never materialized. Apparently, my ex was otherwise occupied, and Sarah knew better than to spell out the details to me.

"I didn't mind Dad ignoring me, Mom. Really," she told me. "With the football game and the party on Saturday, there was a lot going on with Jacob and the crowd." Sarah and Jacob were now dating, and his twin sister Emily seemed cool with the arrangement.

"How's it going with Jacob?"

"I think I'm in 'like' with him," she said, with a little giggle. "I mean, he's funny and cute, and I'm attracted to him—but not in an over-the-moon kind of way."

So, Richard was being a pill as usual, but I couldn't get all worked up over it. With the presidential election looming large, I had much more important items on my worry list.

The polls were a lot closer than I would've liked in the days leading up to the election. I panicked each time I visited Nate Silver's website—which I tried not to do more than once or twice an hour, though I found it hard to restrain myself. I regarded Silver as the undisputed god of election forecasting, and I hung on his every word. He had predicted both Obama's victories with stunning accuracy, but I'd noticed Nate shied away from calling the current race a slam dunk for Hillary.

Very worrisome indeed.

The Chicago Cubs' historic World Series win less than a week ago added to my anxiety. Jack and I watched their dramatic Game Seven victory in a nearby sports bar. While everyone else in the room jumped to their feet and cheered, I shook my head and said to Jack, "This is a bad omen."

"What are you talking about?" he asked.

"Think back to when the Red Sox won the World Series in 2004, for the first time since the Curse of the Bambino."

He knew I referred to the infamous "curse" blamed for keeping the Sox from winning the World Championship for eighty-six years after they sold Babe Ruth to the Yankees in a greed-motivated transaction. To most fans, it was a superstition. But the way I viewed it, a curse was a curse.

Jack shook his head, not yet understanding my analogy.

"The week after the Sox won the Series, George W. Bush went on to win the election, even though a lot of the polls favored John Kerry."

"And this is similar how?"

"Don't you see? The Cubs haven't won in over a hundred years. Their team had a curse too. And this strikes me as a bad sign for the election."

Jack put his hands on my shoulders and leveled his blue gaze on me. "Barbara Gordon: You can't be serious that Hillary Clinton will lose the election because of a Chicago Cubs victory."

"Oh, Jack, when you put it that way . . . I know it sounds nuts. But still, I can't help obsessing over this. Don't forget; you granted me unlimited worrying privileges long ago."

"I'm not sure about the 'unlimited' part. Well, in any case, you've taken full advantage." Jack laughed.

But in the end, I was right to worry this time.

On election night, Jack and I attended what everyone predicted would be a victory party for Hillary. The other members of my happy hour clique had also come—Amy and Red with their husbands, and Carol with her boyfriend Antonio, the pro-Semitic Florentine man she had met on JDate. Four months into the relationship, Tony had started to look like a keeper.

By the time we knew for certain that Hillary had lost, most of the women were crying, while I noted mixed expressions of anger, shock, and disbelief on the men's faces.

"How will the country survive this?" said Carol.

Amy, who always pronounced the glass half-full even in the worst of circumstances, said, "The country has been through other hard times and other terrible presidents. We've always survived, and we will again."

"I don't know," said Red. "There's never been anything like this. I think we're venturing into unknown territory. God only knows what might happen."

Carol said, "I read an article that predicted a Trump presidency would mean the end of civilization."

Amy shook her head. "Now, that sounds a bit extreme. I mean, the end of civilization, honestly?" She turned to me. "Barbara, do you agree with that?"

"Yes," I said through tears. "But only on this planet."

45

LETTING GO

During the months that followed the election, Ma experienced more and more difficulty walking—so in August of 2017, Dr. Sam started making house calls to Tropical Gardens for her quarterly appointments. When he came for her next checkup in November, he appeared taken aback by the extent of her deterioration between summer and autumn.

After Ma lay back in her bed and fell right to sleep after the examination, Dr. Sam said, "I'd like to order a hospice evaluation with the goal of getting Dolly into a program within the next few weeks."

Hospice? I knew Ma had slipped in every way. She was physically slow, cognitively beyond slow, and her social skills were out the window. Still, she didn't seem as bad as Helen in her final days. How could the doctor justify hospice when Ma still knew us (on occasion) and still managed to walk and talk, though with far less proficiency on both counts?

Then I remembered the saying I'd learned from Jack. *If you've met one person with Alzheimer's, you've met one person with Alzheimer's.* I'd always measured my mother against Helen—and since Ma consistently came out ahead, I hadn't yet acknowledged the full extent of her own decline.

It took Dr. Sam to help me face the facts.

"How would you rate her quality of life at this point?" he asked. Dr. Sam knew I took solace in numbers, lists, and rating systems.

"Well, she's not at zero yet, but she's dropping fast."

"Tell me about the quality that still exists."

"I think Ma knows she is well-cared for, and sometimes she'll still smile at a photo or enjoy a treat. But even then, within seconds, the memory is gone, and all she wants to do is sleep."

He nodded. "Dolly has lost twelve pounds since her last checkup."

My surprise at this news further illustrated the extent of my denial. I knew she'd dropped a few pounds, but I didn't think it was anything serious.

"Her appetite's been lousy," I said, "and she has trouble remembering how to eat. Lately, she needs a lot more assistance with feeding." Though Ma might have bellyached about the many varieties of "crap" served up from the Tropical Gardens kitchen, she used to love her food and would polish off her meals with unfailing gusto. Until recently.

"I assume she's incontinent," he said.

"Yes, that's been the case for a while now. They keep her on a rigorous toileting schedule, but even with that, she has a bowel accident most days."

"Does she show any reaction when that happens?"

"She used to be embarrassed," I said, "but not any longer. There's no more control or awareness than you'd see from a baby."

The circle of life.

Dr. Sam went on to recommend that we gradually take Ma off several of her medications. This sent another shockwave through me as I recalled my emotional argument with Vicky last year when she had suggested this same weaning strategy: "I think if they pull back on the meds, it might help to—you know—*hasten* things."

Did Dr. Sam mean we should try to *kill* Ma? Surely that wasn't his intent, but the recommendation still seemed appalling. Seeing the fear in my eyes, he said kindly, "Given Dolly's decline in health and quality of life, and the prospect of this continuing at the current pace, medical interventions should be limited at this point."

"Limited how?"

"By involving hospice, which can guide you through this process, and by reevaluating her medications. My feeling is that we don't want to be treating her in a manner that would extend her life," he said. "I'll come up with a strategy for removing some of her medications in a way that will address this goal without causing any pain or suffering."

I recollected the article I'd sent to Vicky about measuring a dog's health by whether she could still do her favorite things. Then I remembered the activities I'd recorded in Ma's binder, and I realized she never engaged in the items on her own list anymore.

It occurred to me that when it came to this final, diminished stage of life, we treated our beloved pets with greater kindness than we treated our beloved humans. Given our tendency to connect love with possession, we had trouble accepting that love must sometimes lead us to the painful decision to let go.

On the following Monday, Dr. Sam emailed me his recommended medication changes, which I recorded in Ma's binder and reviewed with Cindy. Under his direction, Cindy also scheduled a hospice evaluation appointment for the following week.

Though I found it hard to accept Dr. Sam's advice, I'd come to appreciate his wisdom. When I emailed him back to thank him for all his help, I wrote:

—*This has been a gut-wrenching decision—especially given that my mother sometimes still recognizes us and expresses love. But I've concluded it's not right to give her life-prolonging drugs that may cause her to continue on for months or even years in a state where she no longer has any meaningful quality of life.*

To this, he graciously replied:

—*I know this is a difficult stage of life to be managing. But Dolly has benefited from your diligent care for a long time, and it's been a critical factor in helping her do this well. During this next transition, I'm sure your help will be valuable once again.*

Dr. Sam's final prediction proved to be incorrect, however. In late November, Ma developed a sniffle that started out mild, like most of her colds, but then escalated into a raging infection.

At the hospital emergency room, where paramedics treated her for high fever and breathing difficulties, the attending physician ushered me into a small family waiting room. She motioned for me to take a seat across from her on one of the molded plastic chairs that surrounded a matching white table. My teeth started chattering, even though the room didn't feel cold.

The doctor had dark hair pulled up in a chignon and a heart-shaped face with a compassionate expression. She looked about twenty to my middle-aged eyes.

"Your mother has been diagnosed with pneumonia and influenza."

"There must be a mistake. She had a flu shot."

"I'm sure that's true, but the flu vaccine has been notoriously ineffective this season."

"Oh, right. I keep hearing about that on the news," I said. "Are you going to admit her?"

The doctor tapped her well-manicured fingernails on the resin tabletop. "We recommend a hospice facility where Dolly's symptoms can be managed for maximum comfort." She named a place down the street from the hospital. "They have a bed available right away."

"Doesn't she need an evaluation first?" I asked naively. "We have an appointment set up for next week. Doctor Fairchild authorized it."

She nodded. "I read that in Doctor Fairchild's notes in our online system. He also noted that Dolly is an advanced Alzheimer's patient and that she's declined significantly."

"Yes."

"Given her condition, there's no evaluation necessary. The thing is, your mother's infection is categorized as life-limiting."

Life-limiting? Had this phrase replaced "terminal"? I envisioned a group of public relations gurus brainstorming in a conference room to come up with this new, more positive way to position death and dying.

"I see." I couldn't meet the doctor's sympathetic gaze. Instead, I glanced past her and focused my attention on the waiting room wallpaper.

I continued to shiver. I felt as though I sat on a stage set with another actor, the two of us playing the "how-much-longer-does-she-have" scene we've all watched in a hundred movies and soap operas. It didn't seem possible this could be happening in real life.

Months later, I still remembered that sense of unreality—and even more, I remembered the wallpaper in that room as clearly as if I'd snapped a close-up photo for Ma's binder. It had a muted floral print in light greens and grays, with a thread of metallic silver outlining the trumpet-shaped flowers. I also noticed a light buildup of dust on the color-matched pale green molding.

As the doctor explained how my mother had only a short time left to live, I couldn't stop thinking, *they need to be more diligent in their housekeeping. This is a hospital, after all. No wonder people are dying here.*

Two days later, on December 7, 2017, Dolly Gordon died—before we could journey into that "next transition" Dr. Sam had referred to with such kind eloquence in his final email. Toward the end, Ma was Stage Seven–*ish,* but she never reached the final and most devastating phase of Alzheimer's.

We held a small service with Vicky and me as the only speakers, honoring Ma's wish that her funeral guests should not be subjected to a tedious forum of open-mic eulogizing. She was eighty-four years old.

46

FAREWELL TO FORMULAS

Last night, on the first anniversary of Ma's death, I had a vivid dream about her. Ma had invited Vicky and me to a closing night cast party at Providence Players, and the three of us stood together, laughing like schoolgirls and clinking champagne glasses. I woke up feeling contented and cheerful.

I rolled over on my side to face Jack, who lay awake beside me reading a book, and I described my happy dream to him.

"I'm afraid my dreams about Helen are nightmares," he said. "She always has Alzheimer's, and it's always unsettling."

"Oh, honey, I'm sorry." I brushed my fingertips over the curly gray hairs on his chest and nestled into the warm crook of his arm. He stroked my bare shoulder.

"It is what it is. Another man I once met, a widower, told me it took five years before he could dream about or even remember his wife the way she used to be before the Alzheimer's."

"But Ma's only been gone a year."

"Dolly was always a cooperative patient. Maybe her good behavior even extends to a daughter's dreams."

"Speaking of daughters, I think I'll text Sarah." On this

first anniversary of my mother's death, I wanted to feel close to my own daughter today.

Sarah was a freshman at NYU and thriving. Throughout the summer of 2018, preceding her move to college, I set a personal record for list-making. The packing lists and to-do lists I created, if laid on the ground end to end, would have stretched all the way from downtown Providence to Greenwich Village. With scrupulous care, I also assembled a binder for my daughter, chock-a-block with printouts of carefully researched articles on relevant topics: *How to Drink Responsibly—A Primer for College Students*, *Protecting Yourself Against Date Rape*, and *Creating a Study Plan for Freshman Year*, to name a few.

Every month since starting college, Sarah's had a new love interest. Last month I couldn't remember the newest boyfriend's name. I wondered if I'd started to experience early onset.

With Jack's encouragement, I'd been pursuing my long-time dream of working on children's books. Two years into this writing endeavor, I finally felt I'd achieved real progress.

For the first year, I composed tender stories about cute little animals tucking their babies into bed at night. The babies were always frightened of the nighttime, and the mamas would soothe them with gentle lullabies about the moon, constellations, and other wonders of the sky. My stories came out sappy and unoriginal, and I inevitably chucked the manuscripts into the recycle bin.

Before hitting the delete button, though, I showed a few of my lame attempts to Jack. He read them and told me, "Barbara. You're funny. You have a wonderful sense of humor. Use that in your stories."

Taking his advice to heart, I ditched *tender* in favor of *funny*, and to my surprise, it worked. I developed a family of dogs with quirky personalities that shared a more-than-coincidental resemblance to Vicky, Ma, and myself, and I started to build a series of stories around them. Jack loved the concept and applied his artistic skills to visualizing the characters for me. Once we agreed on a cartoon style that we both liked, Jack created amusing illustrations that brought to life my family of pooches with all their craziness and canine conflicts.

Jack forwarded three of the stories to Marge. One of her old publishing contacts in Boston had a well-regarded children's book division, and Marge submitted our work to him around four months ago. Though we hadn't heard a word back from the publisher, Jack assured me this was a standard operating procedure.

We also entered two children's literature competitions that Jack uncovered through online research. One of the submissions took days to complete, requiring the compilation of numerous supporting documents.

"Whew. That took almost as long as writing the book itself," I said when we mailed the completed entry packet.

"I know. The creative part is fun, but the marketing can be arduous and nerve-racking."

"Tell me about it. You know, when I started writing

children's stories, I thought of it as a casual hobby. This is starting to feel a lot more serious."

"Are you getting cold feet?" he asked. "Because if you want to dial it back"—*that expression again*—"we can call a halt to the submissions and treat it as more of a fun project. Maybe self-publish a handful of copies to share with friends and family."

I thought over this idea. "No, Jack. I think I'd like to try for publication. We won't know unless we give it a shot."

"That's true."

"And you're okay with it either way?"

"Either way, I'm with you. This is a collaboration," said Jack.

"Yes. A collaboration."

This didn't feel like me. The old Barbara would have indeed dialed it back, allowing fear and self-doubt to take over as usual. Strangely, having Jack's shoulder to lean on hadn't made me a weaker woman; it had made me a stronger one. I studied these feelings up close, like someone examining the quality of an expensive dress in a high-end boutique. I nodded to myself, deciding I liked the style and the fit.

Should I worry about not being worried? Perhaps a little.

With Ma and Helen gone, Jack and I were free to travel more. Tomorrow, we would be riding a high-speed Amtrak Acela train down to New York to visit Sarah and attend a performance by Scott, who'd been cast in a new show.

"Do you think he'll be acting in the nude again?" I asked.

"I sincerely hope not. His last play was a bit too experimental for my taste."

That last performance had been made more awkward by the seating arrangements. Jack sat between Sarah and me. I still recall how he squirmed during Scott's nude scenes and kept his face averted from both of us.

This new production turned out to be a holiday revue—much frothier than Scott's usual fare. The location was a downtown Off-Off-Broadway theatre, a step *up* from previous venues. I enjoyed the performance, though attending live theatre always proved an emotional experience for me, bringing back a rush of memories about Ma and her career. Sarah did not attend with us; in fact, at no point in time that weekend did we see Sarah and Scott together, which was uncharacteristic. When I questioned her about it, she gave an evasive response.

"Do you think they've had a falling out?" Jack asked.

"Well, I'm wondering if they've become romantically involved and don't want us to know."

"That interpretation is—well, let's just say it shows a lot of imagination. You might want to stick to children's stories." He grinned as he said this, but in place of the usual twinkle in his eye, I thought I detected a glimmer of concern.

Just, maybe.

We were planning a trip to California for the following March to spend time with Paul, Elise, and the kids over spring break. Jack had found a rental house with a pool in Palm Desert. Dreams of that sunny sojourn would help us endure the brutal onslaught of the New England winter that loomed around the corner.

From California, we planned to drive down to Baja and spend a few days touring wineries and restaurants in the Valle de Guadalupe, the up-and-coming wine region Jack had long wanted to visit.

Though I'd developed a more refined palate and a deeper appreciation of wine with Jack's help, I remained by nature a lowbrow drinker.

"Jack, when we tour the Valle de Guadalupe, would you mind if I don't always do the wine tastings? I'd like to sip a margarita now and then."

"You can sip a margarita whenever you like, sweetheart. It's Mexico." We both laughed.

Ah yes, Mexico. I'd been trying to forget about that. Still a compulsive worrier in many ways, I confessed to being south-of-the-border phobic. I imagined the two of us kidnapped by a drug cartel, felled by a near-fatal gastrointestinal disorder, or hopelessly lost in Tijuana and detained by unsympathetic local *policia*.

As I packed an overnight bag for the New York trip, I reviewed my calendar and remembered another important event coming up next week. On December 12, 2018,

Vicky and Chief would make their debut appearance at Tropical Gardens.

Soon after Ma died, Vicky had to put down her beloved Daisy. The arthritis in the dog's back legs had worsened to the point where she could barely stand. When she stopped eating and underwent a battery of tests, they found a stomach tumor believed to be cancerous. (I wondered if it could have been all those years of snacking on unauthorized human ice cream?)

Even in the improbable event the tumor turned out benign, the vet said Daisy didn't have enough strength to survive the surgery. Heartbroken, Vicky and Martin had the dog euthanized only ten days after Ma's passing.

Those two sad events conspired to make my sister go all soft. She rescued a retriever puppy named Chief and enrolled him in the therapy dog training program. Both mother and dog graduated with honors.

Next week, Vicky and Chief would make their inaugural rounds. It seemed like a fitting tribute to Ma, although I found it ironic that my sister would now be making weekly trips to the memory care facility when I had to drag her there kicking and screaming while our mother was a resident.

A few days ago, when she called to tell me the schedule, she said, "I expect you and Jack to be there."

She *expected* us? You'd think she and Chief were award recipients at a Kennedy Center Honors ceremony. I promised her I'd attend but said I couldn't vouch for Jack's availability.

"What the hell else does he have to do?" my sister

whined. "Besides, if Jack comes to Tropical Gardens to see Chief, he can kill two birds."

"What do you mean?"

"He can book future accommodations for himself while he's there. I hear there's a waiting list now."

Vicky still enjoyed making ridiculous digs about the age difference between Jack and me. Not only did Jack remain sharp as a razor, but he also could have been a poster boy for senior health and fitness—especially compared to Martin, whose primary form of exercise consisted of toting a twenty-ounce can of Bud Light and a family size Doritos bag from the kitchen to the TV room.

But over the last two years, whenever Vicky cracked an old-man joke, I'd smile and say something like, "If Jack wants to live at Tropical Gardens, I'll support whatever he decides. Every day is a gift with that man."

Vicky abhorred sentimentality. Disgruntled, she would say, "Aren't we Little Miss Sunshine?" or "Excuse *me*, I just threw up in my mouth."

Yes, I now found it easy to tune out my sister's taunts about Jack's age. In fact, I'd been trying hard to shed my life-long habit of going by the numbers. I shouldn't need mathematical formulas to compute the ideal age gap for a man and woman seeking a romantic partner or the length of time required to get over a relationship after it ended. The very idea of "getting over" Jack, if the day ever came when I must do so, seemed insupportable.

Because, you see, Jack Winokur was the love of my life. To be honest, I didn't think he would say the same of me. If I added up all the wonderful years he had with Helen before the onset of her Alzheimer's, the numbers didn't work in my favor. (*Uh-oh.* There I was, starting up with the math again.) But I felt okay with that. Truly okay.

Because all things considered, was it terribly important for me to be number one on Jack's list? Shouldn't a close second be good enough?

Now that I stopped to think about it, maybe there didn't even need to be a list at all.

47

A HAPPIER PLACE

In the end, Jack did come to Tropical Gardens for therapy dog day, if only to maintain the peace between Vicky and Barbara—a peace that remained tenuous at best, now that Barbara no longer caved into Vicky's every demand. Jack would do almost anything for Barbara—who remained, by her own admission, a neurotic mess.

He adored her.

The weather for Vicky and Chief's momentous debut was unseasonably warm for mid-December, with the temperature topping out near sixty degrees. The day was blue and cloudless, but with that muted golden tinge that sometimes bathed the New England sky as winter approached and the sun sat low on the horizon.

Dog and handler made a resounding hit with the residents of Tropical Gardens. In honor of the upcoming holidays, they sported matching Santa costumes. Jack had to stifle his laughter when Vicky's Santa hat fell off and landed in a platter of cupcakes—causing her to drop an F-bomb in a voice loud enough to be heard by all, or at least by all who had their hearing aids turned up.

Martin also attended the Chief and Vicky Show, as did three employees from V&M Solutions who obviously valued their jobs. Addressing her private fan club afterward, Vicky revealed plans for a schedule of future costume-themed events: Valentine's Day, Easter, and Purim, explaining this last one with, "We mustn't forget our Jewish residents."

"Do they have Purim costumes for dogs?" asked Jack.

"Oh, I'm sure they do. I'll Google it. I mean, I'll 'Jew-gool' it," she said and followed her own witticism with barking laughter.

After Vicky left with her entourage, Jack said, "I wonder what the residents enjoyed more: petting Chief or listening to Vicky swear."

"It's a toss-up," said Barbara.

"I agree," said Wayne, beaming at Barbara and Jack. "I'm glad to see you two together," he added with a meaningful wink before taking his leave to wheel a patient from the foyer.

Barbara said she'd like to go home, change her clothes, and squeeze in a nice walk while the daylight lasted. "I want to take advantage of this amazing weather while I can. It's supposed to turn cold overnight and maybe even snow tomorrow."

"Would you like company on the walk?" Jack asked, and she nodded in assent. "I'll be over in fifteen minutes." The two had driven in separate cars.

Barbara gave him a light goodbye kiss on the lips. "Oh, by the way, remember that children's book contest we entered? The time-consuming one?"

"Sure."

"A letter came from them in today's mail."

Jack raised an eyebrow. "What did it say?"

"I thought I'd wait for us to open it together. After our walk."

After Barbara left, Jack lingered in the foyer, where he found himself drawn to the familiar potted palm tree that had so entranced Helen during her first months in the memory care unit. He walked over and took one of the fronds in his hand, stroking it admiringly as Helen always used to do, in a sort of private tribute to his late wife.

Jack didn't believe in ghosts, but it almost felt as if Helen's spirit lingered here in the Tropical Gardens foyer. Perhaps it really did. He recalled something Barbara had told him about the religious views of Wayne and his Balinese countrymen. Wayne would believe that Helen's soul had been reincarnated, and she now lived and played as an infant or toddler somewhere in this world or another. If that were the case, Jack hoped his late wife dwelled in a happier place than where she'd been before, one small step closer to Moksha, the final state of enlightenment and liberation from pain and suffering.

But this was not for Jack, or for anyone else, to know. He slowly drew back his hand from the palm frond and followed Barbara out into the soft, warm light of the late autumn afternoon.

THE END

Acknowledgments

There are an estimated six million cases of Alzheimer's in the U.S. today, a number that is expected to more than double by 2050. It will likely touch every one of us in some way over the course of our lives. During the years that my mother, Muriel Port Stevens, suffered from this tragic disease, I often found myself trading war stories and sharing sympathetic reflections with others whose family members were similarly afflicted.

These shared experiences planted the seeds for what eventually became a play and later a novel titled *Stage Seven*, named after the final and most devastating phase of Alzheimer's dementia. The term comes from the Global Deterioration Scale (GDS) developed by Dr. Barry Reisberg, clinical director of the New York University School of Medicine's Silberstein Aging and Dementia Research Center.

The Alzheimer's Association, however, uses a simplified three-stage system to categorize the disease's progression: early-stage (mild), middle-stage (moderate), and late-stage (severe).

The Forgetting: Alzheimer's: Portrait of an Epidemic by David Shenk is an anecdotal history that inspired some of the concepts presented in my novel. This fascinating book helped me to regard the disease in a way that was bittersweet rather than just bitter—a perspective I hope to pass on to my readers.

The songs sung by Jack and others in the novel were "(How Much Is) That Doggie in the Window," written by Bob Merrill and published in 1952, as well as "'S Wonderful" and "They Can't Take That Away from Me," composed by George Gershwin with lyrics written by Ira Gershwin in 1927 and 1937, respectively.

Barbara's favorite TV series, *Sex and the City*, was created by Darren Star and is based on the book by Candace Bushnell.

The sonnet that Jack read to Helen was by William Shakespeare: "Let me not to the marriage of true minds" (Sonnet 116).

In acknowledging the many people who helped me with this work during the past five years, it's impossible to separate the play from the book, as the second would not exist without the first. So, I will start by thanking Winifred Morice, who took a chance on a novice playwright to direct and produce the world premiere of *Stage Seven* in 2018. Hats off to Winifred, Don Sudduth, and the entire cast and crew at the Gertrude Pearlman Theatre for putting on an audience-pleasing production that inspired me to expand the story into a novel.

And, special thanks to the two people who read through countless drafts of both versions. Mary Todd was my editor extraordinaire, the only person I know who is equally adept at giving big picture feedback while never missing an errant comma. And a big thank you to Tricia Hopper for her helpful critiques throughout the development process.

Many others helped shape this story with their comments and suggestions: Leslie Allingham, Elizabeth and

Tish Andrewartha, Katherine Bradford and her book group members (Hedy Carpenter, Jan Fish, and Janet Kubler), Robbie Burke, Amy Gordon, Vic Han, Peter McCormack, Ana Nogueira, Lisa Pasold, Tim and Jane Paulson, Susan Paxton, Sarah Robotham and her wonderful troupe of young actors, and Ann Robson.

I'd also like to acknowledge those who provided additional assistance and support with the theatrical version of the story: Christie Baugher, Steve Giles, Denise Guzman, Anthony Heald, Jack Lovell, Lisa Moeller, Bob Ng, Jonathan Silverstein, Ritas Smith, Gayle Taylor, and everyone who traveled to see the production and to cheer me on.

Thank you to fellow authors Dana Czapnik, Joani Elliott, Dan Gasby, Marita Golden, Daniel Kenner, and Abbi Waxman for their inspiration and their generous comments.

Many thanks to Gordon McClellan, Katelynn Watkins, and the entire DartFrog publishing team for their enthusiasm, their efficiency, and their talent.

I would also like to acknowledge those who gave my mother such loving attention and care in her final years: Carmen Contreras, the late Carol Sceeles, and Dr. Lewis Weiner.

Boundless thanks to my husband, David Olson, my son and daughter-in-law, Jake and Luciana Olson, and all my family and friends for their unflagging encouragement of my writing career.

And last but not least, thanks to Muriel—a great lady who lives on in our memories.

About the Author

Ruth F. Stevens believes in stories that make you laugh and cry. A former public relations executive in New York and Los Angeles, she is a produced playwright and has written hundreds of published articles, but fiction is her love. Ruth lives in sunny California with her husband and she enjoys travel, hiking, hip hop, Broadway musicals, movies, and visiting her grandsons in NYC. *Stage Seven* is her first novel. Visit her website at ruthfstevens.com.

If you've enjoyed *Stage Seven*, please consider giving it some visibility by reviewing it on Amazon or Goodreads. Your feedback will benefit the author while also helping other readers decide whether or not they would enjoy this book, too.

Made in the USA
Monee, IL
08 July 2023

38544489R00218